Sometimes you find love where you least expect it.

All Amanda Mathers wants for Christmas is to travel far from home. To have adventures. What she gets is Luke Post, who's planted as firmly in their town of White Pine as the Christmas trees on his family farm.

Could love be the greatest adventure of all?

Open one chapter each day from December 1 to December 25 and be swept up in the most romantic Christmas no one expected.

The Secret Santa Setup

The Secret Santa Setup

SARAH HUTT

Illustrated by
SARAH LONG

CLARION BOOKS
An Imprint of HarperCollinsPublishers

HarperCollins Children's Books, a division of HarperCollins
Publishers, 195 Broadway, New York, NY 10007
HarperCollins Publishers, Macken House, 39/40 Mayor
Street Upper, Dublin 1, D01 C9W8, Ireland

Clarion Books is an imprint of HarperCollins Publishers.

The Secret Santa Setup

Illustrations by Sarah Long

harpercollins.com
Library of Congress Control Number: 2026936474
ISBN 978-0-06-357330-7
The artist used Photoshop to create digital illustrations for this book.
Book design by Jessie Gang
26 27 28 29 30 LEO 10 9 8 7 6 5 4 3 2 1
FIRST EDITION

For my parents,
who always made Christmas special.
And my beloved family
and the faithful friends who are dear to us,
may your days be merry and bright.

DECEMBER

1

Chapter 1

I'M DREAMING OF A WHITE (PINE) CHRISTMAS

“Amanda, time to get up honey.” I can hear my mom, Janice, calling me through the haze of a cozy, deep, dark sleep. Do I have to wake up? It's so nice under my covers. Her steps are creaking up the hundred-year-old stairs of our Victorian house, getting closer and closer, like Jaws circling a swimmer in that old-school horror movie.

There it is, the knock on the door, and she opens it without waiting for an answer. I don't even need to crack my eyelids to know she's leaning her head in, her dark blond hair (just like mine, but with streaks of silver) pinned up in a no-nonsense bun. I can smell her lotion. She's showered and fresh and put together for her day at the office doing lawyerly things for our small town of White Pine, Vermont. And right on cue, here it comes.

“Honey, time to get up. Don't forget it's December first, that means you need to get your application for your summer abroad program in ASAP, and I want you to email Mr. Sullivan at my office about that internship with the town events department. Summer after junior year is the perfect time for it, it'll look great on college applications, and they need a letter of interest from you this month, so make sure you do it, okay? We don't want to miss this opportunity."

Ugh, I'm barely awake and she's already on my case. Why is she even asking me about the application to my summer abroad program? That's been done for ages. I mean, two weeks at a youth leaders program in Switzerland? You bet I'm not gonna miss that deadline.

But the internship, no way. I'm turning seventeen in April. It's the summer before senior year. I'm not going to spend it stuck in some stuffy office shuffling permit papers. That's how *she* wants me to spend my summer. I have other plans: A travel-anywhere-in-Europe train pass, a backpack, my best friend, Celeste, and, after my two weeks in Switzerland with other "Youth Leaders" ends, spending the rest of the summer exploring Europe, writing in my travel journal, and having a blast!

I guess I should probably figure out when I'm gonna tell my parents that last part . . . ?

I have to save the money for the tickets first. Then, after that, I'll tell them. Either way, it's definitely not right now. It's only December, Christmas is coming, and my brain is still half-asleep.

I'm not sure what sound came out of my mouth from under my blankets; it was somewhere between a yeah and grunt, a "geh."

But it's good enough for Janice, who is clearly already on to the next to-do on her very long list.

"Okay, great. Thanks. Gotta run, honeybun, love you." She closes the door and starts down the stairs.

"Oh, and don't forget that you're driving your brother to school today. He has his cello with him for rehearsal for all the Christmas school stuff. Thanks, bye!" she yells up as she reaches the entranceway.

Bang! The front door, bedecked with a holly wreath and lit all pretty like the rest of our painted-lady house has been since Thanksgiving, slams behind her. As Mom heads off into the early morning darkness, I snuggle a little deeper under my covers, grateful for a few more minutes of peace in my beautiful warm bed.

Gah, December 1. Maybe if I pull the covers up far enough, I can go back to sleep, hibernate through Christmas, and wake up on January 1.

It's not that I don't like Christmas. I mean, I love Christmas, who doesn't? But this is Christmas in White Pine, Vermont, also known to tourists and ski bunnies as "America's Christmas Village." When you picture, like, an old-timey Christmas postcard, with the snowy New England town nestled in the foothills of the Green Mountains, the white historic church, picturesque Main Street covered in twinkly lights, a river running through it, and a glorious fifty-foot-tall (yes) white pine tree with a shining star atop it—that's Christmas in White Pine. And as soon as December hits, it's wall-to-wall tourists from NYC, Boston, and all over

New England rolling into town for their taste of *White Christmas* movie magic holiday vibes. And it can be a lot.

I catch the shuffling of my little sibling, Milo, an unrepentantly annoying sixth grader, trying to ninja his way through my door, ready to pounce. I brace myself under the covers for the ambush. I hear his raspy little voice right next to my ear, "Yo, Brotato, what's baking? Get up. Mom says you gotta take me to school." He grabs the covers and yanks them off me. In the yellow crack of light from the hallway, I see his spiky little black-and-red-dyed Demon Slayer–wannabe head dart out the door. He's giggling, clearly very pleased with himself.

Little twerp, he fired the first shot of the day in our long-running battle to see who can come up with the better bro pun.

"For real, Brozilla? Totally unnecessary, I'm up!" I yell. I hear more giggling through the wall that separates our rooms.

I guess there's no avoiding it. I sit up, turn on my bedside lamp, and survey my room. Past the end of my old four-poster bed, covered in stickers from when I was little, I catch a glimpse of myself in the vanity mirror. Yikes! My long hair is full of bedhead tangles, and as I wipe yesterday's eyeliner from my gray eyes, they drift to the assortment of photos I've wedged into the mirror frame.

At least, I get to spend December with these guys.

I can't help but smile at the photo of me at the lake last summer with Celeste, who's also my next-door neighbor and oldest friend. Her flaming red wavy hair catches the late-day sun, and she's in one of her green cotton, Earth Goddess flowy sundresses, giving a peace sign. We're standing in the sand, the lake at our backs. I'm on one side in my jorts, hair wet, wearing one of my dad's old concert T-shirts with wet splotches from my bikini top seeping through. My tongue is out, and I'm throwing rock 'n' roll hands and being goofy—the polar opposite of Junjun (pronounced like the month but times two), our other bestie, a longtime White Piner by way of the Philippines. He's standing on Celeste's other side.

His dark hair is combed back slick and shining. His robin's-egg blue linen shorts are neatly pressed and topped with a crisp white polo, and he's sporting white-rimmed shades and loafers to complete the outfit. He holds up little heart fingers, tilting his head and lifting his jawline, in a perfect pose. How does he always look so good? It's unfair!

And then, in the foreground, there's Max, our friend since grade school—now Celeste's boyfriend—caught mid–photo bomb diving into our picture. The king of chaos, he's suspended in midair, arms outstretched like Superman, the full length of his tall frame frozen a foot off the sand at our feet. He's shirtless and tan in his swim trunks, ice cream hair flying, eyes closed and dopey grin on face. How can I not love these weirdos?

I swing my feet over the bed, and they hit the cold floor. I wish it was summer already.

I can't wait. We're gonna be taking snaps like that on Lake Zurich and posing in front of fountains in Rome. Well, at least Celeste and I will. I'm going to have to start earning some cash to get those tickets.

And Christmas too. I gotta buy gifts for everybody. How am I gonna afford it?

As I'm mulling over the sad state of my finances my dad, Richard, Dick, Dr. Dick the Dentist, or "Dickie Teeth," lead tenor sax in his dad-band jazz quartet, The Smooth Tones, marches up the stairs whistling "Jingle Bells" in his chipper way.

"Knock, knock, kiddo, it's your favorite Christmas jazz daddio, here to remind you to get your zip-a-dee-bebop moving or you're gonna be late for school." He opens the door and sees me sitting like a zombie on the side of my bed. "Oh, good, you're up!"

My dad is so embarrassing.

But it's a level of cringe so bad I can't help but laugh, which of course is his objective. All of a sudden, I'm awake and smiling at his friendly round face, light brown eyes, and short sandy brown hair, "a little thin on top, but still there," as he likes to say.

"December first!" He leans in the door jamb casually. "Did you know," he exclaims by way of a big reveal, "today is the birthday of revolutionary jazz fusion bass virtuoso Jaco Pastorius? You want to hear some tunes? I can put something on the Bluetooth that'll get you moving . . ."

"Uhhh, I think I'm good, but thanks for today's jazz education." I use a sly sarcastic tone to complete the bit.

"Ah, young acolyte, one day you will see what you are missing, and on that day, you will come to me to learn all about the revolution in music that is fusion jazz. Born out of the 'hard bop' era of the late 1950s and 1960s, this genre . . ."

"Dad, enough! Save it for your patients, you can use one of your jazz lectures instead of sedation. Trust me, it'll put them right to sleep. Anyway, don't you have to get to work?"

"Ouch, a stinging retort from my young wordsmith. Good one. And, yes, you're right, I do have to get to work. Those cavities aren't going to fill themselves. See you tonight for dinner, or are you working?"

For about a year, I've been a barista at a coffee shop in town called Matcha-Do about Coffee, owned and run by my boss, Zoe Huggins. Normally, I would be working, but we are transitioning to a new holiday schedule, and I have the afternoon off.

"Nope, not today. I'll be home by dinnertime." I stretch and slowly start to move.

"Okay. Love you, kiddo."

"Love you, Daddy."

He pulls my door closed and I hear him bouncing back down the stairs, humming to himself. I shake my head and smile as I reach for my fuzzy robe in the pile of clothes on the floor by my bed, slide into my fluffy, slightly raggedy slippers, grab the towel from the back of my door, and head to the shower.

The steamy hot water does the rest of the job of waking me up, and as I'm lathering up my hair, it comes to me:

The coffee shop, duh! I should ask Zoe for more shifts while she's working on the schedule. That could solve my cash crunch.

But what about presents? I still have to get something for my family and Celeste, Jun, and Max. It's a lot.

I step out of the shower and towel off my hair.

Even with extra shifts, this is all gonna add up. I'm never going to be able to afford my train tickets for summer.

I haven't even had any coffee yet, and my overthinking brain is starting to rev. I catch the time on the digital clock on the shelf over the toilet. Oh crap, it's almost 7:45 a.m. I've been zoning out. I gotta go. If I make Milo late for school, Mom will kill me. There's no way that little snake will keep it a secret.

A secret. That's it! Secret Santa!

We'll do a Secret Santa. We'll draw names. Just one person to shop for, instead of three.

I look at my reflection and pause, toothbrush in hand, my mouth full of minty foam, and say, in my best British accent . . .

"You're brilliant, Amanda Mathers! What will you think of next?"

I hustle back to my room, throw on some undies, jeans, big wooly socks, long-sleeved T-shirt, my favorite baggy sweater, and wool beanie. No time for makeup, it's fine. I like how I look. I grab my phone and my journal and stomp down the stairs.

Milo is waiting by the front door next to the antique hall tree, a kind of bench with a high back, a mirror above that, and hooks above that, which are currently overflowing with coats and hats. On the rubber mat next to the hall tree are piles of shoes and snow boots.

Milo's already bundled up and leaning on his cello in its hard case, exasperatedly nonchalant, examining something under his fingernail.

He had time for hair and makeup, apparently.

"Is that my eyeliner and black nail polish? Bro, what even is this look, emo cosplay?"

"You wouldn't understand, you're simply not interesting

enough," he casually flicks away his under-the-nail find.

"Whatever, sixth grader."

"Can we go now? Or else I'm gonna tell Mom you made me late."

"Okay, chill, I'm just putting on my boots. Go in the kitchen and grab my backpack."

Milo sighs but complies.

I sit on the old wooden bench and pull on my snow boots. I put on my winter coat and pat the pockets to check for the keys to my dad's old Volvo—mine to drive since I turned sixteen.

Milo reappears and hands me my backpack and a brown baggie. It has a little heart drawn on it. Mom can be sweet, even if she does nag.

"What kind of sandwich did she pack?" I ask Milo.

"What do you think? Bro-loney and cheese." Milo then literally slaps his thigh and starts cackling again at his own hilarity.

Oh man, I walked right into that one.

I do my neurotic third check that I have everything and reassure myself that I do. Most important of all, I have a plan!

Tomorrow when I go to work, I'm going to ask Zoe for more shifts.

And as soon as I can get all my friends together, I'm going to float the Secret Santa idea.

More cash coming in at work, less going out on presents. Problem solved.

If all goes well, I'll be able to buy my train tickets before Christmas.

Feeling pleased, I turn to Milo. "Yo, Wolfgang Amadeus Brozart, grab your cello, we out."

We both giggle, and Milo nods approvingly and says, "Nice one."

We walk out the door to my trusty old salt-stained Volvo wagon, load in, and back out. The sun is rising through the bare trees and falls on last week's leftover snow, lighting up our lawn in the pale, yellow-gold of a winter morning. It casts its warmth on our pretty street and the old Victorian homes with their painted porches all done up in garlands of green and red ribbons. It's beautiful. And I start to feel pretty good about December.

I mean, I've got a good plan. Christmas is coming.

What can possibly go wrong?

DECEMBER
2

Chapter 2

MATCHA-DO ABOUT CHRISTMAS

Ahhh. Sweet, sweet solitude, and seat warmers!

I sink into my car and lock the doors. My breath turns to steam as I warm my fingers. It's 3:15 p.m. and school's just let out. I start the engine and give it a second to warm up.

Okay, December 2, what else have you got in store?

School wasn't so bad. All the teachers are still groggy from Thanksgiving break so there was nothing too stressful for me to overthink. Except applications.

I gotta remind Celeste to get her application for the young leaders program in before Christmas vacation.

Oh, and Secret Santa! I need to tell everyone about that.

I never got a chance today. Celeste and Max stayed in the chem lab through lunch to finish up a project, and Junjun and I got sidetracked by a yearbook meeting that went long.

I can tell everyone after school tomorrow. Right now, I better get to work or I'm going to be late.

I pull out of the school lot and head toward town. I pop on the radio to the local light rock station. From now until New Year's, they will play only Christmas music, and I will listen to only this station, a mildly embarrassing guilty pleasure I inherited from my mom (Thanks, Janice).

Bing Crosby begins to tell me how he's dreaming of a white Christmas, just like the ones I used to know. . . .

As I crest the small hill on Church Road, the whole village is laid out below me, already glittering with lights and decorations.

There's the white clapboard church with its steeple piercing the winter sky. The paned glass windows of the shops on Main Street glow warmly in the waning evening sun, the lampposts on the stone bridge over the mill-run waterfall are all decked out with wreaths and ribbons, and there's a crisp blanket of icy snow on the grass and the rooftops. With Bing as the soundtrack, it feels like a scene from a movie.

This right here is why White Pine is America's Christmas Village. Even though I've seen this view a million times, I can't help but smile and feel a little more excited about Christmas.

The downside? From the hill, I can already see tourist traffic backing up on Main Street as cars stop to let pedestrians cross. The street parking from the stone bridge to the front of Matcha-Do about Coffee is full.

I know better than to try and park on Main Street in December, and I take a quick right before the shops and sneak around to the municipal parking lot. At the back entrance of Matcha-Do, I see Cheryl Post, the baker who provides all of our pastries, balancing an armload of white cake boxes and struggling to push open the café door.

"Hey, let me get that door for you!" I holler, jogging up.

"Oh, great, thanks, Amanda. You turned up just when I needed you."

I follow Cheryl in through the narrow back hall of the shop, admiring her style. Cargos and a flannel shirt are standard fare in any Vermont town, but she's added her own flair to the look with a long silver wallet chain, her sleeves rolled up enough to reveal the fines lines of well-inked tattoos, and pink hair peeking out from under a neon yellow and peach beanie. She's pretty, probably in her late thirties, and, I think, recently moved back to town from Portland or Seattle or something.

"Hang on, let me help you with the next one," I say as I duck into the storeroom. I drop my stuff, grab an apron, then push open the door into the brightness of the cafe.

"Well, look who we have here, my three-thirty p.m. shift change and my pastries. Right on schedule! That's what I like to see." Zoe Huggins, owner of Matcha-Do about Coffee, is camped out on a stool at the black-and-white-tiled coffee counter, her planner open, jotting down items in her flawless script.

"Hi, Zoe," I say.

"Where you want these, Zoe?" Cheryl continues gamely balancing the boxes.

"Just the end of the bar, thanks, Cheryl." Zoe doesn't look up from her work.

Zoe's also in her thirties. Petite, with brown skin and light brown hair pinned up on one side, she is impeccably dressed in gray wool pants and a white cashmere turtleneck, with understated but stylish nails, jewelry, and makeup. The clean, crisp decor of the coffee shop is an extension of her personal aesthetic and eye for detail.

I like Zoe a lot. She has high standards for everything, including her employees, but always treats everyone fairly. And she gets results. Matcha-Do about Coffee, or Matcha-Do as we call it, is one of the most successful businesses on Main Street. Probably because, in a Vermont town decorated in standard-issue plaid and pinecones, it stands apart for its white minimalist interior decorated with succulents, artfully selected books, cool patterned throw pillows, and well-arranged sofa nooks, all under the glow of a pink cursive Matcha-Do neon sign.

It's always pretty busy, and today's no different. There are people camped at the tables alone, noses in their laptops, and groups of shoppers with their bags tucked under the sofas, taking a load off over a latte.

"Amanda, you might want to check how we're doing on oat milk. I don't think Trevor restocked last night," Zoe tells me.

"Okay, no problem." I take my spot behind the shining, imported Italian expresso machine, put on my apron, and start checking the fridge as Cheryl stacks the cake boxes on the end of the counter.

"Oh, and I posted the new schedules in the break room, so check the board when you're back there, okay?"

"Actually, about that . . ." I pop back up from below the counter. "I wanted to talk to you about the schedule and see if . . ."

Before I even get a chance to ask my question Zoe's onto the next thing. "What'd you bring me today, Cheryl?"

"I got your usual order of croissants and pastries, both the regular and the vegan," she says, arranging the boxes on the bar. "But I also brought you something new to try, something a little special for the holidays."

Finally, Zoe looks up. "What is it?"

"Uh, it's fudge. Christmas fudge." Cheryl awkwardly holds out a small box. "My mom always made it to sell up at the farm, and I thought I'd see if you wanted to try stocking it for the season."

"Oh, that's right, your family has the Christmas tree farm up on Route 9 heading into town," Zoe says, connecting the dots.

"Post Farm!" I interject excitedly. "We used to get our trees there when I was little, but then my mom bought a fake one and that was that."

"Yeah, that happens." Cheryl smiles at me. "Real trees are still better if you ask me, but I'm biased. Anyway, back in the day, my mom used to sell this fudge in a little stand on the tree lot, and it was always a big hit. Do you want to try some?"

Zoe takes the box and opens it to inspect the contents. "Hm. What's this one?"

Cheryl leans in. "That's peppermint dark chocolate, this is gingerbread spice milk chocolate, this is a white chocolate nutmeg eggnog, and I've been playing with my own recipe for a vegan coconut pistachio one. You could try out a small order for the holidays and see how it sells? It goes great with hot chocolate."

"You know, I appreciate your thinking of us, but I'm not sure. I kind of already have my holiday setup dialed in." Before Zoe can say more, I hear the familiar singsongy voice of one of my regulars, Helen Novak, who owns the dress boutique next door.

"Hellloooo, my little Christmas elves!"

"Hi, Mrs. Novak." She's a lot, but I can't help but smile.

"Why if it isn't my favorite barista extraordinaire! *Mandy, there's a minister handy . . .*" she sings. Loudly.

Normally, I hate it when people call me Mandy. But somehow seeing the short, jolly figure of Mrs. Novak shimmying toward my counter, jazz hands jingling chunky bracelets, serenading me with a song from *White Christmas*, I can't be mad. I chuckle at the looks of surprise and confusion on the faces of our other patrons as she finishes her number and smooths the front of her candy apple red chiffon blouse. She lands at the bar with a dramatic exhale.

"Oh, you're just the person I need, Mandy," she says, totally ignoring Zoe and Cheryl, who are also staring bemused.

"The usual, Mrs. Novak?" I try gamely, to keep it professional.

"Oh, now stop that, call me Helen. Well, you know," she says with a sigh, "I usually have my chamomile this time of day to keep me from getting too excited, but oh bless, I've just got done with my window display for the shop. It's a chic-ugly-Christmas-sweater theme! Isn't that funny? I think it's really quite darling. But now I'm just pooped, and I could use a little pick-me-up. How about a dirty chai latte with a double shot, thank you, hon."

I start the drink order as she continues her breathy verbal download.

"Oh, and you know this girl I hired, this Marissa? Always on her phone! No help at all! These college kids home on break, I tell ya. Why can't all the teens be like you, Mandy, so focused and responsible? Ugh, I'm getting all worked up, better make that a single shot, honey."

I chuckle to myself and finish making the drink.

"Mandy." She switches gears again. "Your mom must be just so proud of you. By the way, we got some darling two-piece pajama sets in if you want to get one for Janie. I'll give you the 'White Piner discount,'" she says in a conspiratorial whisper, so the tourists don't hear, using the childhood nickname only the really old-timers still use for Janice Mathers.

"I'll think about it, thanks," I say, handing over her drink. "I'm trying to save money right now. Which reminds me, Zoe . . ."

"Oh no, look at me being so rude!" Mrs. Novak says. "Hiya, Zoe, how's business? And who do we have here?" She gasps theatrically at the sight of Cheryl. "Well, I'll be Rudolf's red nose, is that little Cheri Post, all grown up?!"

"Hi, Mrs. Novak, yeah, it's been a long time."

"Oh, kiddo, look at you . . . you're so . . . colorful!" Mrs. Novak sips her chai and gives Cheryl a once-over.

"That's one way to put it," Cheryl says, smiling, quite bemused and totally unoffended.

"Why, I haven't seen you in an age! Where have you been?"

"I was out west for a while, in culinary school, but I've been back for a bit. You know, since Mom . . ."

"Oh, I was so sorry when your mom passed." Mrs. Novak slows down a beat, lost in a memory. "They sure don't make 'em like Nancy Post anymore, she was a real one."

Cheryl looks down and nods politely. Zoe cocks her head slightly, noticing the change.

"And what's that you got there in the box?" Mrs. Novak asks, changing the subject and nosing between Zoe and Cheryl. She gasps as she brings her hands to her heart in a clenched-fist prayer. "Is that what I think it is? Nan's fudge?"

"Yup," Cheryl replies, smiling again.

"Oh gosh, I haven't had that in forever and it is JUST the best! Zoe, let me tell you, back in the day, when my husband, Ralph, was alive and the kids were little, every year we'd go out to Post Farm to get the tree, and we'd cut our own, you know, not just grab the precuts from the lot, and Cheri, your mom, would have that big fire going and cups of cocoa and that little stand where you'd pay, and she'd sell the fudge? It was all decorated and lit up and we'd hang out by the fire and have our fudge, and it just tasted like . . . like Christmas JOY!" she exclaims, arms outstretched.

The whole coffee shop is rapt now.

"Ahhh, it was just the best." She brings her hands back to her heart. "I miss those days. Haven't got a tree since Ralph passed, you know, no point, it's just me. But, oh, the memories."

Zoe looks at Cheryl and the fudge with renewed interest.

"Well, I was just about to tell Zoe here that we still have that stand, and I'm running my bakery out of the farmhouse kitchen, so there's no reason why we couldn't set it up again and maybe even sell coffee and hot cocoa." Cheryl turns to Zoe. "What do you say, Zoe? Want to do a Matcha-Do pop-up out at the farm? It could be great."

Zoe, a little ruffled at being put on the spot, looks from Cheryl, to Mrs. Novak, to me. "Oh, I don't know . . . I have a system, you know, a way I like to run things . . . adding something new right now . . ."

"Now I'm not one to put my nose in other people's business, Zoe," Helen interjects, "and I know you know what you're doing being the head of the Main Street Small Business Council and all, but you're leaving money on the table if you don't do this. Post Farm is the perfect spot for a stand. It's the main road into town, right before the turnoff to the ski lodge. You put a sign on the road saying 'Hot cocoa, coffee, and fudge,' and you'll grab all the tourists coming into town, and all the folks heading up to ski. I tell you, if I had a stand where I could sell my soaps and little scarves and things out there, I'd be cleaning up. Anyone on Main Street would love a pop-up at that location during the holidays."

"Well, who's going to run it?" Zoe counters, a little defensively. "I already made the schedule for my staff."

This is my chance!

"I could," I interject. "I was actually going to ask you about some more shifts here, but I could easily do them out at the stand. Sounds like there's a kitchen, and we could use the big carafes and do drip coffee and cocoa, not a full menu. I can take the extra tablet to ring people up. It's totally doable."

"That's a lot of work, Amanda," Zoe says slowly. "I know you are one of my most reliable baristas, but still . . ."

Sensing my chances slip away I take a deep breath and cut in. "Don't you always say that a smart entrepreneur is one who doesn't just see an opportunity, but takes it?"

She knows I'm right, but I can tell she's taking a minute to walk through the risks and benefits in her mind. "I guess I do say that."

She's wobbling. She's thinking about it.

Cheryl jumps in. "I'll be in the kitchen most mornings and can help Amanda get set up. And my nephew Luke is her age. He's usually working the tree lot and ringing up customers, so it's not like she'll be out there alone. She'll have plenty of support."

"Well, a couple of people were wanting more shifts, too, so I could cover your regular hours here, and you'd get your normal hours plus extra weekends out there . . . ," she says almost to herself.

Come on. Come on . . .

"Okay, how about this. Amanda and I will take a ride out to your farm during her shift on Friday to see what we're working with. And if it feels like it's not going to pull time or resources from here, well then, we will give it a try." Zoe clicks her pen, back in control of the situation.

Yes!

Cheryl replies, "Great, it's a date!"

Zoe flinches almost imperceptibly at word date. For a moment, she meets Cheryl's bright smile and steady gaze, then almost immediately breaks the look, a little flustered. Zoe snaps her notebook shut and stands for a quick exit. "Sounds good. I have to go update some orders. I'll see you Friday."

"Well, isn't that just wonderful. Christmas magic is happening at the old Post Farm," Mrs. Novak gushes. "I guess I gotta run too. I don't want to leave Marissa alone in the store too long. No sense, this girl, all she does is watch those Tic Tacs on her phone, I tell ya. Okay then, toodle-di-doo. Oh, and don't mind if I do." Mrs. Novak snags a piece of fudge from the open box on the counter and pops it in her mouth. She smiles wistfully. "MMMMMmmm, that's the stuff. Tastes like Christmas," she says before turning on her heel and trotting out the door.

Yes! Yes! Yes! This is gonna be the extra cash I need.

Look out Europe, here I come!

DECEMBER
3

Chapter 3
OH, WHAT FUN!

"Oh my gosh, it's freezing out here," Junjun says, his hands stuffed into his pockets. He's trying to retract his head into the high neck of his peacoat like a turtle so that only his nose, glasses, and tan beanie are sticking out. "Tell me again, why are we standing in the parking lot? And why are we all the way over here by the dumpsters and the snow pile?"

We are standing in a small circle at the far end of the White Pine High parking lot. We all received the same cryptic text from Max last period to meet him in this spot for something that's "Gonna be fire!"

"Celeste, do you even know what this is all about?" Jun bounces in place to warm himself.

"I thought you knew?" Celeste pulls her wool hat tighter over her red curls. "All he told me was that he needed me to take a picture of him for the yearbook, because you told him to?"

"No, I didn't." Jun's voice is muffled by his coat collar.

"I guess I told him," I chime in. "Jun, I said that you wanted all the photos in for pep club ASAP so we could start laying out those pages. We still needed a photo of him in his Bobby the Bobcat suit. I didn't know he wanted to take a new one, I thought he'd just give you one of the ones from the trampoline dunk contest. You know before . . ."

"Before he missed the shot and took a flying dive into the concrete wall in front of the entire school, not to mention his livestream audience?" Jun giggles.

I try to restrain my laughter and instead make some kind of a *snurk* sound.

Yikes, did I just snort?

Now, Junjun's fully laughing.

"You guys, it's not funny," Celeste scolds. "He could have really hurt himself! Thank goodness, the giant bobcat head protected his face from the impact." Junjun is bent over crying-laughing, and even Celeste, in spite of herself, can't keep a straight face.

"Oh, *what* is he gonna do now?" Celeste rubs her hands in their homemade mittens together for warmth. "I better get my camera ready. Jun get yours out too. He's gonna want video of whatever this is for his channel." She sighs and starts digging in her oversized tan vegan leather slouch to fish out her phone.

They do make an odd couple. I mean, how do I even describe Maximus Rex Pearce, a kid who sounds like he's named after three German shepherds? According to Max, his dad actually named him after the main character of the film *Gladiator*. His dad, the Jet Ski–riding, protein shake–drinking, bow hunting, fake-tanned founder and successful owner of Pearce Automotives. But despite his overbearingly old-school alpha dad, Max is a sweetheart. And he's trying to find his own thing to set him apart from the Pearce name. Unfortunately, at the moment, that thing is becoming a YouTube celebrity.

Celeste and Max are super into each other. It's mostly pretty sweet. It bothered me when they became a couple freshman year, but I got over it. We've all been friends since kindergarten, and I guess soft-spoken, witchy-empath Celeste is just the yin to his yang.

Plus, I have Jun. He moved from the Philippines to White Pine in third grade. I remember the first time I met him at school. Even though he was new and could have been nervous, he just smiled, stuck out his hand for me to shake like a tiny businessman, and said, "Hi, you can call me Junjun," and that was it. We've been friends ever since.

Jun and his family are very involved in the Fil-Am community in southern Vermont. He's super proud of his heritage and always invites us whenever there is a traditional Tinikling dance performance or, my favorite, karaoke night. He's upbeat, friendly, super popular and is president of the White Pine High Pep Club, the LGBTQ+ Association Student Council rep, and editor of the yearbook. Without him, I'd be even more hopeless when it comes to hair and fashion and skin routines. He's definitely my best friend. They all are.

"I'm freezing." Jun is clearly ready to move this along. "I'm going to text him and see what the big surprise is. You know I'll do anything for pep club and yearbook, but I draw the line at hypothermia!"

Before Jun can remove his gloves to fire off a text, we see the unmistakable giant furry head of Bobby the Bobcat cresting the top of the ten-foot-high snowpile in front of us.

"Wait, is he holding a sled?" Jun screeches, horrified and amused.

"Hey, guys, it's me!"

Uh, yeah, who else would it be?

By now, a small coterie of kids who spotted Max across the lot are heading over to see what's happening.

"Hey, sweetie!" Bobby the Bobcat waves to Celeste.

"Oh, Max, be careful!" Celeste covers her mouth with a nubby mitten.

"It's cool. I have my bike helmet on under here. It'll be fine." Max straightens his giant costume head and steels himself.

"Okay." Celeste yells up, scared yet smitten.

"Hey, White Pine High! You ready?!"

The small crowd starts to cheer and heckle as Max makes thumbs-up signals with his big furry paws, before mounting his red plastic sled atop the Mount Everest of ice piles. "Let me hear you make some noise!"

The crowd obliges, phones out, recording, ready.

"Okay. One, two, three!" He pushes off screaming "Maximumdanger, like and subscribe!" as he sails down the icy mound.

Celeste snaps a great shot of him, paws in the air, White Pine

High logo on the Bobcat's jersey in full view.

Look out!

He hits a chunk of ice right before the bottom and for two seconds is airborne, before crashing in a roll on the icy verge.

Celeste runs over. "Oh, sweetie, are you okay?!"

Max pulls off the furry bobcat head to reveal his bike helmet and gives the small crowd a thumbs-up. They hoot and cheer and then almost instantly lose interest and disperse as Celeste kneels in the snow to tend to her man. Jun and I circle in too.

"Yeah, I'm fine. Did you get the shot? Was it good? Let me see!" Max is like a puppy waiting for a treat. Celeste hands over her phone. "Nice!"

"And here's the video," Jun says, handing Max his phone.

"Awwww, sick, check out the air on that jump! Bro, you gotta post this and tag me."

"Oh, of course, I wouldn't dream of not!" Jun says sarcastically. "But more importantly, can you walk? I mean, like, can we go now?"

"Oh yeah, I think so." Max stands up a little stiffly in the awkward cat suit, supported by Celeste who's picked up his costume head and is still fussing over him. "Oh no, my sled, I broke it," Max says, deflated. It's cracked in half and missing a giant chunk of plastic.

"Well, you will just have to ask Santa for a new one," Jun says, picking up the shards and tossing them in the dumpster. "Come on, let's go."

Oh, Santa, right!

"Hey, guys, speaking of Santa, I wanted to see how you all feel about doing a Secret Santa this year instead of getting presents for everyone?"

"Well, I still want to get something special for my sweetie here." Max winks at Celeste in a ridiculously over-the-top way that she seems to love.

Jun's and my eyes roll back so far they touch our brains, but we recover.

"Yeah, I mean, you're a couple, you do your couple thing, but for the rest of us, for the group. Secret Santa could be fun! Plus, we can all save a little cash for other stuff, like traveling."

"Oh, I see, this is about your trip," Celeste says gently.

"My trip? It's your trip too!"

"Yeah, you know what I mean." She shrugs dismissively.

"Why not save our cash for summer and still have a fun way to do Christmas together? Is that so bad?"

"Sounds fun to me," Jun says, always an adder. "We can make, like, a party of it."

"Yeah, you know I like to party," Max agrees on cue, limping ever-so-slightly as we reach our cars.

Celeste is contemplative. "I was thinking I wanted to do some kind of gathering for the winter solstice on the twenty-first anyway. We can exchange our gifts then."

"Great, that's awesome!" I'm so relieved I'm already tallying my savings in my head.

"So should we all just come by Matcha tomorrow and do the

names-in-a-hat bit?" Celeste asks.

"Oh no, that won't work. I forgot to mention, and I'll know for sure tomorrow, but it looks like I'll probably not be in the shop most of the month. I'm going to set up a hot cocoa pop-up at the Christmas tree place out on Route 9."

"Post Farm?" Max asks as he pulls off his cat legs and tosses them in the cab of his truck.

"Yeah, Cheryl Post is the baker who does all the pastries for the shop, and it was her idea. I'm pretty excited. I think I can make a ton of tips. If it works out, you guys should all come out and see me."

"Huh, yeah, I guess so, we'll see." Max is oddly reserved all of a sudden. "Come on, Celeste, I think I might need to find some Advil. Jun, you need a ride?"

"Yeah, I'll come with you, my sister has the car today. Bye, Amanda, tell us when you know about your schedule, and we'll plan the Secret Santa name-draw. Text me later. Mwah!" Junjun blows a little kiss, Celeste gives me a wave, and they drive off.

Okay, this is good. Everything is going exactly to plan, I think as I get in my car and crank up the radio to the open scratches of RUN DMC's "Christmas in Hollis" and drive home in the waning afternoon light.

DECEMBER 4

Chapter 4

OH, CHRISTMAS TREES

"Really, Amanda, when was the last time you cleaned your car?" Zoe asks, brushing off the passenger seat of my ancient station wagon.

"I don't know, summer?"

"Yeah, I can tell," she quips, tucking her cashmere camel coat under her as she slides in. "Add a few shells to the sand on your floor mats, and I'll feel like I'm at the beach."

Remind me to never offer a ride to my super-particular boss ever again.

"Take a left up here, and we can skip the after-school bus traffic," she says, pointing to a side road.

I check my mirrors, signal, and comply.

Zoe turns her attention to her phone. I put the radio on low and listen to Brenda Lee rocking around the Christmas tree.

As we reach the edge of town, the buildings start to space out, and there are bigger drifts of old snow along the edges of the road. Neighborhoods turn to open fields, and white hills dappled by bare trees and green pines rise to join the far-off mountain ridges in the distance. We pass the turn off to the White Mountain Lodge. In the thin afternoon sunlight, we see the familiar hulking figure of a large red Vermont barn. A busted, hand-painted plywood sign with a spray-painted arrow reads "Fresh Trees This Way."

"I think we can do better than that," Zoe says, almost to herself.

"Do you want to text Cheryl to tell her we're almost there?"

"I don't have Cheryl's number. Why would I?" Zoe replies a little briskly.

"Oh, sorry, I thought 'cause she's your baker, I mean."

"No, I do my ordering through her website. I don't text with my vendors."

Geez, what's her problem?

"Okay, sorry." I ten-and-two it, eyes front. I see an auxiliary parking lot in a field to my right but make a left turn to park in the smaller lot in front of the huge barn doors. Gravel crunches under my boots when I step out of the car. I notice Zoe, still in her seat, has pulled down the passenger side mirror to quickly touch up her lip tint. She flips it back up and joins me.

"Okay, let's see what we're working with." Zoe pulls on her sleek leather gloves.

The farm is laid out along the road. Beside the barn, the gravel drive continues to the edge of the lawn of the old, white farmhouse. In the center, there is a sizable horseshoe-shaped customer lot. The front door of the house is accessed by a classic farmer's porch topped with two peaked dormers in the low, sloped roof. Bumping out from the front porch, a two-story section of the house features a big bay window. A longer side porch provides cover for another door, probably leading to the kitchen. All the roof crests and dormers are detailed with the kind of decorative wood trim that makes the building look like a real-life gingerbread house. In the front yard, under a bare sugar maple tree, is a wood sign reading "Post Farm" in faded gold letters.

There's nothing in the way of Christmas decorations, aside from a wilted wreath on the front door. It doesn't do much to distract from the chipped paint on the siding. The old house is clearly in need of some love.

At the top of the lot between the barn and the house is a stone firepit ringed by tree stumps for seating. A lonely fire throws shuddering light on the dark clearing that leads to the rows of cut-your-own trees behind it. The warm bulbs of string lights cast a cozy glow. Near the barn side of the lot, there's a plywood stand of fresh-cut trees, and one of those funnel contraptions that they shove the trees through to wrap them in plastic netting. Another plywood rack holds handsaws, stacked plastic sleds, and spools of bundling twine—tools customers can use to cut and transport their own trees. But there doesn't seem to be anyone around at the moment.

Across the lot, closer to the house, is a sad-looking wooden stand. More of a shack really, with an open counter window about chest high. It's lit only by a hanging cage lamp on an extension cord and the orange coils of an ancient space heater. An old-fashioned metal cash register sits on the counter.

Sheesh, not exactly Christmas cozy.

I turn to Zoe to check her reaction and, before anything sarcastic can spill from my mouth, the side porch door opens and Cheryl steps out in a pool of warm light.

"Cheryl!" Zoe yells brightly, waving to her across the lot.

Even in the low light, I can see Cheryl smile and wave back as she jog-walks down the porch steps to greet us. "Hey, you made it!" She's smiling brightly and making eye contact with us both but landing on Zoe.

"Yeah, not so busy though, is it?" Zoe asks.

"Things will pick up after five. Friday night is usually a good tree night, mostly families grabbing precuts. But on the weekend, that's our really busy time, from now until Christmas Eve. People come to cut their own trees and hike and make a day of it. If there's snow, it's even better. Which is why a stand with hot cocoa, coffee, fudge, and maybe a few simple pastry options is a no-brainer."

"And this is where you see us having the pop-up?" Zoe gestures toward the shack with a gloved hand.

"Yeah." Cheryl smiles. "Come on over and I'll show ya. It's bigger than it looks."

We cross the lot to survey the shack. It does feel roomy on the inside—maybe four feet by six feet— but dusty and full of pine needles.

"We used to use this to sell snacks back in the day," Cheryl says, leaning on the edge of the shack's open counter. "Now, people just pay for their trees here."

"Do you use that old register?" I ask, trying to get a closer look. "That thing is cool!"

"No, we have a cashbox. The register just kind of lives in here. It's pretty heavy to move in and out. Honestly, it's probably jammed shut." Cheryl shrugs.

"Too bad. It gives cool, old-timey candy-shop vibes."

"I see you have electricity out here." Zoe changes the subject to the business at hand.

"Yeah, there are a couple of outlets so you can plug in your coffee and cocoa urns." Cheryl looks over her shoulder at the house. "You can either bring them full, or you can do prep in the kitchen. I get here before sunup to prep my orders, so I can even start them if that's easier."

"Okay, Amanda," Zoe says, looking from me to the shack. "Why don't you figure out what we're going to need to dress this up a little bit. If we're putting the Matcha-Do name on it, I want it to be on-brand." Cheryl steps back and gestures for me to make myself at home.

I take a look around as they walk toward the house. I'm not sure Zoe is convinced this whole idea is worth the trouble, but I'm determined to make it work. The extra tips alone could be huge.

The shack has good bones, and the old cash register is really cool. It's covered with fine carved designs, with a crank handle on the side and a glass pane across the top showing a half-raised tab that says "Cash." I think the register is made of brass. Too bad they left it to tarnish.

With a little sweeping, a wipe down, and maybe some fairy lights and shelf paper, I can make the place look a lot better. I'll grab some glass-domed cake stands from the coffee shop to display the fudge and snag some of my mom's black-and-red checkered craft ribbon to tie some pine garlands. It's not like they're short on pine branches. Oh, we could even get some skewers and packaged marshmallows, chocolate, and graham crackers so customers can make s'mores by the fire. I'm starting to get excited by the potential.

I am squatting to check out the shelf space under the counter when I hear a deep, kind-of-stern voice from above me: "What are you doing? Customers aren't allowed back there."

I stand up to explain to whoever it is that I'm not a customer and find myself face-to-face with a set of dark brown eyes.

What was I going to say?

The voice came from a boy about my age. He's tall. His deep-set eyes are framed by dark, thick brows. He has a strong, straight nose, crisp jaw, and a lean, corded neck that disappears into the open sheepskin collar of a tan corduroy work jacket. His dark hair is visible just under the temples of his navy wool cap, and he has a faint shadow of stubble over what I can only describe as impossibly full lips.

Whoever this is, he's hot.

"Oh," he says, seemingly just as surprised to see me as I am him. But it doesn't last long. "What are you doing?" he asks again brusquely.

His totally unnecessary, crappy tone snaps me out of my stupor, and I wind up to tell him exactly who I am and ask him what his problem is when Cheryl returns with Zoe.

"Luke, there you are. I want to introduce you to everyone." Cheryl indicates Zoe and me with a gloved hand. "This is Zoe, she owns Matcha-Do in town."

"Hello, Luke," Zoe says. He gives her his hand to shake.

"And this is Amanda." Cheryl points to me, still standing behind the counter of the shack like a hapless checkout girl at a drive-through. He looks over at me but doesn't even muster up a hello.

You want fries with that, jerk?

"We were just talking about cleaning up the shack here to do a coffee and hot cocoa pop-up," Cheryl explains. "We're going to sell Nan's fudge and some pastries. Amanda's going to set things up and run it."

Zoe sighs but says with a smile, "I'll be honest, Cheryl, I wasn't quite convinced when we pulled up. But, man, you've got a great kitchen in there. The layout of this house is to die for." Zoe is surprisingly animated. "And the porches, it's just aching to be a B and B or a garden café, at least, with the right kind of renovation."

"I know, right?" Cheryl sounds like she's been waiting to hear someone else say this her whole life. "There's a big kitchen garden out the back, and the porch goes all the way around. In the summer, the view of the mountain is spectacular, and I always dreamed of having some kind of farm-to-table breakfast and lunch café. Maybe even rent a couple of rooms on Airbnb in the summer and fall. It could be such a cute spot."

Cheryl and Zoe are clearly running away with dreams of floor plans and menus when Luke interjects, "So, wait, she's gonna be in the shack?" He points his thumb over his shoulder at me like a hitchhiker.

Uh, excuse me, I have a name and I am right here.

"How's this supposed to work? I use this space to ring up."

"There's plenty of space for both, you guys can figure it out, Luke." Cheryl dismisses his concerns with a wave.

"Have you told Hank about this yet?" Luke asks, raising his strong brows for emphasis.

By now the last of the winter sun is gone and the carriage lamps on the barn and house have come on, adding to the flickering light of the fire. As if on cue, a silhouetted figure in a boxy work coat and earflap trapper hat lugging a chainsaw walks out of the trees and steps into the firelight. His salt-and-pepper mountain-man beard and dark eyes glint with the orange of the flames.

Gah! This must be Hank.

"Oh, excuse my brother." Cheryl is unfazed and raises her voice to carry. "Can you put the chainsaw down, Hank? You look like a serial killer. Come over here. I'd like you to meet Zoe and Amanda, the people who are going to do the pop-up we discussed."

Hank sets his chainsaw down by the fire and walks over. Up

close, he's a lot less scary. Shorter than Luke, stocky and strong, he has the same dark eyes, but his seem somehow sad. He nods at us both in lieu of a hello and then stands there silently.

"Hi, Hank, thanks for having us," Zoe says in her all-business way. "This is a good setup you have here, a lot you could do with the place."

I notice the headlights of the cars on Route 9 slowing and multiple sets of orange blinkers flashing as they wait to turn into the lot. The Friday night rush is starting.

"Respectfully, I think things are just fine the way they are," Hank says in a soft low voice. "But Cheryl has let me know the stand is something she wants to do, and it's her house, too, so that's what we'll do."

"Well, great, that works for us." Zoe is ready to wrap up and get started on her to-do list. "What time can Amanda come to set up?"

Hank shrugs before murmuring, "We open at nine, so best be before that."

"That work for you?" Zoe looks at me like, *Don't say yes unless you mean it. This is going to be on you.*

But I'm here for it. This is going to be my way to make the money I need for Europe.

"Yeah, no problem at all," I say, sealing the deal. "I'll be here bright and early to set up."

"Luke, you'll help this young woman with whatever she needs," his father adds.

Luke sighs in a way I find, frankly, a little over the top. "Fine."

"Don't worry, I won't take up much space," I use my most sweetly sarcastic pick-me voice, and Zoe shoots me a look to knock it off, but it seems like the dig went right over lumberjack Luke's head. He is already making his way toward the first evening customers.

"All right then, we'll leave you to it." Zoe slips her phone into her bag and zips it with finality. "It was nice to meet you, Hank."

"You too. See you tomorrow, Amanda," Hank says, looking at me intently. I think he noticed the dig.

Gotta watch where you sling those arrows, Amanda, my dad always says.

Cheryl walks us toward my car. "Don't mind them." She seems to have heard my inner dialogue. "They're just two guys living alone together on a farm. It's a big day if you get ten words out of them. They are not used to company, other than customers." The sound of car doors and the joyful chirps and squeals of kids running toward the tree lot fill the air. "They snap out of it once you get to know 'em."

"If you say so, Cheryl." Zoe raises her eyebrows. "I don't know how you stand it living out here."

"Oh, I don't, I have a place in town, over by George's Pub. I'm just out here all the time to bake. You ever stop in there? George's, I mean?" Cheryl looks Zoe in the eye. "I'm a regular for their Friday night happy hour. It's half-off truffle fries if you ever want to stop by. I'll probably go there in a bit."

"Oh, me? Uh, no. It's a small town and I know all the business owners, so I don't like to socialize downtown unless it's work-related. You know how that is. Keep your private life private." Then she adds offhandedly, "But I do go over to the White Mountain Lodge for a glass of Sancerre from time to time."

"Oh, okay, good to know," Cheryl replies nonchalantly.

Hmmm. Well, what was that I just witnessed?

"Anyway, I won't be here in the morning," Zoe says. "I want to open up the shop, but I'll come by later. Amanda will be here bright and early."

"With Christmas bells on!" I say merrily as Cheryl smiles and turns back to the house.

I unlock the doors and we get in the car. Zoe sits down with a little smile on her face, but then almost immediately starts in on me as soon as she catches me looking.

"Really, Amanda, this car. Not only is the interior filthy, but your hood is covered in pawprints! You have a cat or something?" Her chiding tone is a clear signal to change the subject.

"A cat? No!" I have no idea what she's talking about, but I do know a car wash is gonna have to wait. I have a business to start!

It's going to be a busy day tomorrow.

DECEMBER
5

Chapter 5
DECK THE STALL

It's about 7:00 a.m. and the sun is just rising as I pull into the lot at Post Farm. And I have a good feeling about today. I've loaded my car with cleaning supplies, decorations, paper cups, lids, service items, ground coffee, cocoa mix, and two 100-cup coffee urns.

After we left last night, I took Zoe back to the shop and we planned everything. I guess she worked out a deal with Cheryl to have her provide the milk and some other food stuff. Cheryl will prep batches of hot drinks in the morning before I arrive. At least, that's what Zoe told me when she looked up from their rapid exchange of texts.

I guess she did get Cheryl's number, after all.

It makes life easier for me. Today, I am mostly focused on decorating and setup. I grab the first load from my car and head toward the warm lights of the kitchen porch as a few flakes of light snow swirl in the morning cold.

When I knock on the porch door, I hear a bright "Come on in, it's open!"

Boy, Cheryl sure is chipper this early in the morning. Bakers.

I step into the warmth of the old farm kitchen and am instantly engulfed in the delicious smells of chocolate and cookies.

The kitchen is big, with a large, porcelain double sink under a window that looks out over the back garden and the mountains. There's an old wood cabinet with a marble countertop and little drawers next to the sink that looks like a relic from the original farm kitchen. In contrast, every other counter is stainless steel, and the walls are hung with tools, utensils, and open shelves showing jarred ingredients neatly labeled. Two massive stand mixers sit next to a stainless-steel double oven and range. Cheryl is working at the large butcher block island, carefully icing little shorts and buttons on trays of fresh gingerbread men.

It's like stepping into Mrs. Claus's workshop . . . complete with a grumpy elf. Luke Post sits silently on a stool at the island, warming his hands on a morning cup of coffee. He doesn't look up when I enter. He's dressed in jeans and a white T-shirt. His dark hair, short but shaggy on the top, is mussed like he just woke up. His arms are lean and muscular, and, judging by the way his shirt is stretched across his chest and broad shoulders, hoisting Christmas trees is a great workout.

Oh my God, what is wrong with me? Stop staring at his pecs, Amanda!

He looks at me for a moment. I manage an awkward smile, but he says nothing and goes back to finishing his last sip of coffee.

"Mornin'! I brought the coffee and cocoa." I hold up my bags. "And a bunch more stuff in the car."

"Hi, Amanda! That's great. You can just put that stuff right there next to the coats." Cheryl points to a row of hooks behind me over the ubiquitous snow boot pile. "Luke, go out and help her get the rest of the stuff, please."

I set down my bags, and when I turn back, Luke is standing right in front of me. He is tall, at least six feet, and his brown eyes are intense. He's standing unnecessarily close, and I can feel the warmth of the kitchen flush my cheeks. He smells really good, like pine needles and laundry soap.

"'Scuse me," he mumbles, and reaches one arm past me to grab his work coat, with a flannel shirt still layered inside, hanging on a hook behind my head.

I move aside. He throws on his coat, steps into a pair of lined rubber workboots, and opens the door.

"You coming?" He turns back, and framed in the doorway with snowflakes dancing behind him, it's like he's in a hot lumberjack snow globe.

"Uh, yeah, right." I shake my head to clear it. "Coming." I follow him out. "I'm parked over by the barn," I say.

"That makes no sense. Why don't you pull all the way up to the shack and save us some carrying?"

I feel my face tighten and flush again at his backhanded dig.

"Yeah, okay. Fine."

What the heck? *That makes no sense?!* I parked in the parking lot 'cause I didn't know if it'd be okay to pull up. I didn't want to annoy chainsaw Hank. I'm fuming as I get in my car and drive toward where Luke's waiting next to the stand.

Instead of stopping, I whip a quick sharp right, then back the wagon's trunk right up to him and park with the precision of an astronaut docking on a space station.

"Better?" I ask, shutting my door crisply.

"Uh, yeah." He looks at me a little surprised and confused.

Bet you didn't think girls could drive, either. Am I making sense now?

I am pleased with myself but also notice that I'm kinda crashing out and need to rein it in before I say something I don't mean to.

Relax, Amanda.

The more reasonable part of my brain takes charge. I take a deep breath and recover my calm.

"I thought I could stack all the stuff right here. I'll clean the shack first, then decorate, then set up." I try to take charge.

"Whatever you want," he says while he unloads. "But just so you know, I will need to keep the cashbox in there and may need to get in and out when it starts to get busy later."

"Yeah, sure. I'll leave some space on the shelves." I don't make eye contact.

"Anything else?"

"No, we're good." I look around at the neatly stacked bags of supplies.

"Okay. Then I need to go get ready for my actual job." Luke

turns and heads back to the house.

What is up with this guy? He may be hot, but he has the personality of a lump of coal. It doesn't matter anyway. I'm here for one purpose and one purpose only: make some money to buy my train tickets.

I won't even remember lumberjack Luke's name when I'm sipping an espresso and writing in my journal in a café in Rome.

The next hour and a half go by in a blur of sweeping and scrubbing and organizing and decorating. I manage to get the little shack looking respectable. I line all the shelves with clean white shelf paper and all my cups and essentials are stacked neatly. I scrub the counter and lay a black-and-red checkered runner over it. I also make some really cute garlands with pine branches I found near the cut-tree stand. I frame the window with dangling icicle lights and staple the garland over them. Some extra-large Styrofoam candy canes and gingerbread men from Helen Novak's pile of window display items complete the look. I've got three glass-covered cake stands and white glass pastry trays waiting to be filled with Cheryl's fudge. I tack two wood-framed chalkboards to the rough wood slats above the window. One says "Matcha-Do about Hot Cocoa" in my best cursive to stay on-brand, and on the other is the menu list. With the old cash register on the counter, the whole look is giving old-timey-Willy-Wonka-candy-shop-meets-Santa's-Village.

I'm standing in front of the shack admiring my work, when one of my foam candy canes breaks free of its clear packing tape fastener and falls down.

Shoot. I'm gonna need some wire to keep those up there.

I pick up the giant candy cane and walk over to the tree stand to see if there's anything laying around I can use. Nope. I cross over to the small door on the side of the red barn to see what I can find in there.

Inside, it's the usual farm barn stuff: A tractor, snowblower, snow shovels, big branch clippers, and hardware hanging from hooks on the wall. But it's all big tools. No workbench.

The center of the barn has been partitioned with a temporary wall, and there's a door in it. Maybe through there?

As I reach for the handle, the door opens and Luke steps out.

"Ahhh!"

We both startle, and I lift the giant foam candy cane like a baseball bat, ready to swing for my own protection. Then I realize how crazy I probably look.

"Sorry." I giggle and lower my weapon of mass confection.

"What are you doing in here?" he asks without even cracking a smile.

Oh my God, for real? A random girl just tries to smash you with a giant foam candy cane and nothing?

"I was looking for something to hang my candy cane. Stronger tape or wire or something?"

"There's some in the house. Ask Cheryl." He is curt, exhaling a cloud of steam. "Please don't come into this part of the barn."

So serious. I decide this guy is totally not worth another thought. He's so uptight, it's almost funny.

"Okay, sorry. I didn't realize it was such a big deal. I figured that was a tool room or something." I try to peek over his shoulder through the doorway.

"No, it's not." Luke pulls the door all the way shut. "It's my room. And it's off-limits."

"Bro, you live in a barn?" I am apparently unable to stop my thoughts from spilling out of my mouth.

"Yes. It's a converted loft. And it's my space. Anything you need you can get in the house."

"Okay, understood. My bad, won't happen again." I raise my hands (and candy cane) and slowly back away like I'm leaving the scene of crime.

Sheesh, this guy. The OG—original Grinch. I chuckle at my own hilariousness.

Back outside I see Hank over by the road putting out the sign. Cheryl is inside the stand placing fudge on the cake trays. She's got the drink urns all set up.

"Amanda, it looks great!" She smiles, her hands busy. "I love it. Totally *Charlie and the Chocolate Factory*."

"That's what I was going for!" *Finally, somebody gets it.* "Hey, do you have any wire? I lost a candy cane." I wave the offending giant candy.

"Check in the old kitchen cabinet, first drawer."

I go in the house and open the first little drawer on the wood cabinet by the sink and there it is. Perfect.

Out of nowhere, a gray-and-peach calico cat darts past my feet and stops at the archway between the kitchen and the hall. It sits prettily, tail draped over its feet, and looks at me with probing amber-green eyes.

"Hey, kitty, where'd you come from?" I coo. "Cheryl didn't tell me she had a cat."

I crouch down, hand outstretched, rubbing my fingers together as I inch toward the cat. It casually turns and walks into the hall, then disappears through another archway. I worry about Luke scolding me for trespassing for, like, a nanosecond and decide to follow the cat anyway.

I find myself in a little parlor. There are two damask-patterned gray wingback chairs framing a brick hearth. A painting of the whole farm hangs over the mantle. There's a light blue velvet sofa with quilted throw pillows near the bay window and an oval wood coffee table sits on a hand-knotted rug. On the opposite wall, there's a brown spinet piano and bench.

But absolutely no sign of a cat.

"Where'd you go, kitty?"

Weird. But my curiosity takes hold and I step farther into the room. On the top of the piano, next to a stack of piano books, is a framed photo. I lean my candy cane on the side of the piano and pick the photo up to take a closer look.

"This must be Nancy," I say to no one in particular, wiping a layer of dust from the glass to reveal a formal portrait of a dark-eyed woman in her late fifties with a warmhearted smile.

I put the photo back and look through the books. *Christmas*

Carols for Four Hands. I smile at the memories of my mom and I playing Christmas duets together.

Hmm, we haven't had a chance to do that this year.

I trace a line in the layer of dust on the piano lid. No one's played this in a while.

Probably seriously out of tune.

I lift the lid, hit middle C, and hear it's surprisingly not that bad.

I sit on the bench, grab one of the books, and open to a well-worn page marked with an old photo of two boys bundled up in snowsuits and standing together next to a snowman. They must be about six and maybe ten? I look on the back and see faint pencil handwriting: Rob and Hank, X-mas '82.

Wow, that must be baby Hank, but who's Rob?

The carol on the page it's bookmarking is one of my favorites, "Have Yourself a Merry Little Christmas." I begin to play and I don't really realize I've begun to sing.

Someday soon, we all will be together
If the fates allow
Until then, we'll have to muddle through somehow . . .

"Ahem . . ." Someone behind me clears their throat before I can finish the line.

I whirl around expecting to see Luke ready to tell me off again. But it's Hank, standing in the doorway looking, well, I can't exactly tell. Looking kind of intense.

"Oh, I'm so sorry, I didn't mean to intrude. I was just following your cat, and I came in here and I saw the piano and . . ."

"We don't have a cat," he interrupts my gushing.

Wait, what? I definitely saw a cat.

"Oh I . . . I mean I thought I saw . . ."

"It's nine a.m. We've got the first cars arriving. You'd better get out there."

"Yes, right, of course. Sorry, okay." I am desperate to make an escape or have the ground open and swallow me whole, whatever happens first.

I slink by him, head tucked, speed walking.

"Amanda," he says quietly. I turn back, terrified.

"You forgot your candy cane." He hands me the ridiculous prop.

Is he smiling?

"Thanks!" I reply in a breath. I grab the cane and go.

Fantastic start to your first day on the farm, Mandy.

Oh boy, this is gonna be a long December.

DECEMBER 6

Chapter 6
SECRET SANTA SURPRISE

"We're almost all out of cocoa and halfway through the coffee. Can you start me another?" I yell to Cheryl over the line of red-cheeked, cold-nosed, happy kids and families waiting to warm up with something from the shack. "Oh, and more fudge. Keep it comin'!"

Cheryl gives me a thumbs-up from the porch and heads back inside.

It's Sunday afternoon, sunny, clear, and cold, and the tree lot is bumping. Groups of cut-your-own tree families are trailing out of the woods, dragging their prizes on sleds. They've found beautiful blue spruces and balsam pines, and all kinds of other varieties of tree that I've always lumped together under the general heading of "Christmas."

Hank's hovering near the tree line to guide folks to the shack, and there are a number of college kids and seasonal workers on hand to keep the operation running. There's a cozy gathering of folks enjoying a warm-up by the roaring firepit. From time to time, Hank heads over to add a log and stir the fire. It seems to be his thing. As I was closing up to head home yesterday, I saw him sitting on one of the stumps just staring into the fire like he was trying to divine the future.

Or maybe he was thinking about the past.

Either way, he's definitely a strange guy.

I can see where Luke gets his friendly chattiness.

Luke is across the lot, managing the precut sales, baling, and helping folks tie trees to their cars. I pause to catch my breath between hot cocoa pours and find myself watching him. He lifts a tree on top of an SUV, and as he's reaching to tie it down, his shirt and sweater lift, revealing a set of incredibly toned, smooth abs. There's a dark line of hair tracing from his belly button toward the top of the boxers peeking out from his jeans.

He may not be much of a talker, but he sure is easy on the eyes.

I snap out of it and top off two hot cocoas with some mini marshmallows before ringing up a grateful and exhausted mom. She passes the cups into the grasping hands of her two kids like a robin dropping worms into the beaks of hungry baby birds.

"Thanks so much! This is for you. Merry Christmas." She drops a five-dollar bill in a very full tip jar on the counter.

Woo-hoo! I love the holidays.

"Thank you. Merry Christmas!" I reply to her generosity.

It's been a busy day and my feet are killing me, but the tips are totally worth it. Yesterday was pretty good, but with the sun out and everyone making a day of it, today has been *great.*

My phone buzzes in my pocket. It's Celeste telling me she and Max picked up Jun and they are on their way.

Yay! I can't wait to see them. It feels like it's been ages. Plus, I'm about ready for the break. The sun is getting low, and it seems like the cut-your-own tree crowd is winding down. I should get a second to breathe.

Dang, my phone is gonna die.

I'm pulling out my charger when Luke walks up.

"Can I get the cashbox please?" I reach under the counter and hand it to him to so he can deposit his sales. "I see you fixed your candy cane," he says, not looking up from his task. "The stand looks nice."

Whoa, is bro making conversation? Okay, I'm game.

"Thanks. Too bad you can't get the register working," I add, trying to be friendly. "It's so cool. I tried the buttons and they seem to all work, but the drawer won't pop open. I think the springs are rusted shut. I bet all it would take is some WD-40 and brass polish and it'd be good as new."

He looks at me, one of his dark brows raised in interest, as if this is the first reasonable thing I've said since I met him.

"What?" I say maybe a little too defensively. I have a dad with a tool bench in the garage who likes to tinker, I've picked up a few things.

"Nothing." He resumes his usual stony expression and I let it go.

"You want something?" I ask reflexively. "Coffee or a cocoa?"

There go his eyebrows again, this time both, raised in genuine surprise at the question. He thinks for a moment.

"Uh, yeah, that'd be nice. A hot chocolate, please."

Okay, normal human communication back on track. We're getting somewhere.

I pour him a cup and ask, "Marshmallow or whipped cream? Or both? I know the owner, I can hook you up." Now making it my personal mission to see if I can get Frosty here to thaw.

"Neither," he says, and he grabs a piece of the milk chocolate gingerbread spice fudge and drops in his cup.

"Oh, I see! Now that is the move." I am impressed.

"Yup, it's a Post family secret. That's the best way to eat Nan's fudge. Don't tell anyone."

Oh dang, is he lightening up?

My phone buzzes again. Dangerously low battery. I get back to plugging it in while he sips his cocoa, enjoying a lull in the busy afternoon.

The heavy-duty outlets near the counter are all full with the coffee warmers and the ancient space heater. I only have a short charger and nowhere to rest my phone, so I unplug the heater, move it to the other side of counter, and start to plug it into an ancient extension cord below.

"Don't do that. Are you nuts?" Luke yells like I'm about to stick my hand in a rattlesnake nest.

What the heck? I drop the cord and stare at him, agog.

"What is the big deal?" I demand.

"You can't plug a heater into an extension cord. You could start a fire." His dark eyes are boring into mine.

"Okay, fine, geez." I put all the plugs and cords back the way they were.

"Listen, it's not a joke. You can't be starting fires in a wood shack on a farm full of timber. It's just basic common sense." Luke sets his empty cocoa cup down on the counter with finality.

Oh, this dude is insufferable. This is like Olympic medal–level mansplaining.

"Okay, I get it." I glare at him, hating that he's probably right. But geez, nothing actually happened.

I'm about to wind up and say something quippy to ring the bell for round two when I hear Junjun's unmistakably chipper voice.

"Hey, hey, my hot cocoa queen! We made it. Look at your little Candy Shack, it's soo cute!" he says, landing at the counter next to Luke.

Candy Shack, love it.

"Oh, and who's this?" He pivots to face Luke. "I'm Junjun, you can call me Jun." He offers his hand to Luke for a shake.

"Uh, I'm Luke. I work here." Luke takes Jun's hand awkwardly.

"Wow, a real-life lumberjack!"

Luke finally does smile and looks away bashfully, Junjun successfully disarming him with his pure enthusiasm for everything. Jun then quickly turns to me and mouths silently, "He's so HOT!" then resumes smiling innocently as Luke looks back.

"Hey, Amanda." Celeste walks up to the shack with Max trailing behind, looking at something on his phone.

"Hi!" I wave excitedly.

Luke turns to see the newcomers and his face transforms.

"Max!" he says with a restrained but boyish surprise.

Max looks up from his phone. "Hey . . . Luke. How are you?"

What the heck is this?

Jun, Celeste, and I shoot each other questioning glances as the two guys stand awkwardly facing each other.

"Uh, good, yeah. Man, it's been ages," Luke says, still surprised. "How's your dad, and um . . . Susan?"

"It's April now, Susan was like a stepmom ago. But they're all good, thanks. How's Hank?" Max counters. "He still running around the woods like a little Big Foot in a trapper hat?"

At this, both boys start to genuinely laugh at an inside joke, while we all look on, captivated.

"Yeah, you know it." Luke is grinning widely.

Oh, so he does have a personality!

And an incredible smile.

"What are you doing here?" Luke asks Max. "Come to get a tree?"

"Nah, my dad has a twelve-foot artificial tree. Last year we 3D printed the Nakatomi tower from *Die Hard* for a tree topper, it turned out pretty sick . . ."

"Umm, actually, we're here to visit Amanda," Celeste gently interrupts Max's tangent and gets us back on track. "Nice to meet you. Luke, right? I'm Celeste."

"Yeah, Celeste's my honey." Max gives her squeeze and a kiss on the top of her head.

"How do you guys know each other?" I ask Max, still kind of baffled by the whole scene.

"Oh, we used to hang out all the time when we were little," Max explains. "My grandpa's old hunting cabin is back in the woods there. Before my dad got the spot on the lake, we would be there all the time. We built some sick ski jumps and forts and stuff back in the woods, right, Luke?"

Luke smiles at the memory, and the two boys look at each other fondly.

"That's so sweet," Celeste chimes in. Both guys instantly get self-conscious and stiffen up.

"Anyway, to answer your question, Luke." Jun tries once again to get us back on track. "We came to check out Amanda's setup here, and we also wanted to do our Secret Santa draw." He leans forward, putting his crossed arms on the counter to survey the pastry cases. "Amanda, is that fudge? Can I have some?" Jun says taking off a woolly glove to point at the vegan coconut one. "Mmm, it looks so good."

"Yeah, sure, on the house."

He picks up a piece and makes a show of taking a bite. "That is delicious! Max, you gotta try this."

"Nah, bro, I'm good."

"Anyway, I don't want to stand out here all day, Amanda," Jun says, chewing his fudge. "What time do you get done? You want to go get dinner, and we can do the Secret Santa then?"

"Nah, I can't. I gotta go to some holiday cello recital thing for

Milo. Can we just do the name drawing now? I mean, what do we need, some paper and pen and a hat, right?"

"Yeah, why not? Amanda, give me a piece of paper from your journal and your pen," Celeste says, knowing I keep my writing journal nearby at all times. A pen on the other hand? I'm always misplacing mine.

"I don't have one."

"I have one," Luke says, pulling one out of the top pocket of his work coat. "Here you go." He hands it to me. Wow, friendly interaction. Was that so hard?

I guess he's done telling me off about space heaters.

"Thanks" is all I say out loud.

"Well, I'll leave you guys to it. I should get ready for the next wave of customers."

"No, stay, Luke." Celeste's warm smile telegraphing how much she means it. "Any friend of Max is a friend of ours, right?"

"Totally," Jun says.

I mumble something that I hope sounds like *Yeah, of course.*

"And guess what, I'm going to put your name in here too. It'll be fun." Celeste says, writing their names in her loopy script on the strips of paper she's torn.

"No really, that's not necessary," Luke tries to insist.

"Sorry, too late, it's done." She puts the last of five little folded pieces of paper into her knit hat.

I smile, knowing Celeste so well. She comes off all ethereal moon goddess-y, but when she makes up her mind about something, you better believe that thing is going to happen. And right now, for whatever reason, she wants this.

Celeste brandishes her hat at the group. "Okay, Max, you go first."

"Right on!" Max plunges his hand into the cap and makes a big show of swirling the names around before pulling one out.

"Remember, don't say who you get," Celeste instructs as he pulls out his hand and reads his little paper. "It's a secret!"

Jun goes next, then Celeste, then Luke, reluctantly, all four managing to keep solid poker faces as they silently read the name on the paper.

It's my turn now, and as I reach in, I kind of have a feeling I know how this is going to end.

Oh no, please don't let it be . . .

I unfold my little paper and read the name in Celeste's unmistakable bubble letters.

It's Luke.

Well, that's just great.

"Yay, Secret Santa!" Junjun claps excitedly. "Merry Christmas, everyone! Now I can start shopping."

And it dawns on me. What in the world am I going to get for a guy who hardly speaks, and when he does acts like he can't stand me? I mean what's the perfect present for a dude with the personality of a stale Christmas cookie?

Whose terrible idea was this anyway?

Oh yeah.

Mine.

DECEMBER
7

Chapter 7
NAUGHTY OR NICE?

Monday, lunchtime. I'm mindlessly popping Tater Tots into my mouth, jotting in my journal, lost in thought, as the din of the White Pine High cafeteria carries on around me.

At least the school day's half over. I can't wait for Christmas break to start next week. I like my new gig at the farm, but it's a lot with school, Christmas, and my trip to plan for. This is gonna be a marathon month for sure. Those weekend rushes at the stand are brutal. But, all in all, it is pretty fun running a small business. I'm learning a lot from Cheryl and from seeing how the farm works.

Then there's Luke.

Luke, Luke, Luke, what am I going do about him?

I can't believe I'm his Secret Santa, and I have no idea what to get him. He's only spoken to me like three times, and two of those were to tell me what I'm doing wrong.

But then it was like a switch flipped when he saw Max. He was laughing. And that smile . . .

I mean he must have some kind of personality under all that flannel.

What is his deal anyway? Why isn't he in school like the rest of us?

"Hey, slide over." Jun interrupts my thoughts, sitting down and pulling Tupperware out of his backpack.

"What's for lunch?" I ask.

"The usual, leftovers." His container is filled with chicken adobo, rice, and half an eggplant tortilla. It's cold, but it still smells delicious.

"Jun, tell your mom I'll take her leftovers any day." I pop another tot into my mouth.

"Well, actually, you can come and eat it all fresh." June pauses to put a carefully composed forkful of chicken and rice into his mouth and chew. "I think I told you my lola Ruth is coming with my tita Connie for Christmas, so we decided to host the annual FilAm Association potluck on the twentieth. My mom wanted me to invite you."

Visions of the buffet danced in my head. "Oh yeah, great! Of course, I'd love to come."

"And she wanted me to ask you if you would play piano for the carol singing," he adds.

"Yeah, totally. I'll sing for my supper!"

"And I wanted to ask you if you could come on the nineteenth after work and help me set up?" Jun gives me that smile he knows I can't resist. "She wants to rearrange the living room and move some of the stuff out to the garage."

"Of course, anything for your mom. And your mom's lumpia."

"Did somebody say 'lumpia'? Dang, I love those." Max sets a tray of mystery meat tacos on the table and straddles the bench across from us.

"Yeah, we're having a potluck on the twentieth. You and Celeste are invited," Jun says matter-of-factly.

"Is your lola gonna be there?" Max asks, tearing into his mystery meat. "You know I'm her favorite. She told me last time I saw her."

"Yes, she will, and Max? She says that to everyone."

"Yeah, but, like, she means it with me," he adds smugly.

"What are we talking about?" Celeste joins us.

"How much Jun's grandma loves me," Max explains.

"Of course, sweetie, everyone loves you," she says, patting his face like a puppy.

I swear to God, if he had a tail it'd be wagging.

"Nooo," Jun clarifies. "Not that. I was inviting you guys to our family party on the twentieth."

"The twentieth?" Celeste pauses in thought. "Okay, that's perfect. It's the day before our party, you know, for Yule, the winter solstice."

Max, with recollection dawning, asks, "This some of your witchy stuff?"

"It's not witchy, it's just how European pre-Christian Celtic and Norse people celebrated the beginning of winter." Celeste shrugs, daintily unwrapping a hummus and bean sprout sandwich. "And it's actually why we have things like a Christmas tree, light a Yule log, and decorate with red-and-green holly. These were symbols of endurance through the dark of winter, building up to the longest night of the year. Solstice is the return of the sun, the transition from autumn to winter when the days begin to get longer again. It's a time of great celebration and spiritual cleansing, letting go of the old year and setting intentions for the new."

"I love when you talk about this stuff it's, like, so *Lord of the Rings*, it's like you're an elf queen or something." Max looks at her with unironic awe.

"Max, you are such a secret nerd, but I'll take it. Better than rants about how *Die Hard* is a Christmas movie." Celeste rolls her eyes lovingly.

"That's totally not a Christmas movie," I butt in before Max can stake his claim.

"Amanda, please, for real, you know better than to start this conversation!" Jun pipes up pleadingly.

"You're right, my bad. Max, we can agree to disagree." I put my arm around my best friend. "And, yes, Celeste gives major elf-queen vibes. I do agree with you on that one."

"Super sexy elf queen," Max clarifies.

"Okay, now I'm gonna barf up my tots."

Celeste shoots me a playful side-eye, before turning to Max. "Aww, thanks, honey. Anyway, I would love it if we could all hang out and, like, do some kind of celebration or ritual for the solstice. And then we can do our Secret Santa exchange. What do you think?"

"Yeah, I'm down, you know my intention. Get our butts to

Europe and get out of this podunk town this summer!" My brain circles back to my favorite topic. "By the way, Celeste, did you put your application in?"

"Not yet. I will, but back to the party. I'm just not sure where we can do it." Celeste seems uncharacteristically fixated on logistics. "My parents are having their own thing at our house the same night, so that won't work."

Wait, did she just change the subject on me?

I'm about to rewind to ask her about the application again when Max pipes up.

"Oh, wait, I totally almost forgot! After we saw Luke yesterday, I asked my dad if I could open up the old cabin since we're gonna be out at the farm so much visiting Amanda. It's, like, seriously only a fifteen-minute walk through the woods. He said sure, if we clean it up, and don't do anything he wouldn't do. So basically, we're free to do *whatever*. We can totally have the solstice séance there."

"Not a séance, a ritual," Celeste clarifies. "But, yeah, awesome! That would be amazing! Amanda, can you text Luke and tell him?"

"Tell Max to text him," I say, probably too defensively. "Why would I have his number? I barely know the guy."

"Oh, I figured you'd have it." Jun smiles knowingly. "Since you are working together and he couldn't stop staring at you."

"What, are you high? I've barely said two words to the guy, and he's kinda been a total jerk." I take a deep breath and glare at Celeste. "I can't believe you invited him to be part of our Secret Santa in the first place."

“Aww, chill, Amanda. Luke’s okay,” Max drawls, clearly not appreciating how put out I am about all of this. “I mean, he used to be when we were kids. We haven’t really hung out since my dad got the lake house but, like, when we were eight? He was kinda my best friend.”

“Really? You never told me that,” Celeste says.

“Yeah, he went to a different elementary school than us but, like, all summer long we’d hang out and play in the woods. His grandma would sometimes come out and play cards with Dad and Susan and have drinks. It was kind of hilarious. She was really nice but tough. Even my dad was kinda scared of her. She always kicked his butt at cards. Susan really liked her. And sometimes Hank would come out and like, fish in the pond and take us on hikes and teach us about plants and stuff.”

“Well, what happened?” I ask, suddenly totally intrigued. “Why’d you stop hanging out?”

“I don’t know. I guess Dad and Susan broke up, and then he started dating April, and she wanted to get something on the lake and, you know, we closed up the cabin and stopped going . . .” Max trails off. “I just didn’t see him really after that.”

“Okay, but, like, what about his mom? Where is she? And you gotta tell me what the deal with Hank is, that guy is like a walking jump scare!” Suddenly, all the questions that have been nagging me about the Posts ever since I stepped foot on that farm start to bubble up. “And why isn’t Luke in school with us? Didn’t he go here for a bit? I was looking through the yearbook pictures from freshman year, and I saw him first semester but not after that.”

“Geez, Amanda, stalker much?” Jun says sarcastically.

“I don’t know.” Max seems uncomfortable. “Ask him yourself. It’s not like we talked about that stuff. I just know he had a really weird family situation, and his mom wasn’t around. She lives in Chicago or something, and he’d go out for, like, a week in the summer, but most of the rest of the time he was around. Every weekend in the winter when it wasn’t tree season, we’d hang out. We were just kinda busy catching salamanders and building snow forts and sled jumps and stuff.” Max smiles in his puppy dog way at the memory of what was probably some kind of wicked jump. “It was awesome. He’s actually really good at building stuff. And super funny.”

Luke? Lumberjack Luke, the Original Grinch, Luke Post . . . funny? Clearly, I’ve missed something.

The digital ding-dong of the lunch bell sounds, and everybody snaps out of it.

“Okay, gotta go. Come on, Celeste, we got chem,” Max says picking up Celeste’s tray for her.

“Wait, so when are we supposed to go clean up this cabin?” I ask as everyone starts getting up to leave. “I’m working every day but Wednesdays.”

“How about Friday?” Jun offers. “It’s a half day for conferences. We could go out after lunch and get a couple of hours in before your shift.”

“Okay, yeah, that works,” Max says. “I’ll get the keys from my dad.”

“Oooh, I’ll bring some candles and sage so we can smudge the space and start with some fresh energy!”

"Totally, we're gonna smudge the crap out of it." Max high-fives Celeste before pulling her in for a hug. "I can't wait. It's gonna be sweet. Our own cabin to hang out in this winter!"

Celeste smiles beatifically at me. "Will you tell Luke when you see him, Amanda?"

"Yeah. Sure, I guess, I'll tell him,"

"Great, see you guys later." She walks out arm in arm with Max.

"Don't forget to put in your application for Europe!" I yell after her.

She gives me a thumbs-up without looking back and keeps walking.

Why am I getting a weird vibe about that?

"Oh, I've got to go too. Student council meeting, I'm presenting," Jun says, gathering his stuff. "Okay, love you, miss you, bye-bye, mwah!" He blows me a kiss as he hustles off.

I grab my stuff, down the rest of my soda, and head off too.

It's almost four by the time I get out to the farm, and Celeste wasn't kidding about that "enduring the darkness of winter" business. The sun is fading fast, and the lights above the tree lot are already on. The fairy lights around the shack are giving off a twinkly glow I can see all the way from the parking area.

It's deserted and won't get busy until later when the after-work tree shoppers come through. But I see something move out of the corner of my eye.

"You!" I say to the little calico cat now sitting by the barn doors looking at me like, *Who, me?*

"Where did you go the other day?" I ask, as if it's perfectly normal to have a conversation with a cat. "As a matter of fact, where did you come from just now? The barn? Are you a barn cat?"

I keep talking as I slowly approach the little kitty, trying a few healthy rounds of *psssst pssst pssst* to see if it will be curious enough to come close and let me pet it. She sticks her little nose out for a sniff, and it seems like it might be working. Just as I go in for a head scratch, she startles and runs off into a small hole between the big stones in the barn's foundation.

"Shoot, foiled again! You keep appearing and disappearing, like some kind of fairy barn cat." I try to see where she might be hiding, but have no luck. "I will pet you!" I yell at the barn like a crazy lady, then head toward the Candy Shack to see what needs setting up.

As I get closer, I notice something's different. The old cash register. It's glinting under the string lights, all polished and shining, and I can see the finely engraved details on the surface of the metal. It's beautiful. I punch one of the buttons, and it sends up a little tab in the glass window. I turn the crank on the side, and the cash drawer pops open with a satisfying *ka-ching* revealing the empty compartments of the tray.

He fixed it.

I smile to myself, delighted and surprised.

Huh, maybe Max is right. Maybe there is more to Luke than meets the eye.

I see the lights of a car pulling in and snap out of my thoughts, close the register, and get on with setting up the stand. But my smile stays.

DECEMBER 8

Chapter 8
VERY GOOD FRIENDS

"William, that's enough! If you can't behave, we are not going to get a tree today," a short-tempered dad, still in his work shoes, suit, and tie admonishes an exuberant six-year-old while a younger sister stands by, all bundled up in her ski suit like a starfish.

"Please, Dad, please let me carry the tree, I want to help!"

"No, I need you to just stand there and watch your sister while I pay for this," the dad says, taking out his wallet to pay Luke for one of the precut trees.

Luke.

I still can't believe he fixed the old cash register for me.

I mean I think he did it for me?

Either way, I did not see that coming. And it was kinda sweet.

And now, he's standing in the blast zone of Mount Doom as Work Dad gets ready to erupt.

Probably not a good time to ask . . .

It's not that busy. I'm perched on my stool in front of the heater in the Candy Shack, watching the scene unfold, my journal open, jotting down thoughts with a pen I've snagged from the house. Even though I've seen this same situation play out a couple of different times, it still makes me . . . I don't know if mad is the right word . . . maybe sad? Something in between. It's like, I get it, you had to work today, and now you're picking your kids up from, like, day care or whatever and stopping for a tree on the way home. But getting a tree's not like picking up a gallon of milk. An errand to run. It should be special.

I remember how fun it was when I was really little. I have a vague memory of being out here with Mom and Dad. I must've been about five, because it was just me. No Milo yet. I remember Dad pulling me on the sled through all the trees and they felt GIANT, covered in snow, and the blue sky above us was huge as we winded through the rows. Dad was singing carols and Mom joined in. That's all I really remember, but it's one of those really old memories that live in the middle of your chest that just feel, like, happy. Like love. I guess when Milo was born, it was too much to pick out our own tree, and Mom got the fake one, and we stopped coming.

"William, ENOUGH!" Work Dad shouts, snapping me out of my reverie. The little boy, who is jostling the tree, instantly retreats into himself, lip quivering. His baby sister looks at him, head cocked, and, in just the sweetest way, gives him a little kiss.

Work Dad's just standing there, obviously feeling like crap, and trying to figure out what to do next.

Um, saying sorry would be a good step, bro.

But before he can do anything, the little girl walks over to him and pulls on his coat saying, "Daddy, I made pee-pee." And he just kind of throws up his hands in defeat.

"Okay, come on, let's find somewhere to clean up."

Luke steps in and says, "Don't use the porta potty, you can take her into the house. Just go to the porch and knock, my aunt will show you where to go."

"Okay, thanks," he says, picking up his daughter. "Can he stay here with you for a sec?" the dad asks, pointing to his son.

"Yeah, sure, no problem." Luke isn't thrown by the request. "And I'll get that tree up on the car for you, so you'll be all set."

"Thanks." Work Dad walks away holding his baby in her little pink suit.

Luke turns to the boy, who's still kind of moping.

"Hey, I'm gonna need a hand. You look pretty strong. You think you could help me lift this guy?" He points to the wrapped and netted tree.

And it's like the sun comes out and all is forgotten. The little boy lights up like a Christmas tree and nods his head earnestly.

"Okay, I'm gonna grab this end and you grab the top." Luke gets a hand around the trunk. "Watch out for the needles though. Good thing you have mittens on."

The little boy lifts the top, and in an exaggerated move the whole tree flies straight up, as high as the kid can reach. "Whoa, buddy, you're strong. I was not expecting that!" Luke says, clearly doing all the heavy lifting from the back end of the tree.

The boy instantly starts to giggle.

And I can't help myself, I start to giggle too. Luke looks over his shoulder at me and smiles, his full face lit up and open, and I feel my breath kind of catch in my throat like I just went over the top of a roller coaster.

Wow, he's beautiful.

He turns back to the boy and says, "Okay, you better let me do this part. I don't think you can reach the top of the car, but you see that big piece of twine over there? You can grab it and hand it to me."

"Okay!" the boy says brightly, and runs over to grab the twine, pleased with his assignment.

Luke easily lifts the tree on top of the waiting SUV, grabs the twine from the boy, and starts to fasten the tree to the roof runner in the expert way of someone who's done a task a thousand times.

Then he turns to the kid and says, "I need some help with this last knot. Can you tie your shoes?"

"Yeah. Well, kinda. I can make a knot."

"Perfect." Luke smiles, then he lifts the boy up to let him make a knot in the last little dangling piece of string.

I see the dad start to walk back toward them, carrying the little girl, her mittens dangling from their string inside her coat. She clearly got some fudge from Cheryl while she was inside, judging from the chocolate smudges circling her mouth and all over her fingers.

The dad pauses a moment and watches.

“That’s awesome, good job, buddy. Thanks for the help,” Luke says, setting the boy back down. “This is for you.” Luke reaches in his pocket and gives the boy something I can’t quite see. The boy smiles with delight, then catches sight of his dad and runs up to him.

“Daddy, Daddy, look! I helped with the tree.”

“Yeah, I see that. You did a really good job,” he says, kneeling down to meet his son at eye level. “And I’m sorry about before. Daddy’s just a little stressed. You are a great helper.” He hugs the boy, and all is forgiven.

And, for real, I almost start to cry, it’s so sweet.

The dad stands and shakes Luke’s hand and says thank you, then opens the back seat and loads the kids into their car seats before driving off, leaving Luke standing there, waving goodbye.

And as I watch him, I feel the same warm heavy feeling in my chest that I remember from when I was little. It’s just . . . happy.

Who is this guy?

How is Luke so patient and sweet to a little kid and such a stone-faced grouch with me? I don’t get it.

“Hiya, Mandy! It is I, your faithful and stylish purveyor of fine ladies wear!”

“Mrs. Novak! What are you doing here?” I say, surprised to see Helen Novak walking up to the shack wearing a bright purple, quilted, floor-length winter coat with big brass buttons, a purple, faux-fur headband, and jade green leather gloves. An impossibly large multicolored handbag is slung over her shoulder.

“Well, I was driving into town—I’m closing for Marissa tonight, she's got some kind of an appointment and has to leave early. Anyway, I saw your shiny new Matcha-Do about Hot Cocoa sign on the side of the road and wanted to stop and see how things are going," she finishes with a sparkling smile.

I realize I was totally zoning out and Mrs. Novak is still chatting.

"I tell ya, I miss you, Mandy. My four p.m. teatime is just not the same without you. That Trevor is not near as good a listener as you."

Ooops.

But I'm off the hook when Luke walks over to say hi.

"Well, wrap me in paper and put a bow on top, is this handsome young man Lucas Post?" Mrs. Novak gushes.

"Hi, Mrs. Novak!" Luke says, smiling and looking down bashfully.

"Wait a minute. I need to take a step back and get a good look at you." She places a hand lightly on Luke's strong shoulder and holds him at arm's length. "How is this possible? You're all grown up! And so tall. And so good-looking," she says the last part in an exaggerated almost-growl, giving his shoulder a squeeze.

Oh man, poor Luke, so awkward.

"Don't you think so, Mandy?"

May a comet fall from the sky, hit the Candy Shack, and put me out of my misery.

I feel my face turn as red as the barn, and all I can do is smile uncomfortably and pray that she stops soon. But then I sneak a look at Luke. He's even more embarrassed than me.

"What a fine young man you've turned out to be, dark eyes like your papa but tall like your mom! How is Annabelle, still in Chicago teaching?" Mrs. Novak gives Luke a considered look.

"Yup, yup, she's good, thanks," he replies gamely.

Now, I really feel sorry for the guy. He is clearly regretting his choice to come over to say hi.

"What can I get you, Mrs. Novak?" I ask, trying to come to Luke's rescue. "We don't have chamomile, but the hot chocolate is delicious, especially with a piece of the fudge you like," I say, distracting her from more personal questions. I mean Luke can be a grouch, but no one deserves the embarrassment of one of Helen Novak's well-meaning interrogations.

"Well, yes, that sounds just delightful, thank you." Mrs. Novak turns her full attention on me. Mission accomplished. "I think I will have my afternoon treat here instead of in town. Don't tell Zoe on me now!"

"I wouldn't dream of it, Mrs. Novak!" Relieved, I pour a hot cocoa and add a healthy dollop of whipped cream, something I know she likes.

"Mandy, please, we've discussed this, call me Helen. Oooh, and you remembered I'm a whipped-cream gal and not a marshmallow lady, although I will be if I keep eating all these sweets!" She laughs uproariously at her own joke.

Luke, sensing the danger has passed, surprisingly leans on the bar to stay awhile, appearing to enjoy the sometimes embarrassing, always entertaining bundle of energy that is Mrs. Novak.

"Mmmm, that's good," she says, sipping her cocoa. "That's why you're the best, Mandy, you remember the details! I tell ya, Luke, Mandy here is something special. One of a kind, this beautiful girl."

Uh-oh, code red, code red! She's rearming for another round of torture, and this time I'm in the hot seat.

"Not like the other kids, our Mandy."

I feel like he notices me starting to squirm and then, in a total break of character, a sly smile comes across his face, and he starts to egg her on! "Oh yeah, how so?"

The jerk! And after I saved him! Though, low-key respect. It's a move worthy of Milo.

"Well, for one, she's whip-smart and, two, she's such a good listener." Mrs. Novak is delicately stirring her whipped cream into her hot cocoa.

I shake my head modestly.

"It's true, Mandy! Why do you think I always come to get my tea from you? You have a really great way of listening and saying just the right thing. You have a genuine way with words. I guess it's 'cause you're always scribbling in your notebook. It's the writer in you. Whatever it is, you're a dear heart to listen to the cares and worries of an old lady and then find something smart and kind to say. You're an old soul, Amanda Mathers."

I'm too touched by her sincerity to be embarrassed anymore. I'm always getting scolded by my teachers and parents and even my friends for talking too much, saying stuff I should probably keep to myself, letting my mouth work faster than my brain. So it feels, well, nice to hear someone say that I'm not always getting it wrong. Sometimes I can say the right thing at the right time.

"Thank you, Mrs. Novak," I say softly.

"Well, I'll take it all back if you don't get with the program and start calling me Helen! Now how much do I owe ya?" she asks, digging around for her wallet in her giant purse.

"Um, that's five dollars, please," I say, regaining my composure.

She hands me a twenty-dollar bill, and I ring her up on the old register and then wind the crank and get the satisfying *ka-ching* as the drawer pops up open.

"Well, will you look at that!" Mrs. Novak says. "Isn't she a beaut! Where'd you get that?"

"Oh, it was Dad's great uncle Jim's. He got it ages ago," Luke explains.

"It looks like he just got it yesterday. It's in beautiful condition. That must be over a hundred years old."

"Well, yeah, I did fix it up a bit. Changed a few springs. But mostly all it needed was WD-40 and some brass polish, and it was good as new." He echoes my line from the other day and flashes me, honestly, a very genuine smile.

I start to smile back, catch myself, and look away self-consciously.

"Oh, well now." Mrs. Novak's eyes twinkle as she looks from me to Luke and back again.

Please don't say anything, please don't say anything, please, please, please don't say anything . . .

She smiles and looks at me like the cat that's got the whipped cream, but simply says, "Well, how nice. Here's to that register overflowing with all the resources you need to make your wonderful, big ideas happen." She sips the last of her cocoa and plops her empty cup on the bar. "Now, Luke, how's about you take me over there and help me find a small tree for my house. You know I haven't had one since Ralph passed, but I don't know . . . all of a sudden, I'm feeling pretty Christmassy. I guess it must be you two young people and the hot chocolate just cheering me up."

Phew. Made it out unscathed.

But not quite. She reaches over the counter, puts her hand on mine, leans in, looks me dead in the eye, and says in a low, smiling voice, "I just have a feeling you two are going to be very good friends."

She winks, turns, and takes Luke's arm as he escorts her over to the trees.

What the heck does she mean by that?

But deep down, I think part of me already knows.

DECEMBER
9

Chapter 9
WHAT THE FUDGE!

"Phew, it's hot in here!" I take off my big sweater and hang it on a coat hook in the kitchen. It's Wednesday afternoon, and it's supposed to be my day off, but Cheryl caught me on my way out yesterday and asked if I wanted to come make some extra cash helping her with a big fudge order. Which is how I find myself in the toasty warm Post Farm kitchen, inhaling the intoxicating aromas of sugar and spice and everything nice.

Cheryl's standing over two big pots of bubbling fudge, checking the temperature on the candy thermometers inside.

"Okay, two hundred thirty-five degrees. These are just right," she says, and pulls the pots off the stove to dunk them into a waiting ice bath in the big sink. She starts directing me as she stirs the pots.

"So, here's the deal. I've got the first few batches of fudge ready over there on the counter. And I've got sixty of these little boxes that need to be assembled." Cheryl points to a stack of flat folded paper boxes. "They're just big enough for two pieces of each flavor—candy cane dark, gingerbread spice milk, eggnog white, and vegan coconut pistachio. You need to build the boxes, line them with paper, fill them up with fudge, and then seal them with one of these stickers," she says, pointing to a roll next to the boxes.

"Oh, these are super cute!" I pick up the stickers and admire the sage green and hot pink logo. The pink exactly matches Cheryl's hair, which is currently tucked up under a neon green bandanna.

"'Sweet Cheryl's Confections,'" I read aloud. "I like that!"

I sense the unmistakable influence of Zoe Huggins.

"Yeah, you like those? Zoe hooked me up with her designer and helped me with a name," Cheryl says, smiling a little.

Is she blushing?

"It looks like Zoe. She has a great sense of style."

"Yeah, she sure does, and so smart about business. She's pretty awesome," Cheryl almost-but-not-quite gushes. "Anyway, that's the job! I suggest you set up a station on the island, and we can stack the packed boxes in the pantry. I'm going to start on the next few batches of fudge." Cheryl turns back to the pots in the sink.

"Got it!" I say, spinning my long, blond hair into a high bun like a ballerina, and tying it up with one of the elastics that's permanently on my wrist. I bring everything over to the island and start to set up my space when I notice an old portable dial radio with an antenna on top of one of the cabinets.

"Does that thing work?" I ask, pointing to the radio.

"The radio? Yeah, it probably does."

"Can I turn it on? It might make the time pass if we had a little music."

"Sure thing." Cheryl smiles.

I reach up to turn on the small brown radio and play with it for a minute trying to figure out how it works.

"You turn the volume knob and that turns it on."

Crazy, I bet they probably have a landline phone hanging from the wall somewhere in this house too. I turn up the volume and hear some static. I adjust the tuner, which slides a little orange marker across a bunch of numbers in a window in the bottom, and there it is! The unmistakable sounds of Nat King Cole . . .

Chestnuts roasting on an open fire
Jack Frost nipping at your nose . . .

I head back to my spot and start to pull on a pair of food prep gloves when I look over at Cheryl in front of her pots by the sink. Her back's turned to me and her head is cast down. I can't tell, but I think she might be crying.

"Are you okay?" I ask.

"Yeah, yeah, I'm fine." She takes off her gloves and grabs a paper towel to wipe her eyes before turning toward me. "I was just thinking of my mom. That was her radio, and we always had it on when we baked together, especially at Christmas."

I smile and just listen.

"She would have loved this. The kitchen, warm and full of good smells, making fudge with carols on the radio." Cheryl's eyes shine with tears, even as she smiles at the memory. "It's what she lived for. She just loved Christmas."

"You must miss her a lot," I say, and get back to building my boxes, and her to her next batch of fudge.

"Yeah, I do. It's hard being here without her. I mean, it's sad because the house is sad. There's no way she would have let the boys get away with not decorating and lighting up the porches, and no tree in the front window?" Cheryl sighs. "I mean come on, we're a Christmas tree farm!"

"Why don't you do it?" I can't stop myself from asking.

"Well, it's delicate with my brother," Cheryl says carefully. "I don't want to overstep. He's been running things for so long. You know, I got out. I went out west and started my own life, went to culinary school, and he stayed and took care of everything. And he always supported my move, he never made me feel bad for not being here. But he's been through a lot, and when Mom died, we all worried it might just be too much for him. So I came back to help, and Luke decided to do school remotely so we could keep an eye on him. He's doing okay, but I have to go slow. I can't just start changing things all at once. Family businesses, they can be complicated.

"Anyway, you don't need to know all the drama, 'cause there's plenty of it," she says cryptically. "I'm just glad to see this kitchen full of life. And your Candy Shack. It's really great how you fixed it all up, Amanda. Mom would have adored that. I just wish I could convince Hank to do more. We'll see. Maybe next year." She pours her fudge into the waiting pans and walks them over to a large fridge on the far side of the kitchen to finish cooling. "My point is, I'm glad you're here. And I think it's good for Luke too. I was never in favor of him getting his GED remotely. I mean, he's seventeen. He needs to be with other kids, but he wouldn't have it any other way. Losing Nan really hit him hard, too. She basically raised him after his mom left, so . . ." She catches herself saying too much again. "But never mind that. I'm just glad he has someone his own age to talk to."

"Really? 'Cause it doesn't seem like he's been that thrilled to have me around."

Although, it did feel like the ice was melting a little yesterday . . .

"Nah, that's just him. He's quiet, maybe a little set in his ways. And spending all day with Mountain Man Hank for company, your social skills get rusty." She takes a dig at her big brother and laughs. "Trust me, he definitely likes you." She smiles knowingly.

Why does everyone keep giving me that look!

But some part of me is pleased to hear it.

Why do you even care, Amanda? It's not like you're looking for a boyfriend. You got plans, remember!

I try to refocus back on my work, but when I look through the little plastic window of one of ten sealed boxes I already made, I notice I totally messed up.

"Oh shoot, I just realized I forgot to add the vegan fudge!"

Nice job, Amanda, zone out much? My inner critic pipes back up for an encore.

"I'm sorry, Cheryl, I'm such a dope."

"Relax, honey, it's no big deal," she says soothingly. "I got plenty of boxes and plenty more stickers. As my mom always used to say when we were cooking, 'Cheryl, if you fudge something up, don't panic, just fix it.'"

I laugh. "Okay, if you say so. I promise not to fudge the next one up."

I start to undo my work when the kitchen door opens and Luke walks in, stomping the snow off his boots and shaking off the cold as he hangs up his coat. "It's pretty slow out there, thought I'd see what you guys are doing."

"Perfect timing," Cheryl says. "You can come and help Amanda."

"Oh," he says, stopping in his tracks, looking at me like he's seeing me for the first time. "You look different."

I realize he's only ever seen me in my winter coat with a beanie over my hair. But now I'm wearing one of my old T-shirts with the cut collar. It's hanging off my shoulder, showing the maroon lacey strap of my camisole. My silver hoops are dangling against my bare neck.

"Um, yeah, it's hot in here." I say wiping my forehead on my elbow crook, because my hands are wrapped in giant fudge-covered plastic gloves.

Cheryl says, "Indeed, it is," in a teasing way that makes Luke shoot her an unamused glance. "Anyway, you are just in time. I'm gonna put you to work. Why don't you build boxes and Amanda can fill them?"

"That sounds better than whatever system you have going on here," he says, pointing to my reopened boxes, their stickers torn in half.

And there it is. That condescending, smug tone that gets right under my skin and makes me want to fight him! "Listen, if you think you can do better . . ."

"Take is easy, I didn't mean anything by it." He holds his hands up in the universal symbol for *yo, chill.* "I just meant, it would help if we had a system." He speaks slowly like he's trying to calm a barking dog.

"Oh . . . okay. Yeah, a system sounds good," I say, regaining my composure.

"Amanda, you are hilarious." Cheryl chuckles, amused by the whole dynamic. "You're like this pot of fudge here, always running at a low boil. And don't get me wrong, that's not necessarily a bad thing, it's what it takes to make the candy set. But you know what ruins the fudge? Letting it boil over. That's why you have to always keep an eye on it and learn when to turn down the temperature."

Luke cracks a cautious smile, and I smile too. "Ugh! Yes, I know. I do have a tendency to boil over. I also talk to myself in funny accents and occasionally have been known to talk to plants and animals. I'm sorry," I say with an exaggerated hangdog expression, my fudgy gloved hangs dangling at my sides, feeling a little weird at being called out and deciding to lean into it and spill all my quirks.

My name is Amanda Mathers, and I'm a hotheaded weirdo, nice to meet you!

But to my relief both Cheryl and Luke seem wholly unfazed. "Talks to animals, who does that remind you of?" Cheryl says to

Luke, who smiles and chuckles. Then he sidles up next to me at the kitchen island and starts expertly assembling the flat boxes.

"Who?" I ask, looking back and forth at them both, eager to be let in on the joke.

"My mom," Cheryl says. "Nan was known to talk to the birds at her bird feeder." She points at an empty feeder hanging outside the kitchen window. "She used to feed deer down at the edge of the yard too, and she gave them all little names and would say hi to each of them. It was one of her many quirks."

"Yeah." Luke laughs to himself as he works. His arm is warm when he softly brushes against me to reach for the next box, but he doesn't miss a beat. "Remember, Simon, the squirrel that would always steal all the birdseed from the feeders?"

"Ha! How could I forget? Mom would open the kitchen window and spray him with the sink hose to get him off of there! You never saw a squirrel jump so fast, and she'd be yelling, 'Simon, you little . . .' Well, I'll let you fill in the rest." Cheryl laughs.

"Yeah, and he'd always come right back," Luke adds, chuckling at the memory. "She couldn't stand that squirrel stealing her bird food." He looks right at me, grabs a piece of fudge from one of the boxes I'm filling, and pops it in his mouth.

"Hey!" I elbow him in the ribs lightly.

"Oww," he says dramatically. "I think Amanda's fudge is about to boil over again."

"Knock it off and get to work." I am trying to keep my face very serious and businesslike, even though I'm starting to think it's not my temper that's got me heating up.

"Or what?" he asks, totally deadpan. But there's something in the way he looks right into my eyes, with just a hint of a smile on his lips.

Wait, is bro, like, flirting with me?

"Or I'll . . . ," but before I can say anything else, he pops a piece of fudge into my open mouth, and I have no choice but to enjoy the delicious chocolatey goodness, and stop talking.

"Ooh, that was a dirty move," Cheryl says, deeply amused.

"Yes, a dirty trick," I say, still chewing. "But I'll forgive you if you give me another piece." I hold up my gloved hands to signal that I need to keep them sanitary for food prep. He carefully selects another piece and holds it up for me to bite, a second too long, then quickly pulls it away.

Oh yeah. Definitely flirting.

But I still give Luke a small hip check and sly smile for good measure.

Yeah, I can flirt too.

He laughs. We get to work.

Cheryl goes back to rinsing a few dishes in the sink. She's looking out the window, lost in thought. "My mom and her birds and squirrels." She chuckles to herself. "So funny. Don't even get me started about her cats."

Wait, did she say cats?

DECEMBER
10

Chapter 10
IT'S A DATE

"One hot cocoa please, extra marshmallows." Celeste has arrived at the Candy Shack!

"Hey! Where did you come from?" I step out from behind my counter to give my bestie a hug. "I feel like I haven't seen you in ages."

She's all done up in winter wear with her vegan fur-lined boots, her homemade knit cap and scarf, and an eco-print, natural dyed satchel full of holly and berries, fir branches and pinecones, looking like a walking Pinterest page.

"I walked over from the cabin. Max dropped me off so I could see what we need for cleaning up tomorrow. He had to go back to town for his dad's Christmas photo shoot for the dealership. I think April hired a stylist. It's a whole thing. Anyway, I told him to pick me up here so I could visit you."

"Works for me. I'm happy for the company." I hand her a

steaming cup of cocoa. "How was the walk over?"

"Beautiful, uhhh," she says expressively. "I just felt like I was bathing in the forest and communing with the spirit of winter while I gathered things for my Yule altar. The cabin's got a big old stone hearth so we can decorate the mantle when it's all cleaned up. It's gonna be perfect for the solstice."

"Cool, was it a long walk?"

"No, like fifteen minutes. There's a path through the woods that ends right at the tree line by the pond."

"There's a pond over there?" Geez, I realize I haven't really explored this place. I've just been in my little Candy Shack the whole time.

"Yeah, it's small and pretty snowed-over, but it's there. Right behind the big red barn. That's such a cool building, by the way, have you been in there yet? You can't see it from here, but on the other side there are these big windows and a chimney pipe. Looks like the top floor is a converted loft. It's really cool."

"Uh, no, it's kind of off-limits. It's a whole thing."

Or is it still, I wonder.

Luke has definitely been warming up. It was fun hanging out with him yesterday. I caught myself thinking about him the whole ride home, teasing me with that piece of fudge . . . Totally flirting. I was thinking about him while I fell asleep too. That glimpse I got of his stomach and his arms . . .

"Uh, yoo-hoo, Amanda? Where'd you go? Disassociate much?"

"Yes, sorry." Busted. "And by the way, can we please just go back to calling it daydreaming? I was just thinking of something else, it's not that deep. Anyway, what were you saying?"

"I was saying how nice it was walking over. There were all kinds of birds in the woods, I saw a pair of cardinals and even a red-tailed hawk, which as you know . . ."

"Is your favorite bird, yes, I know," I say, teasing. "It must be a good sign that we're opening the cabin." Celeste smiles beneficently toward the white winter sky at that. "By the way, did you happen to see any cats as you were walking up?"

"Cats? Uhhh, no. No cats. I mean, why would they be out in the woods?"

"I don't know!" I say, getting instantly agitated. "I keep seeing this cat, but every time I ask about it, everyone here says they don't have a cat. Then, yesterday I found out Nan, Luke's grandma, used to feed a bunch of stray cats over by the woods. But Cheryl says they haven't been around since she passed away, which was, like, two years ago. So I'm totally doubting reality. But this fairy barn cat seems to be there every time I turn around!"

"Hmm, well, cats are powerful symbols of the spirit world. I mean, the ancient Egyptians worshipped them, Mesopotamians . . . They show up in Norse mythology and are important symbols all over Asia. And I mean, come on, we still worship them, all anybody really does online is watch cat videos. Maybe this cat is like a spirit guide or something." Celeste considers my predicament seriously. "What color was it?"

"Orange and gray splotches."

"That's a calico. They are usually females and are considered a sign of transformation, good fortune, and new beginnings. I don't know, Amanda, you may very well have a fairy barn cat watching over you. Wouldn't that be amazing?"

"Hmmm, I'm not quite convinced, but I like the thought."

There are a few folks starting to arrive for precut trees, and Hank appears on the lot to take care of the customers. Luke must be doing his online classes or something. I haven't really seen him since I got here this afternoon.

I pour a few hot cocoas, but otherwise it's pretty chill. It's nice to have Celeste to hang out with. "So, anyway, tell me more about the cabin. Is it in bad shape?"

"No, just needs a good airing out, dusting, and sweeping. The furniture was all covered, and the mice hadn't gotten into much. We turned the water back on and everything worked, electric heaters came on, so it shouldn't take that long."

"That's awesome, it's really cool Max's dad is letting us use it."

"Honestly, I was amazed he did. He's been really putting the pressure on Max to spend more time 'learning the family business.'" Celeste puts air quotes around this last part. "Max must have made some kind of deal with him to get him to go for it. All the pressure stresses him out so bad, and that stresses me out! Every time Max tries to talk about college or doing something else, his dad's like, 'What for? I built all this for you, you can run it, what do you need college for?' It's like he can't fathom that Max might want to figure out his own thing, and it makes me just so grrrr."

Celeste is not a huge fan of Max's dad, who loves to give her a hard time about her new age "nonsense," as he calls it.

"You know what, I'm glad Max has you. You see him for who he is, and that must mean a lot."

"Thanks, Amanda. That's really nice of you to say," Celeste says, touched.

"Why do you sound so surprised?"

"I don't know. You usually just have some kind of mission you're on, and that's all you focus on. Something's different about you. Maybe it's this place, and all the trees, and your fairy barn cat. And your tall dark lumberjack . . ."

"Don't even start! Everybody's been giving me weird looks and winks and vibes about him. I swear nothing is happening. He's only, like, just barely talking to me, so you can stop trying to make out like there's something there, 'cause there isn't. Besides, you know better than anyone, I am not looking for anything that's gonna keep me hanging around town. We're supposed to travel! Remember?" But she doesn't take the bait. Instead, she just he shoots me a knowing look. "That! That's the FACE! Stop making that face! Why is everyone making that face when they mention Luke?"

"You mean the tall, superhot, super-ripped lumberjack that you have spent the last week staring at?" She starts laughing and making an even weirder, smiley I-know-something-you-don't face.

"Celeste, I swear to God, I will cover you in whipped cream if you don't stop it! Nothing is happening!"

Now, she's straight up laughing at my total crash-out, and it's all turned into a big bit.

Do I really even believe that? That nothing's happening?

Maybe there is a little something happening. Standing next to him yesterday, side by side, working in the kitchen, being so close to him, it felt just really . . . nice. Like, comfortable. Like, familiar or something. It's hard to describe, so I don't try to.

"Anyway, thanks for before, for what you said about me and Max." Celeste has caught her breath, and she has her serious face back on. "He's just so important to me. And he's so supportive of everything I'm into. You know that chem project we did?" She asks, excited in a way I don't usually see. "It went really well, and I have been loving my env-sci classes. It's like all my interest in plants and herbalism is not just some trend, it's real science. It's chemistry and botany, and I really like it. Ms. Chen says that I should look at the environmental science program at UVM. They have all kinds of internships and summer programs . . ."

"Wait a minute, hold up. Summer program? What are you talking about? You're doing the young leaders program with me! You're gonna do the arts leadership track, I'm gonna do intercultural leadership and communications, and then we're gonna travel around Europe, that's the plan."

"There it is again, your mission," she says dully.

"What? No, it's not my mission. It's a plan we made together." *I mean, isn't it?*

"Yeah, it is. I'm just kidding," she says off-handedly. But somehow, I'm not convinced.

"You put in your application, right?" I ask tensely.

"Not yet, but . . ."

"Celeste, come on! You promised!" I'm feeling my pot of fudge start to boil.

"I will, okay? I just haven't yet. Can we drop it? You have customers."

A couple of kids come up waving a nice crisp twenty their mom gave them for snacks and hot cocoa, so I get it together and do my job. Refocusing on pouring the drinks calms me down a little, but I notice I'm still agitated. I can't believe it. She really sounded like she was gonna back out on me.

Drop it, Amanda. Turn that heat down.

Dang, that thing Cheryl said yesterday really stuck with me. I know nothing good ever happens when I boil over. I just don't always know how to turn down the temperature. And I feel like Celeste is taking some serious digs at me, like I'm being pushy or something. *My mission . . .* Where did that come from?

I change the subject.

"Anyway, what time should we meet tomorrow? Are we leaving from school?"

"Yeah, that should work!" Celeste brightens, relieved to be moving on. "But we will need to bring some brooms and mops and stuff. I guess I can grab one from my house, but then I'll have to take it to school."

I see Hank across the way organizing the stacked trees. "Maybe I could ask if we could borrow stuff from here? They have a bunch of tools in the barn. Even a leaf blower."

"Oh, that would be great. But for real," she says, lowering her voice, "you're not even just a little bit creeped out by that guy? He's so intense! I don't know if I'd want to ask him for directions, let alone anything else."

I think about my conversation with Cheryl yesterday. "No, he's okay. I think he's just kinda quiet and keeps to himself. I mean, Luke's fairly normal and Cheryl's great, and their mom sounds like she was amazing. He can't be that bad."

"Hey, Celeste, check me out, I'm wearing makeup!" We hear the beep-beep of a horn and the unmistakable voice of Max, who is pulled over at the side of the road and hollers at Celeste from the open window of his truck. Yup, he is wearing makeup, and a horrendous shiny blue suit and skinny matching tie.

"Oh, right, the Christmas card shoot. Nice contouring, Max, looks great!" I yell, giving him a thumbs-up. He checks himself out in the rearview mirror and gives a big cheesy grin and a thumbs-up back.

Celeste is just smiling and shaking her head at her sweet, goofy, lovable boy. "Okay, well, that's my ride. See you tomorrow. Text me if you can get the stuff from Hank, okay?"

"Okay, bye," I say, as Celeste trots over the truck and climbs in. Max leans over to give her a big kiss.

Okay, I get it. They are really cute together.

I notice Hank looking at them and then surprisingly, he wanders my way.

"You wouldn't have an extra cup of coffee back there, would you?"

Whoa, conversation.

"Yeah, of course. Anything in it?"

"No, just black's fine." I hand him the cup. "Was that Ron Pearce's boy?"

"Max, yeah, that's him."

"Well, he's all grown up," Hank comments. "That's quite a truck."

I just nod.

"I remember when he was just a kid running around in the woods with Luke. He'd always end up in the dumbest situations."

"Yup, definitely sounds like Max." I laugh, the ice officially broken.

"I remember one time down at our pond I had to pull a snapping turtle off him. He wanted to see if they actually snap, or if it's just a myth. I guess he found out," Hank says, chuckling a little at the memory. "He was lucky it was a small one, or he would have lost a finger. But, boy, was he howling." Hank kind of shakes his head, smiling.

He actually has a nice smile, the kind that crinkles all the way up to his eyes. If his mountain man beard was white, it would totally be giving Santa Claus. And I realize this is the first time I've seen him smile.

"That checks out. Actually, speaking of Max, his dad is going to let us open up their old cabin, and my friends and I are gonna go out and clean it up tomorrow before my shift. We were wondering if, maybe, if it's all right with you . . ."

"Spit it out, what do you need?" he asks warmly.

"Umm, could we maybe borrow some brooms and rakes and things from the farm? That would save us bringing everything to school. We could just grab it all when we get out here and then bring it all back when I come to work."

"Yeah, that's okay with me. Just put it back the way you found it."

"Absolutely, of course. Thank you so much."

"You can go in the barn and take what you need."

"The barn? Um, it's okay to go in there?"

"Yeah, sure, why not? Like I said, just put things back where you found them when you're done."

"Okay, great, thanks! I'll go look now." I make to leave the shack.

"Amanda," he says, calling me back into the conversation.

"Uh, yeah?"

"It's Amanda Mathers, right? Your dad's that saxophone player in that band? And he's got the dentist office in town." I laugh out loud, and Hank looks instantly confused. "Was I being funny?"

"Oh no, I'm sorry, it's just my dad would be so happy that you know him as a sax player first, dentist second. He's going to love it when I tell him about it."

"Your parents know you're working up here?"

"Yeah, of course. Zoe also sent them an email and explained to them what we were doing to make sure they were on board."

"And your mom is Janice Mathers, right, the town lawyer? Her dad was Tom McKay?" Hank continues.

"Yeah, that's her," I say.

"And she's okay with you spending so much time up here?"

"Yeah, totally." This conversation is taking an odd turn. "I mean, she would rather I work somewhere in the municipal building with her, but, yeah, she's been okay about it, why?"

"No reason. Just curious," he says, clearly done talking about it. "Go on in and see if what you need is in the barn. If not, I have some more tools in the basement of the house. Just let me know."

"Okay, thanks."

All right, maybe I spoke too soon about him not being weird, I think as I open the door to the barn. Before I flick on the overhead light, I see that the door to Luke's side is open. I leave the light off and move a little closer to peek inside.

There's music playing, an old record. I think it's Chet Baker. (My dad would be thrilled!) There's a warm light coming from the room. I see an old wood-burning iron stove and beat-up corduroy couch, and on the far wall is a workbench. There are all kinds of cool models hanging over it, like three-dimensional hollow cubes and infinity steps made of thin wood, that look like they never end when they spin on their strings. Luke is sitting at the bench in his T-shirt, his back to me, leaning over something, totally unaware, just lost in whatever it is he's doing and he's humming along to the melody.

He seems so happy.

All of a sudden, there's a crash behind me—a metal snow shovel tips over and I see a flash of fur. Fairy Barn Cat darts by, stopping in the light of the open door. Her eyes shining like mirrors, she looks right at me.

"There you are!" I scream, totally forgetting I was just low-key spying on Luke. "Come back here!" Fairy Barn Cat darts into the shadows—to where I have no idea—and is gone.

By now, Luke is at the door, totally confused. "Amanda?" he says, flicking on the light. "What are you doing in the dark?"

He seems kind of amused, but then realizes the music is still playing and self-consciously pulls the door to his cozy little world closed behind him. He asks again, but to my relief it's clear he's curious, not mad. "What are you doing?"

"Oh, your dad said I could borrow some tools to take to Max's cabin so we could clean it up tomorrow, but then this . . ."

"Max is opening up the cabin?" He switches from curiosity to excitement.

"Uh, yeah, we're gonna fix it up, you know, for while I'm working here, so we can have a place to hang that's close by."

"Oh, cool," he says, clearly interested.

"I mean, do you want to come and help? We could load everything in my car tomorrow before our shifts start—I have the afternoon off school—and then I can drive us over there."

"Uh, yeah, yeah, that would be fun," he answers, like he means it.

"Okay, great, it's a . . ."

Don't say it, don't say it, Amanda Mathers, don't make it weird!

"It's a date," I say, and he starts to smile and I start to smile back, and it's at that moment that another snow shovel slowly slides from the spot where it was leaning on the wall and lands in an epic clatter.

"Yeah, I think you are definitely gonna need some help transporting these tools." He laughs.

"It wasn't me, it was the cat!" I say, defeated.

"But we don't . . ."

I don't let him finish.

"I know, I know, you don't have a cat!"

DECEMBER
11

Chapter 11
IT'S COMPLICATED

"That's the last bag," I yell to Luke, who has been tossing the trash bags I hand him off the porch of the cabin and onto the snow.

It's a simple, old-fashioned, two-room cabin with a long front porch, set in a pretty clearing in the woods surrounded by tall pines, near a feeder stream to Gully Crick. There was a fresh dusting of snow last night, so the whole scene is trimmed in three inches of powder, looking like a Bob Ross painting. According to Pearce family lore, Max's great-grandpa built the cabin himself from a mail-order kit and then handed it down to Max's grandpa who finally handed it down to Max's dad. It's a charming and much more modest house than the cathedral ceiling, five-bedroom, lakeside timber McMansion Max's dad has now.

Inside there's a galley kitchen with a sleeping loft over it. There are a dining area and a small bathroom on one side and two small bedrooms on the other side. In the middle is a big open living space with a stone fireplace and solid wood mantel. The dirtiest part of the whole clean-up was dealing with the fireplace, which had some debris that must have made it down the chimney. Otherwise, the sweeping, dusting, and washing hadn't taken very long at all.

At some point, one of the Pearce men insulated the cabin and added electric baseboard heating. After taking out the trash, airing out all the rooms, and smudging generously with sage by Celeste to clear any negative energy, we finally close the doors and crank the heat to warm everything up.

"Ahhh, that's more like it," Junjun says, plopping down on an old leather sofa in front of the hearth and a freshly made fire, laid but not lit. "You know, when Max said 'hunting cabin,' I was afraid this place would be full of dead animal heads with glass eyeballs staring at me, but it's not so bad."

"Yeah, other than the antler wall sconces, and that painting, it appears no animals were harmed in the making of this cabin," I say.

The decor that is still here is mostly wooden cross-country skis and snowshoes hanging on the wall, and an old-timey etching of a distressed-looking dog swimming through a rapid river, hanging over the mantle. There are also a couple of brass lanterns, and some end-table lamps in dire need of new bulbs and shades, but that's about it.

"Okay, I found a box with some plates and cups and things in the loft," Celeste says, stepping out from the kitchen, "but there's no blankets or towels. They probably wouldn't have survived the mice anyway, so we'll have to bring some over tomorrow."

"Yeah, no biggie. We have tons of stuff at home. I can ask my mom," Junjun says. "So what do we do now? Where are the boys?"

We hear a rumbling below us and pounding on the floor under our feet. A tortured voice screams, "Fresh brains, fresh brains!" followed by the muffled sounds of Max laughing, reliving every cabin in the woods zombie horror flick he's ever seen.

"As you may have guessed, they are in the crawl space seeing what else is down there," Celeste says like an indulgent teacher describing a couple of her preschoolers.

Jun smirks. "Seems like they have picked up right where they left off."

It has been sweet watching Luke and Max reconnect. And, honestly, seeing a whole other side of Luke.

He's actually not the total Grinch I thought he was when we first met.

The two of them have a lot of funny stories about this place. Max has been saying, "Remember that one time," on repeat since we got here, and each story usually ends with him crashing into something, falling off something, or some other kind of general destruction.

Earning his handle @maximumdanger since before there was Instagram.

"Oh, awesome!" We hear Max's muffled exuberance from beneath the floor. "Luke, look what I found!" There's a whole lot of shuffling and scuffling like a hoard of crazed raccoons under our feet, then the sounds of footsteps stomping up the porch followed by the thumping of snow boots at front of the door. Finally Max throws open the door and steps inside, Luke trailing behind, with what looks like a coffee can in one hand.

"Look what we found!" Max holds up an old wood and steel Radio Flyer sled. The wooden steering bar is cracked in half. "It's my old sled, *Rosebud*."

"Why's it called that?" I ask.

"I have no idea. Hank came up with it." Max holds the sled up and stares at it admiringly like a long-lost friend.

"Me and Luke used to build the sickest ramps and jumps and take her off them. It was so much fun."

"Lemme guess, you made the jump too high and crashed, and that's how you broke your sled," Jun says in his sweet sarcastic way.

"Uh, no, not at all, that's not what happened," Max says earnestly.

"Really?!"

"Yeah, it wasn't me. Luke did it."

"Yeah, my bad." Luke raises one hand sheepishly for full comedic effect.

"Oh, and look what else we found! Luke show 'em." Max puts the sled out on the porch and closes the door.

"Uh, it's a time capsule," Luke says, revealing the rusted coffee can with TIME CAPSOL scrawled in black crayon. "Max and I hid it in the crawl space when we were, like, eight? Apparently before we learned how to spell, at any rate. I can't believe it was still down there."

"Well, open it." Celeste beckons Luke to come closer. "I want to see what treasures you put in there!"

Luke kneels in front of the wood coffee table across from where Celeste, Jun, and I are sitting are sitting on the couch, and Max sits criss-cross applesauce at the other end of the table. Luke opens the can and dumps the contents.

"Oh, fire, my Pokémon!" Max says, shuffling through some well-worn cards.

"Ooh, look at all the cool rocks!" Celeste digs through an assortment of sparkly granite and marble finds. "This greenish one is talc, I think. Very good grounding energy."

"What's this?" I pick up a ball that's actually a piece of construction paper folded like a thousand times. I unfold it and see what appears to be the block print scrawl of eight-year-old Max.

"'Dear Luke,'" I read aloud. "'By the time you read this letter, it will be the future. You will be an architect in Chicago, and I will be famous. I hope we will still be best friends. Yours truly, Max.'"

"AWWWWWWWWWWWWW!" Jun and Celeste coo in unison.

"Oh my God, it's sooo sweet I'm gonna cry, you guys." Jun fans his eyes with his hands.

"You two are so cute!" Celeste says, squeezing her hands in little fists under her chin like she's looking at baby bunnies.

Both guys are visibly squirming but are being good sports and even crack a smile at each other. I'm still hung up on the note.

Architect in Chicago? Where'd that come from?

"Well, this has been great," Luke says in the exaggerated way of someone clearly trying to make an exit. "But I should probably get back to work."

"Oh yeah, I probably have to go too." I check my phone for the time and see a text from my mom.

> Hope you're having a good day. Don't forget about the internship application. xo

Ugh, the best part about being at the farm all the time is I have barely seen my mom and have managed to avoid this conversation so far. I "like" the text to buy myself some time and hope that she'll forget about it by Christmas.

"I should go too. I have choir rehearsal. Can you guys give me a ride back?" Jun says to Max.

"Sure, no prob."

"Maybe we can hang out tomorrow night after you guys get done at the farm. I can grab some stuff from home, and we can cook dinner out here," Celeste says.

"That could be fun, very cabincore. What should we make? Something in a cast-iron skillet!" Jun says, already planning the party.

"Oh, totally, but we should cook outside," Max says. "I've been wanting to do some wilderness survival, like, off-grid living content. This is perfect. I got this. I'll bring the food, we'll cook everything over an open flame, I can narrate, it'll be . . ."

"Fire?" Jun says.

"Exactly!" Max says.

"I was thinking more like knit sweaters and stew, but that works too," Celeste says diplomatically.

"Hmm, I wonder if my dad has any elk steaks left in the freezer?" Max has his finger to his chin, pacing like a movie director planning his next big shot.

Celeste blinks. "Can we have some vegetarian options, please?"

"Okay, I'm gonna leave you guys to whatever this is. I still have to put back all the tools we borrowed, so I'm gonna go."

"I'll help you," Luke says, all too happy to get a move on.

"Thanks." I smile, and we all trudge outside leaving Max, Celeste, and Jun to their planning.

Luke and I start collecting brooms and shovels and bags of trash and head to the side of the cabin where my Volvo is parked.

"Architect in Chicago, huh?"

"Yeah, that was the plan," Luke says with an exaggerated sigh. "I was just a small-town kid with big city dreams. . . . But, hey, sometimes things don't work out the way you planned. I mean, Max is working on it, but I don't think we can say he's famous yet."

"Maybe his living-off-the-land content will do it." I chuckle.

"He should probably stick to ski jumps."

"I don't know. Celeste would definitely prefer he makes content where he's not in danger of breaking a limb." I open the trunk and starting to load in.

"Yeah, that's funny. Max has a girlfriend. Last time we hung out, girls were still gross."

"Yes, they are a strange, but very cute couple." I watch Luke instinctively organize the tools and bags in the trunk, like it's a game of Tetris.

"What about you? Do you have a boyfriend?" he asks, not looking up from his work.

"Me? Nah, not in the cards. I have other plans. You know, small-town girl with big city dreams," I say theatrically as he gives me a curious look, closes the trunk, and moves toward the passenger seat.

Luke picks up my bag and phone and makes to hold them in his lap for the ride back to the farm. "Oh, you can just put that stuff in the back," I say.

The car is cold and the windows almost instantly start to fog up. I'm acutely aware of how close he is as he turns his broad shoulders toward me to deposit my things on the back seat.

"Um, you're buzzing. Looks like your mom is calling you." He turns back, holding up my phone with Mom's picture lighting up the screen.

"Don't answer it!" I gasp. "I'm not trying to talk to her right now."

"Okay, sure," he says, putting the phone in the cup holder and then buckling in as I pull out onto the snowy gravel drive through the woods and head back to the main road to the farm.

We drive in an awkward silence for a few minutes and then Luke asks with genuine concern, "Is everything okay?"

"Yeah, it's fine. My mom is just on my case to do this application for a summer internship, and I don't want to do it. But I haven't really gotten around to telling her yet."

"Why not? What's the big deal?"

"The big deal is it's not what I want to do, okay?" I say with way too much temper. "She wants me to do some, like, stupid town government internship, and I don't want to. I want to travel! I have my own plans for the summer that don't involve sitting around White Pine. That's her thing, not mine. And I'm going to tell her, it's just complicated." I realize too late that I am totally letting the fudge boil over.

"Sorry I asked," Luke says sincerely.

"No, I'm sorry. It's just I feel like ever since last summer, she's been on me about college and my future and how I should be thinking about applications and stuff, and honestly, it's stressing me out. I don't know what her deal is. I don't want to think about that stuff yet. I just want to, like, enjoy my time with my friends. And for summer, I mean, I wanna do things that interest me, not what she thinks I should do because it looks good on applications. Or because it's what she did and that's all she knows. It's like she can't even imagine that I have different interests!"

"Well, what do you want to do?" Luke asks.

"I want to travel! I want to get out of White Pine and see stuff, you know? I want to have, like, adventures and have good stories and write about them, like, real things that happen, not just stuff I make up. I want to have some kind of experience that happens anywhere but here."

"You don't like it here?" he asks carefully.

"Of course I do, I love it. White Pine is my home. But I feel like it was my mom's home first and everyone in town knows her, and they know my dad the dentist, and they know my brother and they knew my grandpa and, like, they all just assume they know me. And I don't even know me, and I just want a chance to do my own thing for one second and find out. That's why I'm going to go to Europe this summer. I signed up for an exchange program in Switzerland. There are all kinds of tracks, and I'm doing communications, which my parents are okay with because it looks good on college applications, and Celeste is gonna do the art leadership program. Then, as soon as the program is over, we are going to go travel. That's why I've been working so much at the stand. I'm saving up for my train pass. So I can finally get the heck outta this town."

He listens in silence, and I start to worry. I did the thing I do, where I say too much and don't think.

"I'm sorry, that probably doesn't even make sense," I say, trying to smooth things over.

"No, I get it. I do," he says with a sincerity that piques my curiosity.

"That's right, you wanted to be an architect in Chicago. Was that for real or, like, a 'I want to be an astronaut' kind of thing?"

"No, it was for real, it *is* for real. I mean, I guess it was, but not anymore."

"Why not? What happened?"

"Um, it's complicated."

"I mean, how complicated can it be? There are probably all kinds of good programs. If that's what you wanted, why don't you just . . ."

"Remind me again, why haven't you told your parents about your backpacking plans?" he says, interrupting me and sounding a little irked.

"I told you, it's complicated!" I instantly fire back, before realizing the well-laid trap I just faceplanted into. "Okay, I get it. Point taken. I'm sorry. It's none of my business. Sometimes I just get excited and get ahead of myself. I don't mean anything by it."

"It's okay," he says gently. "I actually like that you have stuff that you're into and get excited about, like writing and traveling. I mean, I think it's cool."

I keep my eyes on the road, momentarily flustered by the compliment and itching to fill the silence.

You 'actually' do, huh? I'm about to say sarcastically but instead decide to just listen.

"It's just that Chicago is where my mom lives. And so, living there and, you know, being an architect, it was an idea I had when I was little, that's all. But it's tied up with family stuff. And as you may have guessed from spending any kind of time with my dad, stuff in my family is . . ."

"Complicated," I finished for him.

"Yes, complicated."

By now I'm approaching the left turn to pull into the lot. I slow down and signal. It's not that busy. The Friday night after-work rush hasn't started, and Hank's sitting alone by the fire, giving it his daily thousand-yard stare.

"But I really do think it's cool that you want to travel." I can feel the energy of Luke's eyes on me, and I struggle to keep mine on the road. "Sounds like the trip of a lifetime." There's a touch of envy in his voice.

"Yeah, I hope so! It's kind of all I want, and I'm totally willing to do whatever to make it happen, you know?" I hazard a quick glance his way, and his eyes are still on me, his intense expression hard to read. "But first, I have to survive Christmas! Less than two weeks left and all this will be done, and I can get my tickets," I say resolutely as I pull in the lot and park.

"I can put the tools back. You probably need to set up the stand." Luke breaks his long stare and gets back to the tasks at hand.

"Okay, yeah. Thanks," I say. "I appreciate it."

And as I watch him walk away toward the barn, carrying a trash bag in one hand, brooms in the other, I suddenly realize that after Christmas I'm not going to have any reason to come up here.

Or any reason to see Luke.

And as much as I'm excited about summer, I don't think I want Christmas to be over just yet.

DECEMBER
12

Chapter 12
THE FIRE IS SO DELIGHTFUL

"Okay, all done!" I am putting away the last of my service items. "I just need to wash out the drink urns, but this is ready to go," I say handing the day's receipts over to Cheryl in the warmly lit kitchen of Post Farm. "Thanks so much for getting these to Zoe."

"Sure, no problem." Cheryl wipes her hands on her apron and takes the pouch. "I live right off Main Street so it's easy enough for me to connect with her and settle up on my way home. In fact, I should probably get going, she and I are actually going to meet over at the lodge tonight and grab a quick drink."

"Oh yeah?" I am not doing a very good job of hiding the interest in my voice.

In more than a year of working with Zoe, no one, I mean *no one,* at Matcha-Do has ever met anyone Zoe's dating or heard any kind of mention of any part of her personal life, even though it's a coffee shop and everyone who works there loves to chat. Like, I could write a book about my coworker Trevor's last five dates. (Headline: They were not great and according to him there are no datable guys in town.) But Zoe is always hyperprofessional with everyone, especially her employees, and never spills anything. So I can't help but be a little intrigued that she and Cheryl are getting together for drinks.

"Yeah, you know, just to hand off the receipts. She's gonna be up there anyway, so I figured we could meet there." Cheryl plays it cool.

"If you say so."

"Hey now, watch it!" She swats me playfully with the pouch. "What are you up to tonight anyways?" She changes the subject. "There's some leftover pastries in the pantry if you want to take them home to your family."

"Actually, I'm headed over to Max's cabin, he's going to attempt some kind of a cookout. So, you know what, I will take those pastries. It may be good to have some backup snacks, knowing how most of his schemes work out. I'll tell Luke to grab them."

"Luke's going with you?" Now, she's the one doing a terrible job of hiding her interest.

"Yeah, you know, he's friends with Max, and there are a couple of us just hanging out over there. So he's coming." She gives me the FACE—eyebrows raised, knowing smile, like oh-something-else-has-been-cooking-in-this-kitchen.

"Hey, *you* watch it!" I say. "It's really not a big deal."

"Uh-huh, if you say so . . ." But she's still smirking. "I'm gonna go freshen up." She hangs up her apron and heads to what must be her old room upstairs. "Have fun tonight!" she says with a wink.

"You too," I tease back in my best singsongy voice.

Ugh, I guess I deserve that, I think as I empty the last dregs of cold coffee out of the urns and wash them out in the big sink. I can't tell if I'm actually annoyed at Cheryl for the FACE or annoyed at myself for feeling excited at the thought of hanging out with Luke again. I mean, it's not like I like him. Like, like-him like-him, and I'm not trying to do the whole boyfriend thing like Celeste. But he is kinda growing on me.

And let's be real, I do catch myself looking at him a lot. To be fair, he does stand right across from me all day while I work so it's hard not to notice him. But he's also just kinda hypnotizing to watch. He's so tall and fit, and he moves so effortlessly. Picking up trees and tossing them up on cars, taking his jacket off when he gets hot. And then just hanging out in his flannel like an L.L.Bean model.

I swear the other day he got out a hatchet and, like, legit chopped off the end of a tree like a lumberjack. I thought I was gonna fall off my stool. And he's definitely lightened up a ton. He clearly likes to flirt. And I can't help myself. I'm totally having fun flirting back. But I don't think it really means anything.

Or does it? I wonder if he likes me? Like, likes-me, likes-me? I think as I finish washing the pots and start to dry them.

I mean he *is* always coming over for coffee, and I swear he doesn't even finish half of it. I think he just wants to, not chat really, but just hang around. When it's slow and I'm writing in my journal, he sort of hovers, leaning on the counter, drinking his coffee and not saying anything. It's nice. I kind of forget he's even there. But one or two times, I've definitely caught him looking at me. He looks away quickly, but I can still tell. It's like I can feel where he had his eyes on me. It tingles.

What if he was looking at me right now, and he just walked up and kissed the back of my neck, right on the spot where it meets the top of my shoulder, and then he puts his hand around my waist, and pulled me against him . . .

The sound of the door opening snaps me out of it, and I spin around to see him walking in, stomping snow off his boots. I stare at him as though he can read my not-quite-appropriate thoughts and he just . . . smiles. And oh wow, there are those tingles again.

Oh my God. I totally like him.

The revelation rings through my brain like bells on Christmas morning.

"You ready?" he asks.

"Uh, yeah, I've just got to put these away." I fumble to recover and thank my lucky stars that Luke's not a mind reader.

No, no, no! Get a grip, Amanda! He's just a guy you work with, and you're just gonna hang out with mutual friends. That's all this is.

"Cheryl says there's some pastries in the pantry if you want to grab them." I put the urn into one of the cupboards, wipe down the sink, and hang the dish towel.

"Yeah, I found them," he mumbles through a mouth full of Danish. "I'm gonna load up now, 'cause you know whatever Max makes is definitely gonna be sketchy."

Huh. Great minds think alike.

We each take our own cars over since it's already dark and starting to snow a little. We pull in at about the same time and park in front of the cabin. There's warm light coming from inside and the sconces on the porch cast a pool of yellow light on the snowy ground. We can see everyone huddled around the glow of a small fire over by some tall pines near the tree line.

"Okay, but if this is, like, a wilderness survival video, then where did you get the hot dogs?" Junjun asks as Luke and I walk up to the fire. "It's not making a lot of sense."

Max is standing next to the fire loading hot dogs onto some long pointy sticks he clearly carved with the multitool he has hanging from his belt. He's decked out in several hundred dollars worth of top-of-the-line outdoor gear and has a headlamp on his head, which is casting eerie shadows across his face, like he's in a low-budget horror film. Jun is squatting across from him, holding his phone at a low angle, trying to get Max, the fire, and the hot dogs in the shot. Celeste is sitting on a log behind both of them, looking cold and pretty over it.

"Yeah, I guess, but, like, it doesn't really matter. It's like wilderness survival–inspired, you know? I mean, like, if you were really out in the woods trying to survive, you probably wouldn't be looking at your phone for content anyway, you'd be trying to call for help, right? Or at least be looking up how to build shelter." Max taps his temple like *think about it*. "Oh, hey, what's up, Luke!"

"Hi, Luke," says Junjun.

Luke waves at them, crosses his arms, and settles in to watch the show.

"Um, hello, I'm here too!" I say, but the boys are already back to their filming. "Sheesh, how you like that. A new guy comes along, and all of a sudden I'm invisible," I say in mock offense. But I get no laugh from Celeste, who is clearly sulking. "How's it going?"

"As you can see, you have arrived just as the talent and director are working through some creative differences," she says stonily.

Uh-oh.

Celeste is a sweet, kindhearted, patient, nature-loving flower child, but heaven help you if she gets hungry. This is a code orange. We need to feed her fast. "Luke and I brought some of the leftover pastries from the stand, you want some?"

"What I want is for us to wrap this whole thing up and just go back to town and get some pizza!" Her voice crescendos to a slightly unhinged yell, definitely loud enough for Max to hear. But he just nods and waves and then continues to pile wood on the fire and discuss the right angle to capture him roasting his weenies.

Oh no, code red, code red!

"Okay, yeah, we can do that," I say gently. "But why don't we just go to the truck and grab you something to hold you over, okay? It'll just be a second." I back away from Celeste slowly.

"We gotta hurry." I grab Luke's elbow, pulling him toward me like a coconspirator, and speed-walk him urgently back toward his truck.

"What's the deal?" He is bemused, letting himself be dragged along.

"We have to feed her fast, or we're all in big trouble! This girl gets HANGRY. We have, like, ten seconds before she blows her top. We gotta get some carbs in her!"

He stops in his tracks and starts to laugh. I lose my grip on his elbow, my hand slides down his arm, and I end up holding his hand and yanking on it like a kid in a rush to see Santa.

"Why did you stop? And why are you laughing! This is serious. It's a pastry emergency." I start to laugh at the absurdity of the whole thing.

He walks slowly up to me, closing the gap between us, and I realize he's still holding my hand, and it's warm in the chilly air, and he's really close, close enough to kiss, and I instantly let go of his hand, to make it not weird.

"Seriously, you don't have to worry. This whole thing will be done in like a minute, and everyone can go eat."

"How do you know?"

He gently grabs me by both shoulders and turns me around. "Just look, what do you notice?"

I take a moment to regard the ridiculous tableau in front of us. Max is next to his now-raging campfire, its light making shadows dance on the snowy tree branches above him. Jun is still squatting down by the fire, like a nature filmmaker capturing footage of an elusive species. Celeste is huddled on the log, knees pulled up, arms crossed, rocking herself for warmth or in agitation, I can't tell which.

"Did you read that short story in middle school by the guy who wrote *White Fang*?"

"You mean Jack London?"

"Yeah, that's the guy, and the story was about a guy freezing in the winter and he has to build a fire."

"Oh, you mean 'To Build a Fire'?" I say obviously. "Yeah, I read it. Why?"

"You think Max did?" Luke watches Max squat down low to riff to the camera in an intense close-up.

"I mean, yeah, I guess. We were in the same class. But, like, why?" I am confused, looking at Luke and then back at the scene, when I notice one of the pine branches above Max, heavy with snow, bending ominously.

"Ohhhh."

"Give it like thirty more seconds, and Max is gonna have some excellent content for his blooper reel," Luke says.

"Oh man. Should we tell him?"

"Naaah," we both say in unison, and it takes about three more seconds for the melting snow to slide off the branch, dumping snow all over Max and snuffing out his "survival fire."

"Ahhhhh, my hot dogs!" Max squeals in a heartbroken scream.

"Bwah ha-ha-ha-ha-ha!" Junjun drops to his knees, losing it, as Max just stands there covered in snow going, "So cold, so cold, oh, so cold."

"Yes! Finally! Can we go get pizza now?" Celeste springs to her feet and starts to brush the snow off Max with her mittened hands, while Jun is literally keeled over, wheezing, trying to catch his breath from laughing so much.

"You're still filming, right?" Max says. "You got that?"

"Oh yeah, I got everything," Jun says, standing up and dusting snow off his knees.

"Sweet!" Max has already completely recovered. "Okay, then let's go get some pizza!"

"Yay! I'll go lock up." Celeste trots off to the cabin, suddenly full of energy.

"I guess he doesn't have to worry about putting the fire out," Luke quips, laughing.

"Amanda, I'm riding with you, I have dibs on your seat warmers." Jun walks toward us while looking down at the blue light of his phone and giggling to himself. "I can't wait to post this. 'maximumdanger hashtag-fails.'"

"Uh, I guess I'll head back then." Luke turns toward me, his keys in hand, gesturing back toward his truck.

"You're not coming with us?" I say, surprised.

"Yeah, let's go! I'm starving." Jun gets into my car, still preoccupied with his phone.

"I don't know. I didn't want to intrude on you and your friends." Luke looks down at me sheepishly.

"What are you talking about? They're your friends too." I say it like it's a plain fact, because it is. "Come out with us," I add, gently touching his hand with mine.

"Yo, Luke," Max yells as he heads toward his truck, arm around Celeste, who has now regained her human form and is smiling at the promise of imminent food. "I got hella change for the pool table, we got first game."

"Yeah, okay," he yells over my shoulder at Max.

"Okay," he says softer, now directly to me, and I feel him wrap his fingers around my hand and hold it, for just a moment. "Let's go."

Oh yeah, I think he might like-me, like-me too.

DECEMBER
13

Chapter 13
WINTER WONDERLAND

"Come on!" Luke says, grabbing my hand and pulling me out of the Candy Shack playfully. "It's still early enough, no one will miss us if we make it quick. Besides, Cheryl said she'd set up and cover for you for a bit. She's in a surprisingly good mood today!"

I guess drinks went well last night.

"Okay, fine, but let me get my snow pants from the car, I don't want to freeze. I'll meet you by the barn in a sec."

"Okay," he says, releasing my hand and backing away. "See you in a sec."

I don't know what's happening with Luke, but I'm not gonna lie, I like it.

It's Sunday, and I haven't had a day off all week and am not really feeling like slinging hot cocoa today. There's a fresh dusting of snow on the ground, the sun is up, and it's cold and clear. Luke wants to walk back to the cabin to grab Max's old sled from the porch. "For no special reason . . . ," he said cryptically when he proposed the idea, and I'm totally down for a distraction.

I guess I know who Luke has for Secret Santa.

I'm glad somebody's thinking about Secret Santa. Or any kind of Christmas prep. I've been so busy I haven't even started, and I still have no idea what to get Luke. Even after almost two weeks of seeing each other every day, he's still kind of a mystery. Definitely not your typical almost-eighteen-year-old guy. I did find out that much last night. His birthday's coming up in January.

He's not on socials and doesn't seem to have a ton of friends. The only time I've seen him take out his phone was to trade numbers with Max and Jun last night so they could go skiing.

Why didn't he ask me for my number?

I was a little annoyed at that and was gonna say something, but I didn't want to make it weird. But here we are hanging out anyway, so I guess it didn't matter.

"Right-o, Amanda, your challenge, should you wish to accept it, is to find out what to get your Secret Santa," I say out loud to no one in my go-to old British man accent. I open my trunk and pull out my spare snow pants.

Weather-ready, that's part of the deal if you are going to be driving.

I can hear my mom's voice in my head chiming in with the reminder. Of all the funny voices and bits that take up space in my overactive brain, Mom reminders are probably the least fun.

I sit on the edge of the open trunk, slide out of one of my boots, and, in a delicate, yoga-like pose, attempt to slide one leg of my snow pants on over my jeans without letting my sock touch down and get soaked. I'm mid-balance when I hear a little *meow*.

"I guess I wasn't just talking to myself. Where are you?" I say to the parking lot.

Fairy Barn Cat appears from behind a snow pile near the barn across from where I'm parked and gives me her cocked-head little look.

"Aha, well, hello there, Madame. Warmest greetings of the festive season to you, my good kitty," I say, bringing back the old Brit.

Fairy Barn Cat trots up in her dainty little way and sits in front of me, just out of reach of course, and meows again.

"Ah-ha. I see what you're up to, waiting until I have no shoes on to come nice and close so I can't chase you! You devilish little minx!"

But the cat just looks at me with curiosity.

"You know that one of these days, I'm going to see you at just the right time, and I'm gonna coax you over, and then I'm gonna pet you. You know that will happen, right?" I tell the cat in my own voice now.

The cat just looks back at me and starts licking her paw and rubbing it over her ear like a little washcloth.

By now, I've managed to get my snow pants and my other boot on, and I slowly start to creep over toward the cat. "I'm gonna pet you, kitty, it's going to happen," I say slowly, stretching out my hands, when she suddenly looks up, meows, and darts off.

"Drat! Foiled again. I will have my pets, Madame Kitty, you mark my words!" I say loudly in British while waving a fist in the air, when I turn to see Luke standing at the corner of the barn, staring at me like I'm, well, just a little insane.

"Oh, don't mind me." I close my trunk and own my weirdness. "Just talking to invisible cats."

"In a British accent? Okay, you have definitely been working too hard. You're starting to crack up," he teases.

I reach down and scoop up a ball of snow and chuck it his way, which he easily dodges. He looks at me in put-on shock and says in a playful warning, "Careful, don't be starting something you can't finish," before he trots ahead and disappears behind the barn.

I laugh and run after him. I round the corner and am stopped in my tracks by the view: a gentle snowy slope down to the pond, the formal rows of Christmas trees disappearing into the horizon off to my right, and the little dell in front of me bordering on the wilder woods, with the clearing of a small trail leading in. The whole scene is positively sparkling with icy crystals of fresh snow reflecting in the morning light, the diffuse cottony clouds breaking to patches of blue in the sky above.

"Wow." I am taken aback by the beauty of the scene. But the peace is broken when I feel a splash of cold, loose snow across my face, and Luke bounds off down the hill, laughing like a ten year old.

"Ugh, I can't believe it! You dirty little . . ." I shout, galloping down the hill after him into the woods. "It's ON!"

Dude has seriously underestimated me. I have a sixth-grade brother. I don't play when it comes to snowball fights.

Luke slows just inside of the woods, turns with his hands up, slowly backing away to manage the distance between us, laughing and saying, "Okay, truce! Truce! I'm sorry, I couldn't help it."

"Fine." I lower my weapon, a well-packed snowball locked and loaded in my right hand. "But I will get you back when you least expect it," I say in a perfectly calm voice so that he can't tell if I'm serious or flirting. Honestly, neither can I, so I just start to smile and he smiles back, and we walk along the path side by side.

The ground rises up a gentle slope to our right, and the sun casts dappled shadows on the snowdrifts between the trees. To our left is a gully that cradles an icy stream. The only sound is the crunch of our boots on the dry snow. The wind in the pines blows a light dusting of fine crystals through the morning sun.

"It's beautiful," I say, looking at the glowing snow surrounding us like fairy dust. "I never really noticed how snowflakes can hold a thousand colors of light. It feels like I'm walking through a poem."

"Hmmm," Luke says peacefully, walking slowly. "You have a nice way of describing things."

"Thank you," I say, pleased at the compliment.

"I guess that's why you are always writing in your journal, huh?"

"Yeah, I guess so." I think about it for a second. "I really like words," I add. "I mean, I like finding the right words to paint a picture of what I see. And it kind of blows my mind that the words I choose can paint that same picture in someone else's mind when they read them. It's like magic." I kick up little dustings of snow as I walk. "Plus, it kind of calms me down to write. As you may have noticed, there's a lot happening in my brain most of the time."

"Oh yeah?" he says nonchalantly. "I hadn't noticed, I mean other than the strange old British man that apparently lives inside your head."

"Shut up." I playfully slap him on the arm. "His name is Sir Reginald Dillpickle, and I just find it entertaining to do, like, little bits and characters. If my brain is going to be running constant commentary, at least I can keep it interesting."

"Your brain is constantly commenting on things?" he asks curiously.

"Yeah, isn't yours?"

"Um, no. Not really. I mean, I guess I've never thought about it. If I had to describe it, I'd say I think more in pictures than words. I like to see how things fit together, and notice patterns, and how to connect shapes. Probably why I like to make things and work in the shop."

"In the barn?" I ask, my curiosity bubbling up again.

"Yeah, it's kind of my woodshop-slash-workroom. My grandpa used to teach my dad and his brother, Rob, how to make models and things, and my dad taught me when I was little. I like to mess around in there. You know, fix things."

"Like sleds?"

"Maybe," he says playfully.

"Where's your uncle Rob? He doesn't help out on the farm?" Any hesitation I had about asking too many questions has faded away.

"No, he doesn't live nearby. Florida, we think, but he and my dad stopped talking years ago, and he kind of dropped out of the family. He just took off around the time I was born, after my grandpa died, and he never came back."

"I'm sorry," I say. "That must have been hard."

"I mean, not for me. I never really knew the guy. And my dad won't talk about it. But it was definitely hard on Cheryl and my grandma."

"Nan, the fudge lady?"

"Yes, the fudge lady," he smiles at her memory. "She wouldn't talk about it much either, but I definitely know it made her sad. Especially around Christmas. Most people probably couldn't tell because she loved Christmas, you know, and always made a big deal with lights and decorations, but I could tell. She'd sit at the piano and play a couple of songs, and sometimes I'd hear her cry. But she never wanted to let anyone see her doing it. Especially not my dad."

"That's really sad." I remember the faraway look Hank gave me when I was playing the piano. "You must miss her a lot," I add gently.

"Yeah, I do. But, you know, she loved these woods and this place, so I feel like she's kind of still around."

I stop and once again take in the quiet magic of the sunny

white woods. "It is a pretty special place."

He stops next to me. "Can I show you something?"

"Yeah, sure."

"Okay, but you gotta trust me."

"Well, now I'm not so sure . . . ," I say in mock skepticism.

"Just come over here." He guides me by my shoulders to a bank of fresh snow. "Now turn around, and we'll just flip your hood up like this." He lifts the hood of my ski jacket. "You ready?"

"Ready for what?" I ask, just as he gives me a light shove and I flop over on my back into the soft snow like I'm about to make a snow angel. Before I can protest, he flops down next to me.

"Now who's crazy? What was that . . ." I start to admonish him.

"Shh, just lay there and look up." He is absorbed in something high above us.

Irritated but intrigued, I let my head fall back on the cushion of the snow and look up.

I can see the black branches of the bare trees, dusted in snow, next to tall green pines reaching for the blue sky above me, swaying in sync with the loose white clouds that are moving and shifting on the breeze, revealing bursts of sunny blue sky as they pass. The snow cradles me like a baby and in my snow clothes, I don't feel cold. I feel connected to the ground and the sky and the trees. I'm aware of the slow rise and fall of my breath as well as Luke's, rising and falling in visible puffs of steam next to mine.

"This is what I do when I miss her," Luke says. "I lay in the snow and look at the sky and listen and just kind of breathe." He pauses. "And it's like she's still here. You know? I mean, she spent almost her whole life here on this mountain, and my grandpa, and his dad and Uncle Jim and my whole family, even my mom for a while. They were all here. And it's like some part of them is still here somewhere, and when I lay here, I don't feel lonely. I just feel like I'm part of something bigger than me. Like I belong here."

I just listen as he talks, relaxing into the rhythm of my breath, and I feel peaceful. Like I belong here too. Or, at least, to the mountains and pines and snow that's my home . . . White Pine. And I realize I've been dreaming of traveling and seeing the world for so long, I kind of forgot how beautiful the place that I live actually is. I guess I can understand why someone might have a hard time leaving it. And it makes me wonder why they would.

"Chicago, right? That's where your mom is?" I ask.

"Yeah, she's an anthropology professor at the University of Chicago," Luke says, still looking up and watching the clouds go by.

"Do you ever go see her?"

"I mean, I did when I was little, like every year. But somewhere around middle school, I just didn't really want to go anymore."

"Why not? Do you not get along?" I ask gently.

"No, it's not that. She's fine. I mean, I wouldn't say we're close, but we get along fine. It's just, you know, my life is here and she's more like Cheryl, like an aunt or someone who sends me birthday cards and checks in pretty regularly. But my grandma raised me, so I just don't feel like putting on some kind of a show just 'cause she's my mom. I love her and we keep in touch and that's about it.

Although, she wants me to come visit her more and call. But with my dad, you know, it's . . . I don't know." And all of a sudden, he starts to close back up. "I don't even know why I'm telling you all this stuff." He snaps out of his reverie and starts to get up. "We should probably get going anyway. I'm sure it's starting to pick up at the lot."

I sit up, surprised at the change in tone and feeling like I've just woken up from a strange dream. "Sorry if I upset you. I didn't mean to pry." I look up at him, now standing over me.

"No, you didn't. I just, I mean, I don't really ever talk about all this stuff. I don't know why I am now," he says, looking thoughtful. "I guess for someone who never stops talking, you are actually a really good listener."

"For someone who never talks, you actually have a lot to say," I volley back, smiling.

"Yeah, I guess I do." He's looking down at me, the trees and blue sky now crowning his smiling face. "Come on," he says, stretching out his hand, "I'll help you up."

I take his hand and he gives me a tug to my feet, totally underestimating my size and his own strength. I fly up and he catches me, arm around my waist, holding me tightly, chest-to-chest, eye-to-eye, and for a second, time seems to stop as we stare at each other.

No, don't do it, don't do it, Amanda. It will ruin everything.

Too late, I think as I drop a handful of snow down the back of his collar and run off toward the cabin.

"Told you I'd get you back!" I cackle hysterically.

"Oh, *that's* a dirty move." He shakes the snow from out of his shirt, in total shock but clearly impressed. "You better run," he says, lobbing a snowball my way.

"Last one to the cabin is on Santa's naughty list." I turn and taunt him playfully.

And he smiles at me and I smile back, as we race to the cabin, snow under our boots, the winter sun on our faces.

DECEMBER
14

Chapter 14
THE WEATHER OUTSIDE IS FRIGHTFUL

"Whoa, it's really starting to come down out there," Cheryl says as we finish Candy Shack cleanup in the warm and cozy Post Farm kitchen. "It looks like there's a little sleet in the mix, and that wasn't part of the forecast. I'm glad we're closing early 'cause I don't like the idea of you driving home if it's icy."

"Yeah, neither does my mom. She's texted me like a hundred times to ask if I'm heading home yet. If it's okay with you, I'm gonna get going."

"Yeah, that's fine, but if you give me ten minutes, I'll follow you out. I'm headed back into town and I'll drive behind you, make sure you get back safely."

I get out my phone to text Mom with the update, and as I do, the back door opens and Hanks steps in, shaking big, wet, sloppy snowflakes off his hat and coat on the mat by the door. Right behind him is Luke, who does the same.

"I don't think anyone's driving anywhere tonight," Hank says. "We just dropped one of the guys over by the lodge, and it's nothing but black ice out there. Plus, I heard on the radio there's a weather advisory, and they're telling everyone to stay off the roads until the sleet stops. There will definitely be a delayed school start tomorrow." He nods with finality. "It'd probably be best if everyone stayed here. We got plenty of space. Cheryl can drive you in tomorrow in the truck, Amanda, and you can come back for your car when they have everything cleared."

Oh, man, Mom is going to freak out.

She was already kind of on my case about the weather this morning when I left for school, but they were only predicting a couple of inches, so I told her it wasn't a big deal. As if on cue, my phone starts to buzz.

"This is my mom calling, I better take it and tell her what's going on. Excuse me." I step into the hall where a table lamp is casting a warm yellow glow.

"Hey, Mom."

"Where are you? Are you driving? You know you shouldn't drive and talk on the phone," she scolds.

Uh, you called me remember? This is going to be a fun conversation.

"No, I'm still at the farm." I'm trying not to sound testy. "I was just talking with Hank, and he said the roads are really bad and there's a sleet and ice advisory. He offered to let me stay here, and Cheryl will take me to school in the morning in the truck, and then I can get a ride out after school to get the car."

“Ugh, I knew this would happen,” she says with an exasperated sigh. “I just knew I should not have let you go out there today.”

“Mom, I didn’t decide the weather. They weren’t predicting sleet. I mean it’s not my fault.”

“Yes, of course, I know. I just have some meetings tomorrow that I’ll have to move to give you a ride, but we’ll figure it out!” She tries to tack on a chipper tone after she’s already made clear how annoyed she is. Then she says the thing she’s really worried about. “I just don’t like the idea of you staying out there all by yourself.” The unease in her voice is clear.

“Mom, I’m not by myself.” I lower my voice so the Posts don’t hear. “Cheryl’s here and Luke and Hank.”

“Cheryl’s there? Where will you sleep? Will she be nearby?”

“What? I don’t know. Yeah, probably, she still has a room here, and it’s a big house, and Luke sleeps out in the barn, and I think Hank’s room is on the ground floor, so I’ll probably be upstairs? Why are you being so weird about this?”

“It’s not weird to want to know where your child is sleeping when they are staying at a strange place, all right?” she says defensively. “I’m not happy about any of this. I just want you home when the weather’s bad! But I guess I have no choice.” She sighs, trying to recover herself. “Just call me when you are on the road tomorrow, okay?”

“Yes, okay.”

“Promise . . . ?”

“Yes! Fine!” I catch myself snapping and feeling instantly guilty. “Look, I’m going to go. Do you want me to have Cheryl call you or something so you can talk to her?"

"No, that's not necessary. I trust your judgment."

Really, you sure?

"Okay, bye, Mom."

"Bye, honey, love you."

"Yeah, I love you too," I say, and hang up the phone, letting out an audible sigh.

Man, my mom stresses me out so bad sometimes.

"Everything okay?" Hank carefully leans around the corner so as not to startle me.

"Yeah, my mom is just a little nervous about the storm and me not being home."

"Well, it's parents' prerogative to worry," he says matter-of-factly. "We all do it, whether we tell you about it or not. Come on back in. I'll fix us some dinner."

Hank cooks?

"Okay, thanks." I follow him back into the kitchen. "And thanks for letting me stay."

"Don't mention it. We're glad to have you. And these two are tired of my cooking," he says, eyeing Luke and Cheryl as we walk into the kitchen. "So I'm looking forward to lots of compliments from someone new."

I giggle at that and notice Luke squirming in embarrassment at his dad's, well, dad joke. I guess the Posts are not that different from any other family after all.

About an hour later, we are sitting around the kitchen island, surveying the remains of a massive meal of chicken, baked potatoes, veggies, and some of Cheryl's delicious jalapeño cheddar corn biscuits. "I'm totally stuffed. That was delicious, Hank, thank you so much. That chicken was so good." I heap on the compliments as instructed while clearing the plates and handing them to Luke who's rinsing and loading the dishwasher.

"Yeah, a lot better than Max's wilderness hot dogs the other night," Luke adds, prompting us to exchange a look and chuckle.

"What's that all about?" Cheryl asks.

"We don't want to ruin your experience of watching the video."

"Just search maximumdanger," Luke says, "You'll see. Totally worth it." We look at each other again and start cracking up.

"Okay, if you say so." Cheryl shares a bemused look with Hank and then leaves us to our inside joke.

"You getting tired, Amanda?" she asks after we finish the last dishes. "I made up the bed in the upstairs front room, and there are fresh towels and a new toothbrush for you. I left a pair of my old sweats and a long-sleeved T-shirt to sleep in too. I can show you where it is when you're ready."

"You mean Nan's room?" Luke asks, his tone shifting.

"Yes," Cheryl says firmly. "It's warmer than your old room and neater. Or do you really want Amanda staring at your middle-school-era Avengers posters and all your D&D stuff?"

"Wait, what?" I am kind of giggling. "You're a D&D nerd?"

"Oh, I can't believe you, Cheryl." Luke is clearly unamused.

"Relax, everybody's a little nerdy in their own way." She waves him and his embarrassment away.

"It's true," I say, trying to save the day. "I had a really long, like, longer than it should have lasted, Disney princess obsession. I'm talking matching pajamas and slippers and dress-up dresses. I know it's hard to believe considering how cool I am now," I say with mock bravado. "But it's true."

Cheryl smiles, and Luke lightens up a little at the thought of me dressed as Ariel, but still shoots an unamused look at his aunt.

"Anyway, don't worry, Amanda, we put away most of my mom's things a while ago, and the room is very much our guest room. But I guess, you know, for all of us, it'll always be Nan's room."

"Well, I really appreciate you giving me a place to stay. Thanks again."

"What do you say we go in the parlor and light the fire?" Hank chimes in from out of nowhere.

"Really?" Cheryl is clearly surprised, as if she's seeing a long-lost friend. "We haven't done that in ages."

"Yeah, you know Mom always said, nothing better than a warm fire on a stormy night. And maybe, Amanda, you'd play the piano again," he adds.

"Um, yeah, I suppose I could." I'm feeling a little shy all of a sudden.

"Dad, I'm sure Amanda's tired and wants to go to sleep." Luke is clearly uncomfortable with the idea. It's like his stone-faced Grinch alter ego is back, and it's so hard to get a read on the dynamic that I have no idea what I'm supposed to do, so I decide to follow Luke's lead.

"I do have school tomorrow . . ."

"Of course," Hank says politely. "Just a thought. We should all probably get some rest," he adds, though it feels like he's a little disappointed.

"Okay, come on, Amanda, I'll show you to your room." Cheryl secures my exit.

"Good night," I say to Hank. "And thanks again for dinner."

"Good night." I try to catch Luke's eye and get a read on what's going on. But he just mumbles a good night and goes to get his coat and boots to walk over to the barn.

"Don't mind him," Cheryl says calmly as I follow her up the stairs. "I think this is a lot of change for him for one evening."

"What do you mean?"

"I mean, we haven't had anyone to dinner or sat in the parlor by the fire since my mom died. It was just kind of too sad because she loved to entertain. So, I think having you over and laughing and joking . . . Let's just say I haven't seen Luke open and chatty like that in a long time. And I haven't seen Hank like that in even longer! So I'm guessing it's all just a little bit much for Luke."

"Oh, I didn't mean to upset anyone." My brain starts to anxiously spin a highlight reel of mess ups.

"No, sweetie, it's not you." She stops in front of a closed door at the end of a long hall and turning to me. "Honestly, you are the best thing to happen around here in ages. You're like a big, bright, goofy, outspoken, funny, smart, chaos fairy, and exactly the kind of positive energy we need to shake things up around here." She gives my shoulder an affectionate squeeze.

That is, by far, the weirdest compliment I have ever gotten. But I kind of love it. And I can't help but smile.

"This is your room," Cheryl says, opening the door to a cozy front room with a dormered window, built-in bookshelves, and an old four-poster bed just like mine, covered in a faded but lovely geometric quilt. There is a small table and rocking chair across from it, lit by a reading lamp. "I'm just down the hall if you need anything, and the bathroom's at the top of the stairs. There are more blankets in the closet." Cheryl smiles once more. "Good night."

"Good night," I say as she shuts the door softly, and I find myself alone in Nan's room.

After changing and dipping out to the bathroom to brush my teeth, I climb into the big bed under the fluffy down duvet beneath the quilt and finally have a moment alone with my thoughts.

Well, this is a strange turn of events.

I realize that even though I'm usually good at sleeping away from home, with the sleet tapping on the windows and the wind making the old house creak, I'm feeling pretty far out of my comfort zone.

Mom was right. I should have just gone home after school today. What am I doing here? What am I doing period? I always make such stupid decisions, say stupid things. Disney princesses? I can't believe I told them that.

There it is, my anxiety highlight reel, greatest hits edition, all cued up and ready to play all night. I just need to take a deep breath and settle down. I'll fall asleep and it'll be morning. The storm will be over and I'll be fine.

I wish I had something to take my mind off this. Of all the days to leave my journal at home.

That's when I hear just the faintest little noise—a very quiet *meow*.

There it is again, definitely a meow, but where is it coming from? I turn on the lamp, get out of bed, and listen. I can still hear the sleet on the windows, but I also hear something else—scratching, and the *meow* again, now a little more urgent.

I go to the dormer window that looks out onto the low, flat porch roof, raise the shade, and there, cold and wet, is Fairy Barn Cat.

"Oh my goodness, poor baby, we gotta get you inside!" I raise the sash and let the cat climb through. This time, Fairy Barn Cat does not play coy: she jumps right in and immediately starts to make figure eights through my legs, purring loudly.

"We need to get you warmed up." I grab the bath towel Cheryl left at the end of the bed and bundle the cat up in it, which she gladly allows. I hold her to my chest to keep her warm. She reaches out her nose to mine for a sniff, then closes her eyes, smiling, and gives me a little bop across my face.

"Well, how do you like that? You sure can be friendly when you are avoiding a sleet storm." I get a *meow* in reply. I'll take it. "Now, let me see if I can find you another blanket, and I'll make you a bed on the rocking chair."

I carry the bundle of kitty over to the closet, put her down, and open the door. There's not much inside, a few old cardigans, and a lambswool-lined corduroy work coat that must have been Nan's. It's well worn, and the pockets are sagging open, and I can see something inside the one closest to me. Curiosity gets the better of me, and I reach in and pull out a bandanna and several individually wrapped mini candy canes.

Huh, so that's what Luke must be giving to all the little kids. He keeps candy canes in his pockets, just like his grandma did.

The discovery is so sweet and sad it almost makes me cry. I put everything back in the pocket and respectfully press it closed.

I look up and see a stack of quilts on the shelf above the hanging rail, and as I reach up for one, Fairy Barn Cat starts shuffling around at my feet, just inside the closet. I grab a quilt and then squat down to see what she's gotten herself into.

On the floor just inside the door is a cardboard box with the flaps worn out and loosely folded over. Fairy Barn Cat is pawing at them in the playful way of all cats obsessed with cardboard boxes.

"What are you into, get out of there," I say, sliding the box out into the light to see if the cat has scratched anything.

The box is open and inside are photo albums and some memorabilia. "Kitty, you can't be scratching on this." There are a few papers on the floor behind the box where the cat must have pulled them loose.

I pick up an old, yellowing paper with a child's painted handprint turned into a turkey. The written message reads: *For Mommy and Daddy, From Luke, Happy Thanksgiving.*

Huh, I guess Luke's mom was still around for holidays when he was little. I thought this was Nan's stuff.

Maybe it doesn't matter whose stuff it is. You probably shouldn't be looking at it anyway!

I do realize as I sit on the rug in front of the closet, with the storm raging outside and the warm cat curled up next to me, that I'm crossing over into all-out snooping. But with my anxiety still raging, I decide that flipping through a few family photos albums could be a good distraction from a full-blown panic attack. So I forge ahead.

I grab one of the albums from inside the box, gently tuck Luke's drawing inside the cover, and turn to open the first page.

The first photo is of a young couple sporting backpacks, in front of the Parthenon. The man has the dark eyes of a Post. That must be Hank. And the woman is fair, very tall, with blond hair in a ponytail and sunglasses. Huh, I wonder if that's Luke's mom.

The caption reads *Hank and Annabelle, Backpacking Greece.* There are several more of the young couple, probably still in college or just after, all over Europe.

Oh, wow, these aren't Nan's old albums. It looks like they're Hank's.

I know I shouldn't look but, by now, curiosity has total control. The pictures are amazing. Hank is young and happy and indulging in plenty of goofy tourist poses. My favorite is him beaming, the camera angled so it looks like he is holding the Eiffel Tower in the palm of his hand.

And he is clearly head-over-heels for Annabelle. There is photo after photo of her looking out over the Seine, blond whisps blowing across her face, serene smile. Annabelle sitting in cafés, shades on her head, looking tanned and content over a coffee. A couple of bikini pictures of her walking out of a teal blue Mediterranean. She was really very beautiful, and Hank sure had an eye for capturing her.

Wow, this is exactly the trip I want to take!

How funny Luke's parents did it.

I get to the last page of the album, and a postcard slides out. It's of the Sears Tower with the word CHICAGO in big letters below. I flip it over to read the message:

Dear Hank and Luke,

Can't wait for you to join me out here. I found a perfect apartment for us. Tell Luke how excited I am to take him to his first Cubs game.

Love to my boys, A.

Oh, wait a minute. They were all supposed to go to Chicago together.

What happened?

I suddenly feel kind of sick and pretty ashamed of myself for snooping. I put everything away how I found it and slide the box back into the closet. Fairy Barn Cat looks up at me wondering why I'm fussing and disturbing her sleep. I scoop up the kitty, quilt and all, and plop her at the end of the bed. I climb in and turn off the light as the storm continues to batter the windows.

"Well, at least one good thing came out of all of this." I stroke the cat as she turns circles on my stomach. She makes a few biscuits before curling into a ball and landing on my chest.

"I finally get to pet you. Told you I would. I'm glad you are my friend, cat." It's the last thing I say before her warm weight and purring lull me into a deep sleep.

DECEMBER
15

Chapter 15
FAMILY TREE

"Did you know there were actually two versions of this Christmas carol?" Dad is driving the family car, fully loaded with Mom, Milo, and me, to Post Farm, Frank Sinatra's smooth crooning voice on the radio singing "Have Yourself a Merry Little Christmas."

Through the years, we all will be together
If the fates allow
Hang a shining star upon the highest bow . . .

"In the original version sung by Judy Garland from the musical *Meet Me in St. Louis*, that last line was *'Someday soon we all will be together, if the fates allow. Until then, we'll have to muddle through somehow . . .'* "

Dad's singing voice is almost as smooth as Sinatra's.

"Frank thought it was too depressing, so he changed it to the version we just heard." He takes a beat. "What? No response? No, 'How interesting, Dad?'" Another pause. "Well, I think it's interesting," he mumbles, and we all ride in a semi-sulky silence, Milo on his Switch, Mom texting urgently on her phone for work, and me staring out the window.

I hate not driving myself.

Normally, I tune out of my dad's jazz lectures, but this one actually is interesting, since this particular Christmas carol keeps coming up. It's the same carol Nan had bookmarked in the piano book, with the photo of Hank and Rob. It might have been the song Luke heard her play when she thought she was alone. Except hers was the original version. The sad one. And after everything I've been learning about the Posts, it sounds like they've been "muddling through" for a while now.

I didn't see Luke when I got up this morning. I didn't see the cat either for that matter. I don't know how she did it, but when I woke up my door was ajar and the little sneak was gone.

Fairy Barn Cat, you are a mystery.

But at least I know she is real. My blanket was covered in cat hair.

I slept well, and Cheryl was really sweet getting me to school in Hank's big truck. I was glad for the ride, because the roads were still pretty hairy.

School was fine, but all day I just kept feeling, I don't know, sad, I guess? Just realizing how much Luke and everyone at the farm have been going through. And then they were all so nice, feeding me and putting me up.

And then you totally invaded their privacy by snooping around.

I feel bad about looking through Hank's album. Not my finest moment. Which is why I was hoping after school Max could just give me a ride to get my car, I could do my shift, go home, and, like, avoid eye contact with Hank. But my mom *insisted* she come and say thank you herself. Then my dad had the great idea to use the ride out as an excuse to get a real Christmas tree this year, so here we all are.

"Wow, this place sure has changed," Dad says when he pulls into the lot. "Geez, Janie, we haven't been here in ages, have we?"

"Huh?" Mom seems distracted when she looks up from her phone. "Yeah, not since Milo was born. It does look a little less sparkly than I remember it when Nancy and Joe used to run it. But is that your little stand, Amanda?" She points to the Candy Shack as we park and get out. "It sure brightens the place up."

"That's it," I say quite proudly. "I decorated it, set it up, and have been pretty much managing it myself. Zoe says it's been adding a nice little bump to her holiday numbers. It even brought a few new ski lodge customers to the shop in town."

"Well, good for you, honey," Dad says. "Way to take initiative. I'm so proud of you."

"I guess that explains why you've been spending all your time here," Mom adds.

Geez, would it kill you to just admit that I started something myself that had nothing to do with you?

My mom has been so uptight all afternoon. I can't tell if she's mad at me for getting stuck out here last night, or if it's because I haven't done her internship thing yet. Whatever it is, I feel like she's looking to find something wrong.

"Do you only sell hot chocolate, or do you also have Bro-bble tea with extra Bro-bba?" Milo asks dryly as we walk up to inspect the stand.

"Nope. Weak. Zero points, gonna have to do better than that," I say, reminding my little brother of the rules of engagement for our long-standing bro-pun game.

"Hey, says here you sell fudge." My dad points at the chalkboard menu. "Do you only have chocolate, or do you also sell Bro-nilla?" He makes a face like, *How you like that one?*

"Oh no," I say, "no, no, no, no, no, no, no." I shake my head.

"Ehhh!" Milo makes a buzzer noise. "Negative one hundred points, Dad. Really, just terrible."

"What? I don't even get points for effort?" Dad is hamming it up.

And we both just shake our heads smiling at the old goof.

"Can you at least hook me up with a hot chocolate? What's a guy gotta do to get a drink around here?" He comedically slaps his hand on the counter of the Candy Shack just as Luke walks out of the kitchen with a full urn of cocoa.

"Oh, hey, let me help you with that," I say, rushing up to the porch, trying to get to him before my parents do.

"Nah, it's okay, I got it." His tone is friendly, and he seems to have recovered from his tense mood the night before. "Is that your family?"

"Yes, and I apologize in advance for anything ridiculous they may say. Especially my dad."

This gets a smile out of him, and I smile back. When we reach my family at the Candy Shack, all three of them are smiling at us, making the FACE!

This is going to be so embarrassing.

"Well, hey there, need a hand with that?" my dad asks Luke, sizing him up.

"No, sir, I'm all set." Luke puts down the urn and turns smoothly to shake my dad's hand.

"Sir? No need to be so formal, you can just call me Dr. Mathers," Dad says in mock seriousness. "I'm just kidding, call me Dick."

"Very nice to meet you. I'm Luke Post."

"Nice to meet you, Luke. I'm Janice, Amanda's mom," Mom inserts herself and offers her hand. "You must be Hank's boy."

"Yes, ma'am."

"It's okay, Janice is fine," she says warmly. "So, tell me, Luke, how old are you?"

"Mom, what the heck?" I say in a nervous low whisper.

"Oh, I'm just wondering what school you go to and all that, you know," Mom adds nonchalantly.

"I don't go to school," Luke says.

"That's sick," Milo whispers in awed respect.

"This is Milo." I point toward my weird little emo sib. "We're not actually related. He was switched at birth."

"Whatever, your nose growing much, Bro-noccio?" Milo fires back.

"Whoa, good one," my dad says, and gives my brother a preposterously cringe high-five, which Luke laughs at.

"That's a nice smile you got there. Who's your dentist?" Dad can't help himself.

"Now hold on a minute," Mom interrupts, still fixated on interrogating Luke. "You're out of school already? Now I really need to know, how old *are* you?"

Oh God, it's all just so mortifying.

"I'm seventeen. And, no, I haven't graduated," Luke says politely. "I'm close, but I've been doing my GED online and will probably finish next semester."

"Well, okay. But still, online GED? I've heard really mixed things about some of those programs . . ."

"Mom, we're here for a tree, remember?" *Not to analyze Luke's academic career. If I don't stop her, she's gonna want to see his grades next!*

"Yes, of course. Can't blame a mom for being curious who her daughter is spending all her time with, right?" she says sweetly.

I can't believe her.

"Yes, a Christmas tree, right! Let's get a tree!" She dials up holiday cheer, like flipping a switch.

"I'm happy to help you with that," Luke says, thankfully ignoring her last comment. "Did you want to grab one off the lot or go cut your own?"

"Well, you've got to get to work, right, sweetie?" Dad says to me.

"We wouldn't want to go cut one without you, so I guess we'll just grab one off the lot."

"Bummer, I thought I was going to swing an ax," Milo says.

"We use a saw actually," Luke says, "but I'd be glad to take you out. It's Tuesday and we had a storm last night, so it's not going to be that busy until later. You can come out too, Amanda. It should be fine."

"You hear that, sweetie? How great!" Dad is bouncing on his toes with fatherly excitement.

"Well, no, I really shouldn't. I mean someone has to finish setting up."

"Just text Cheryl, she'll cover for you. It'll only be a half hour or so," Luke counters.

"What about you? Don't you have to set up and . . . get things done?" I add, trying to avoid prolonging Luke's exposure to my family.

"Oh, don't worry about me," Luke says in total deadpan. "This is not my first Bro-deo."

"There it is!" my dad exclaims.

"Nice one," my brother says, nodding his head, deeply impressed.

My mom just laughs. "You're funny," she says, putting a hand on Luke's arm and then turning back to shoot me a little raised eyebrow.

Oh boy.

"Well, let us away!" Dad says dramatically. "Into the wilderness to hunt for our tree, like our forefathers!"

We cross the lot, grab a sled and saw, my dad and Luke in the lead, the rest of us trailing behind.

"So, tell me, Luke, do you like jazz?"

"Yeah, sure. My dad's great uncle had a lot of records, so I listen to them when I'm working on projects. He was mostly into big band, Tommy Dorsey, Basie, and Ellington, but he did have some Miles and of course Coltrane, Rollins, and Bird."

"Good lad!" my dad shouts, slapping Luke on the back in pride. "There's hope for the next generation!"

As they continue to banter, Milo jumps in the sled for a free ride from Luke, who obliges, and my mom hangs back and quietly says to me, "*Now,* I understand why you're spending all your time out here. He's cute." She gives me a playful nudge. I can't help but smile sheepishly.

It's the first thing she's said to me in ages that wasn't a reminder or deadline, and all of a sudden I just want to tell her everything, about Secret Santa and Fairy Barn Cat, laying in the snow, finding the album, and how confusing it's all been because I think I really like Luke, and I think he really likes me. But how we're also kinda just friends, and that I wish she and I could talk like we used to. But instead, I say, "Yeah, he is cute," and smile as we wander into the pristine rows of trees.

"I see it! That's the one, everybody. I see her. She's a beaut!" Doing his best Clark W. Griswold, my dad points ahead at a seven-foot-tall, full, beautiful Christmas tree. "Onward!"

A half hour later, we are pulling the great tree in the sled back to the lot, Dad and Milo beaming like conquering heroes. My mom and I even managed to sing a few carols. I figure I got to peek into Luke's family life, it's only fair he gets to see mine, Christmas carols and all.

He took the whole outing in great stride, listening to my dad's jazz rants, even promising to come see a gig, and talking D&D and comics with Milo, his former nerdy interests giving him serious cred with my sixth-grade brother.

Cheryl is in the Candy Shack and Hank is manning the cut trees when we get back, but as Luke predicted, there aren't a ton of customers on the lot yet.

"Thanks so much for covering for me, Cheryl," I say as she steps out from behind the stand to say hello. "Um, this is my family. My mom and dad, and my brother, Milo." She shakes hands with everyone.

"Hello, Mathers, looks like you found a good one!" Cheryl points to the tree. "And thanks for lending us Amanda here. She's been just a treat to have around."

"Speaking of treats," my dad says, "are you the person responsible for all the incredible fudge Amanda's been bringing home?"

"Guilty as charged," Cheryl replies.

"Well, as a dentist with a sweet tooth, I have to thank you on two levels. Not only is your fudge my favorite holiday indulgence, but you're keeping me in business! I'll be filling some extra cavities in the new year. Keep up the good work!" Dad dials up his dentist jokes to the next level.

Cheryl just chuckles until my mom interrupts the banter.

"Hello, Hank," my mom says, noticing Hank has wandered over while we were all chatting.

"Hello," Hank replies.

"It's good to see you."

"It's good to see you. It sure has been a while." Hank looks at my mom intently. She holds his gaze with equal intensity.

Wait, what?

"Um, you know my husband, Richard, and this is Milo." She breaks their eye lock to introduce everyone.

"Hank," my dad says with a nod, shaking his hand and striking an oddly professional tone.

"We just wanted to thank you, both of you"—Mom turns to include Cheryl— "for looking out for Amanda yesterday. We really appreciate it."

"Well, it's nothing you wouldn't do for Luke if the situation was reversed, but of course, it was our pleasure. That's a good kid you got there. Smart and takes initiative." I blush at the out-of-nowhere compliment from Hank.

"We sure can say the same for you," my dad adds warmly. "Thanks for your help with the tree, Luke."

"No problem," he says, but is also clearly glad of the praise. "I can get it wrapped up for you and, if you pull up, I can get it on the car," Luke adds.

"Will do. Come on, Milo, you can ride shotgun."

"Sweet," Milo says.

"Thanks again, Hank." My dad shakes Hank's hand firmly. "Glad to see things are going well. Good to meet you, Cheryl."

Dad shakes her hand too. "Keep that fudge coming!"

"Nice to meet you, Dick," she replies, chuckling.

"And I'll see you at home." Dad kisses me on the top of my head and then walks off to the car with Milo.

"Bye, Dad!"

"Oh, before I forget, what do I owe you for the tree, Hank?" Mom reaches in her purse to get out her wallet.

"Oh no, it's on the house," Hank replies, hands up, waving away her offer of money.

"Come on now. I can't let you do that, especially after you took such good care of Amanda."

"Like I said. For you, Janie, it's on the house," Hank insists, giving her that long look again.

"Thanks, Hank." She shakes his hand again warmly. "And thanks to you too, Cheryl."

"No problem Mrs. Mathers. Great to finally meet you."

"See you at home after your shift, honey," she says, giving me a kiss. "Drive safe."

"Okay, Mom."

Whoa . . . Janie? Nobody calls my mom that, except old, old friends and Dad. Holy crap. My mom and Hank used to be friends!

DECEMBER
16

Chapter 16
HANG A SHINING STAR

Finally, a real day off. Well, if you don't count the time I spent at school. But it's two days until Christmas break, so school is a breeze. Starting this weekend, though, I will really put some hours in at the stand, and by Christmas, I'll have plenty of cash for my summer train tickets. But right now, I'm glad to just have a cozy night at home.

It's about 5:00 p.m. and I am already in my sweats. Dad has band practice, Milo is in his room, and I have been vegging on the couch in our living room since school let out. But I'm feeling a little restless. I make a cup of peppermint tea and wander into the dining room where our beautiful tree is standing unadorned in the front window. I can't help but smile thinking of our outing to get it. Milo was hanging on Luke's every word like a puppy, and Dad sure liked him. Even Mom was pretty chill. It was kind of like bringing a date to meet your family for the first time. But it was Luke.

At least now he understands why I'm so weird!

My family's weirdness didn't seem to faze him one bit, and that makes me smile too.

The box of lights and decorations are all stacked on the table, but it's clear that's as far as my mom got with decorating yesterday. Maybe I'll help out. I turn on my speaker, put on an Ella Fitzgerald album, *Ella Wishes You a Swinging Christmas*, one of Dad's favorites, and start with the lights.

Always plug them in first to see if there are bulbs that need replacing before you hang them up. It'll save you taking it down and starting over. There's one of Mom's reminders, popping into my brain.

Mom. I can't believe Mom and Hank know each other! I definitely need to get to the bottom of that.

Right on schedule, I hear Mom's keys in the front door. I guess now's my chance.

"Hi, I'm home, anyone here?" she calls from the front hall where she's putting down all her stuff.

"In here," I say.

"Well, look at this cozy scene." She leans around the archway into the dining room. "You're doing the tree! Oh, and you plugged the lights in first, great."

"Yup, you trained me well," I joke.

"Hey, come on, I'm just trying to teach you things that I learned the hard way and save you a few steps!"

"I know, I know, I'm teasing." I start to wind the lights around the tree.

"Give me a second to change outta my work clothes and I'll come help you."

I get the lights in place and then start sorting through the ornaments.

Aww, there's my favorite, a little wooden toy chest with wooden toys inside. I flip it over and it says "Janie '79." It was my mom's when she was little.

And here's one I made out of Popsicle sticks and Elmer's glue. It's a sled. Must have been from when I was in kindergarten. I pop it up on the tree.

"Okay, I'm back. What do we have?" Mom asks, sliding the ornament box her way.

"Awwww, I love this one!" She pulls out a little baby footprint in clay labeled "Amanda's First Christmas."

"My baby feet were pretty dang cute," I say.

"Yeah, I remember when I first held you, I was just so fascinated by your tiny little toes. They were just so small. Gosh, how was that sixteen years ago!" She's smiling to herself and examining the ornament in her hands. "And then you wouldn't suck your thumb, you'd always put your foot in your mouth."

"That hasn't changed," Milo comments as he walks through the hall past the dining room to the kitchen.

"Hey, be nice to your sister!" Mom chides. "She has the power to drive you places!"

"Yeah, don't forget it!" I add, piling on.

"And don't load up on snacks, I'm going to cook dinner when I'm done here!" Mom yells after him as she hangs my dainty little baby foot somewhere in the middle of the tree. It reminds me of Luke's handprint turkey.

"Hey, Mom?"

"Yeah, sweetie," she says absently, digging through the box and finding more of her favorite ornaments.

"I noticed Hank called you Janie yesterday. Do you know him or something?"

"Hank Post? Well, sure, we went to high school together," she says matter-of-factly.

"Wait, really?! Why didn't you say anything?" I ask, astonished.

"I don't know. It didn't occur to me to mention. That was a long time ago and we weren't, like, friends or anything."

"You were too cool?" I tease.

"No, actually, the opposite. He was a year older than me and the captain of the basketball team. He's not as tall as Luke, but he was fast and could really shoot. All the girls had crushes on him."

"Wait, what? Hank? You're kidding!" I picture his earflap hat and chainsaw. Not exactly heartthrob material.

"He wasn't always the way he is now. He was smart and funny and really outgoing," she says, like she can read my mind, and hangs another ornament.

"Did *you* have a crush on him?"

"What, me? Pffft, no. Although we were on the debate team

together and we used to lock horns from time to time. I loved arguing with him. I think it's what made me realize I could be a good lawyer."

Oh, you totally had a crush on him.

Suddenly, her face changes, overcome with a wave of tenderness, as she reaches delicately into the ornament box.

"Oh, Dad . . . ," she says, pulling out a small, hand-painted wooden angel from the box. There's a handwritten '98 on the bottom, the year my grandpa died.

"Miss you," she says softly, then gives the angel a tiny kiss and hangs it near the top of the tree.

I don't say anything. I just watch my mom. I never got to meet my grandpa. He died when my mom was still in college. I only ever got to know him through her stories, and he seems like a really incredible person. He was a union rep at the mill till they closed it, then a history teacher at White Pine High School, and then finally a town council member. Mom always said he inspired her to work for the town and give back to White Pine. I realize Mom wasn't that much older than I am now when she lost him. I wonder why I never thought of that before.

"You know Hank lost his dad not long after Grandpa died," she says as if reading my mind. "Sadly, we did have that in common. I remember Hank had graduated from college and was traveling when he was called home. That was the first time I met Luke's mom, at the funeral." She's lost in selecting and hanging ornaments, like airing old memories on a laundry line.

"You knew Luke's mom?" I can barely hide my curiosity.

"Not very well. I met her a few times. I mean, it's a small town and the young people who stayed would go out and socialize. So I saw her around. She was really pretty and tall. And smart, too, I remember that."

"So what happened? Why did they split up?" I ask, now totally invested.

"I have no idea and frankly it's none of my business. But I do know that it wasn't their plan to stay in White Pine. I think they came back to help Nancy and Hank's older brother, Rob, with the farm after Joe died. Next thing you knew, Anabelle was pregnant and it looked like they were staying. But maybe a year or two later things went sour."

"Why, what happened?" I have given up any pretense of decorating and am hanging on every word of the small-town lore.

"I shouldn't really be telling you all this. It was gossip around town, so I'm not really sure how much truth is in it, but word was Rob got the farm in some serious financial trouble. Took out some big loans against the land. And when it all came to light, the brothers had a falling out and Rob left. I remember reading in the paper they sold a bunch of land to the ski lodge around that time, so that must have solved some of their financial worries. But Hank wasn't the same after that."

"How so?" I ask carefully.

"Well," she scoffs, her eyes on the tree. "That's about the time Hank started getting kicked out of all the bars in town. He was banned from George's for a couple of years because his drinking was so out of control. And then I stopped seeing Luke's mom around. I guess she just had enough and left. On the one hand, you can't blame her for going. But I can't imagine leaving my child behind." She sighs. "Though who am I to judge?"

You clearly are . . .

"Anyway, it's all ancient history." She snaps out of the memories and surveys the tree. "I have to be honest. I did have my hesitations about you spending so much time out there, Amanda." She looks at me closely now. "But Hank seems okay. And I'm glad to meet Luke. He seems like a nice boy." She can't leave it at that, though. "But not being in school . . . I don't think that's the right direction for the smart young man he clearly is."

"Well, it seems to be working out for him," I say, a little defensively. "The farm is doing well and he likes it there." Man, I hate it when she gets judgmental like that.

"Honey, I know you like the Posts, but trust me: Leaving school, being cut off from friends and sports and clubs and normal teenage activities, and taking on all the stress of a family business when you're so young, it's not good for him. He should be thinking about college, getting a chance to figure out his own path. He clearly has so much potential."

I almost do a spit take with a mouthful of tea. Does she even hear herself? That's what I've been trying to do, find my own path, and all she wants me to do is follow in her footsteps and do this stupid internship.

"Well, I think he can figure out his own life, and if he wants to stay in White Pine, it's none of our business," I say sharply. "I mean, you got out and came back. How bad can it be?"

I feel like I see my mom actually recoil. My words have landed like a slap.

"I came back because my mom needed me. Because I lost my dad, Amanda. And I thank my lucky stars that you don't really understand what that feels like. Once I was back, I realized that my dad had dedicated his whole life to this town because he loved it so much. And I made my own choice to do something to give back, because this community mattered so much to him. And it matters to me. And your father came with me and supported me. And that's why we made our life here. I didn't start drinking and falling apart, even though I sure wanted to. I put my energy into making a difference and contributing to something bigger than myself. And I've done my best to give you every opportunity to use your potential to find ways to do the same. But I guess you can't understand that. Or I wouldn't be hearing from my colleague that you still haven't sent in your internship application letter."

"I'm sorry, Mom, I didn't mean to . . . ," I say weakly, feeling all the cozy Christmas vibes we had going disappear from the room, like someone opened a window and let in the winter chill.

"You know what, honey," she says, taking a deep breath and speaking in an intentional calm, "it's been a long day, and I still have to start dinner. Why don't you finish up here, and we can talk about this some other time." She avoids my eyes and makes a quick retreat to the kitchen.

"Okay," I say to the empty room.

Forgot to watch the temperature of that fudge, Amanda.

It sounds awful, but sometimes I forget that my mom has feelings too. And deep down I realize I just hurt them.

But it's kinda not my fault. She's so judgy and thinks she knows what's best for everyone!

That does drive me nuts. And she just never seems to take what I think and want seriously. And who is she to decide what Luke should do with his life?

"I'll be famous, and you're going to be an architect in Chicago . . ." Wasn't that what Max's note in the time capsule said? And Hank's album. Hank and Anabelle got to travel the world, go to school, and it seems like Luke has never really had that chance. He obviously had dreams of other things.

Maybe Mom has a point.

I finish hanging the rest of the ornaments. It's a beautiful tree. And it was so fun going out to get it together. Mom, Dad, Milo, and me, and Luke, too, out in the snow, sun shining. Everyone was laughing and happy.

I look in the box and there's only one ornament left. The yellow stained-glass star for the top.

Hang a shining star upon the highest bow . . .

I think of my dad singing that line from Frank Sinatra's version of that song yesterday, And somehow I don't want to put it on yet. It doesn't feel like the right time. I should wait until everyone's here, until that Christmas feeling is back. Then it'll be right. And I can tell Mom and Dad about my trip, and they will understand that I'm just trying to do my own thing, like Mom said. And it'll all be all right.

Won't it?

Until then, we'll have to muddle through somehow . . .

I realize my carols are still playing, and Ella's singing the original.

And have yourself a merry little Christmas now.

I leave the star on the table, turn off the music and the overhead lights, and go to my room, leaving the not-quite-finished tree glowing in the darkness.

DECEMBER
17

Chapter 17
CANDY CANE CRUSH

"I think I'm traumatized by hot dogs ever since Max's cooking," Jun declares, sitting down at our usual table in the cafeteria. He steels himself. "No. I cannot let him ruin this for me." He takes a bite of one of the two hot dogs he has on his tray. "You're not eating?" he asks between chews, noticing my untouched tray.

"Nah, I'm not really hungry."

I'm still feeling bad about how things ended with my mom last night. She was quiet at dinner, and she still popped her head in my room before leaving for work, but I didn't get a chance to . . . well, say sorry, I guess.

"What's wrong with you? You seem awfully quiet considering there's only one more day of school tomorrow, and then it's Christmas break!" Jun beams over his second hot dog. "I am soooo ready."

"I don't know, just tired I guess," I say, trying to shake off my holiday blues. "What are you going to do this weekend?" I try my best to sound merry and bright.

"Uh, hello? Sunday is our party. You didn't forget, did you?" Jun scolds me.

"Oh, yeah, of course. No, I didn't forget."

I totally forgot.

"And you are still coming to help me set up on Saturday after work, right?" he adds, pinning me with a stare.

"Yeah, of course, happy to help. I haven't seen your folks in ages."

"Okay, good. I thought Saturday I could do some shopping earlier in the day and start setting up late afternoon, and you can just come when you're done at the farm. Lola's already here, so there will be plenty of food. You can eat dinner with us. By the way, did you get something for your Secret Santa yet?"

Oh crap, I forgot about that too. What am I gonna get Luke?

"What are we talking about?" Celeste joins us, setting down her tray.

"Secret Santa," I say with all the cheer I can muster.

"Oh yeah! I'm super excited," Celeste says. "I have the best idea for mine. And Max says he does too. He seems really into the whole thing. I'm kinda surprised he hasn't spilled who he's got yet. He's totally keeping it a secret!"

"Well, I'm just putting it out there, to whoever my Santa may be," Junjun says, "I am in desperate need of some moisturizer. My winter skin is out of control."

"Your request is acknowledged, though the identity of your

Secret Santa is not confirmed," Celeste says with mock formality.

"Oh, and Amanda can you let Luke know too? Like, just in case he's my Secret Santa? You know what, never mind, I'll just text him. I wanted to invite him to the party on Sunday anyway," Jun says, pulling out his phone.

Wait, Jun and Luke are, like, texting? Why don't I have his number?

I feel an odd pang of jealousy bubble up. "Oh, while you're at it, remind him that we're going to do our Secret Santa exchange at the cabin on the solstice—that's Monday. Whenever he and Amanda are done with work, they can just come over," Celeste adds.

Um, I'm right here? Is Luke now the point person for plans with me? What is happening?

"I was thinking we can decorate the mantel and light a Yule log." Celeste is on a roll. "In keeping with the solstice rituals I've read about, we can all write out what we want to leave behind in the old year and our intentions for the new one and then drop the papers in the fire. And after, we can exchange our gifts," she adds, clearly excited.

"You want me to text him all of that?" Jun looks overwhelmed.

"No, of course not, just remind him about Monday," she says. "You can too, Amanda, when you see him. You haven't forgotten, right?"

"No, of course not!"

Strike three, forgot about that too. What is going on with me?

Honestly, I'm starting to feel kind of overwhelmed. There are a million things happening, school's almost over for break, and

I have been so focused on the Candy Shack and Luke and the Posts, and then fighting with my mom about Luke and the Posts, and now Luke is like everywhere—Secret Santa, parties, hanging with my friends—gah! It's like I forgot why I was even doing all this . . . my study abroad program and my backpacking trip!

"Hello, is there anybody in there?" Junjun is waving his fingers in front of my eyes to snap me out of my long stare. "I'm trying to say bye. I have to run and wrap up some student government stuff, and tomorrow pep club is doing a holiday party thing at lunch. But I'll definitely see you Saturday for party setup, okay?"

"Yes, definitely."

"Okay, bye!" he says cheerfully and dashes out of the cafeteria.

"You okay, Amanda?" Celeste asks after Jun leaves. "You seem a little spaced out."

"Yeah, I was just thinking I've been so busy I haven't even been thinking about our trip. I should check my bank balance, with my tips and this week's check, I think I should be pretty close to having enough for my train tickets. What about you? Did you get your application in for the leadership program? It sounds like spots for the Arts Leadership track are almost full," I say.

"Yeah, about that."

Uh-oh, this isn't gonna be good.

"I've been meaning to talk to you about this, but there really hasn't been a good time," she says carefully. "I know this means a lot to you, but I'm not going to go."

"What?! Why not?" I practically shriek, drawing bewildered stares from the rest of the cafeteria.

"Well, I talked it through with my parents and, first of all, it's a lot of money. And you know I'm not that focused on art anymore. I'm actually more interested in environmental science. There's a program at UVM I can do that's cheaper and closer to home . . ." Celeste sounds excited, but I'm freaking out.

"And closer to Max," I say. "That's what this is about, isn't it?"

"No!" Celeste says vehemently. "I mean, it's part of it. This is our last summer before senior year, next summer is going to be all college and stuff, and is it that wrong that I don't want to spend the whole summer away from him?"

"What about me? Don't you want to spend the whole summer with me?" I am starting to lose any connection to time and space and totally making a scene.

"Amanda, chill. You're, like, yelling!" Celeste looks around at the other students who are blatantly eavesdropping on our conversation.

"Of course, I'm yelling! My best friend just threw me and our plans under the bus for her boyfriend. Like, how cliché. You know my parents probably won't let me go now? Backpacking, I mean. You know that's probably not gonna happen for me, because of you."

"What is your deal? You don't have to be mean. And you haven't even told your parents about your backpacking plan. You have practically been lying to them about the whole thing, so if they don't let you go, that's not on me," Celeste fires back. "I told you I wasn't a hundred percent sure about the whole idea yet, but you just plowed ahead. So yeah, I'm sorry if this isn't what you want to hear, but it's my decision. And last I checked, best friends support each other," she says, grabbing her bag and getting up to leave.

"Yeah, last I checked, that's exactly what they're supposed to do," I spit back.

"I can't even with you right now. I have to go. I'll see you . . . when I see you." Celeste gets up and leaves.

The rest of the afternoon is a total blur. I replay our fight over and over.

How could she? We had a plan!

Last period was study hall, so I just straight up ditched and drove to Post Farm on autopilot. All I want is to get lost in my job, so I don't have to think.

"You're here early," Luke says, walking up to the Candy Shack as I'm lifting one of the heavy urns on to the counter. "Here, let me give you a hand with that," he says, coming in close and trying to grab the handles.

I realize, as upset as I am, I'm instantly consoled by the sight of Luke. But somehow it doesn't come out that way. "It's fine, I got it," I say testily.

"Okay, my bad." He backs right off, clearly a little hurt.

"I'm sorry." I turn to him, realizing my toxic mood is spilling over everywhere. "I got in a fight with my mom, then a massive fight with Celeste." I sniff. "I'm just having a really bad day." I keep my head down, avoiding his eyes. With horror, I realize I actually might cry.

I'm staring at my own toes when I hear the crinkle of a wrapper and a little candy cane appears in my field of view.

"You want one of these?" he asks gently. "They usually cheer up our younger customers when they are having, you know, big feelings," he says using his best teacher voice.

It's one of his pocket candy canes. Now I really am going to cry.

I take the candy cane but still can't bring myself to look at him. Instead, I launch myself at him, burying my face in the front of his sweater and wrapping my arms around him inside his open jacket in an awkward, sloppy hug.

"Whoa," he says, and I can feel him hesitate in surprise. But only for a moment. He closes his arms around me, holds me close, and hugs me back. I just breathe in his smell, pine and soap, and I feel how warm he is, and I feel safe.

He drops his head down and rests his chin on my head and breathes deeply. I can feel his ribs expanding and the taut muscles in his back. I feel a shudder of pure energy from the crown of my head all the way down into the bottom of my stomach, and I hold him just a little tighter. I feel him press closer in response, and I know that if I look up right now, his face will be so near to mine that all I would have to do is close my eyes and . . .

"Ahem." Cheryl is standing behind me. "Hate to break this up, but a little help?" She's got the other large, very full urn of hot cocoa in both hands, and we are blocking the counter where she needs to set it down.

"Sorry!" Luke and I scatter like we were hit by lightning. "I was just having a bad day. And Luke gave me a candy cane," I say awkwardly, holding it up like a kid showing off a lollipop after a doctor visit.

"Oh yeah, that's a classic. My mom always had her little candy canes at the ready to 'put a smile in the heart of special people,' as she would say to any kid who needed cheering up on the lot. Nice to see you've kept up the tradition, nephew," Cheryl says, giving Luke a wicked side-eyed smile that makes both of us start to turn red.

"Uh, yeah," he manages to mutter.

"I got the rest of this, Cheryl." I eagerly take my spot beyond the counter and plug in the urn. "Thanks for the help."

"No problem, hope that little bit of sugar puts a smile in your heart," she says. "The candy cane I mean." She saunters back to the house, chuckling a little to herself.

"Oh yeah. Right," I say, and I start fiddling with the candy cane wrapper to avoid eye contact with Luke.

Oh, this is gonna be awkward.

But, actually, it's not. When I look up, Luke is still standing there, looking at me with a sly little smile on his face.

"What?" I ask, almost giddy and trying not to smile. But he doesn't answer, he just reaches into his pocket and starts unwrapping his own little candy cane.

"Why are you looking at me like that?" I can't hide my massive smile and nervous giggle.

"It worked," he says, popping the candy cane in his mouth, with the cool bravado of a cowboy chewing on a toothpick in a western saloon. "The candy cane, it cheered you up. Works every time." He smiles and turns to walk back to his tree stand, like he's riding off into the sunset.

Yeah, that's not what's got me smiling, I think, taking a long look as I watch him walk away.

DECEMBER 18

Chapter 18
SWEET DREAMS

It's officially winter break! I'm free! School is out, I'm in my car with my seat warmers cranked, my radio is blasting Donny Hathaway's "This Christmas," and I'm singing at the top of my lungs:

Hang all the mistletoe,
I wanna get to know you better
This Christmas . . .

I'm jingling all the way through a flurry of snow, past the pretty lights of town, to Post Farm for my shift at the Candy Shack. In spite of everything, I'm feeling pretty merry. Celeste and I managed to avoid each other all day, and I'm still super mad that she just bailed on me. Jun pulled me aside and tried to broker a truce, but I let him know I'm not there yet. And I'm sure by now Max has heard all the gory details from Celeste, but we've all been friends so long he's pretty good about not getting in the middle of stuff between us. So none of it has been able to dampen my mood heading into two weeks of vacation. I'm feeling kinda . . . good.

Maybe that has something to do with Luke?

Not gonna lie, that hug has been playing on repeat in my brain since yesterday. Last night, it was low-key impossible to sleep. I kept thinking about how I fit perfectly inside his arms, my head on his chest. The way his body felt against mine. The crazy all-over chills I got when he held me tighter. I can still feel them just thinking about it. And I'm 100 percent positive he felt it too. It's kind of nuts. I mean, Luke Post is so not part of my plans, but there's something about him I just can't get enough of.

Okay, enough, Amanda, eyes on the road!

I realize I'm daydreaming and snap out of it to focus on the drive. Yes, Luke is definitely part of my good mood. But it's more than that, and more than winter break. I think I just made up my mind that I'm not gonna let Celeste stop me from taking this trip.

I mean, forget her, if she just wants to hang around town for a *guy*, even if it is an awesome guy who is one of my best friends and they are super good together, fine! Do that! I'm gonna do me! And I'm not gonna let anyone get in my way.

"You're not down for the count yet, sweetheart, you still got some fight in ya!" I say out loud in a grizzled old boxing coach voice.

Whoa, that's a new one. I shall call him "Coach." And Coach

is right, I'm not gonna just give up when I've worked so hard. I'm going to find a way to make this trip happen.

You can have brains, and you can have talent, but if you don't have persistence, you're not gonna get anywhere you haven't already been.

Now that's a voice I recognize. Zoe's advice always seems to cut through the noise in my head. She trusts me with the Candy Shack, and I feel like if I could figure out how to set up and run this little business, I can figure out how to get myself to Europe, with or without Celeste.

"Speaking of Zoe . . . ," I say out loud as I make my now very familiar left into the Post Farm lot and see her car already parked. "Wonder what she's doing here?"

The lot's quiet, but it's Friday afternoon and Christmas break has begun—it will be busy soon enough. There's no sign of Hank or Luke, so I head over to the kitchen to get what I need to set up the shack.

"Please help me understand your hesitation about this?" I walk in on Zoe addressing Cheryl across the kitchen island where she is busy cutting up a fresh batch of fudge. Zoe continues in her I'm-being-very-calm-but-I'm-not-going-to-let-up-until-I-get-the-answer-I-want voice. "I've done all the legwork, the small business council is going to cover any incidental costs, all the businesses are on board, the ski lodge will cross-promote it, and you said yourself you have all the stands just sitting in the barn. I'm not seeing the downside," she adds sincerely.

"Zoe, I told you, it's complicated," Cheryl says, pausing her work, putting her hands on the table and meeting Zoe's very intense gaze.

Are they fighting?

"Umm, hi," I say, making myself known. "I can come back later if I'm interrupting something."

"Hi, Amanda. No, not at all." Cheryl greets me warmly, clearly relieved that I am, in fact, interrupting something. "Zoe and I were just talking through some business. But we can finish this conversation later," she says, putting the emphasis on the word later.

"Of course." Zoe is clearly not ready to press pause on their discussion but takes the hint. "I wanted to catch up with Amanda anyway."

"Yeah, sure, I just have to get the drinks out if you want to chat while I set up?" I grab one of the drink urns Cheryl has ready for me.

"I'll get the door for you. And I'll see myself out," she adds with a little pepper for Cheryl's benefit.

Oh yeah, they were fighting.

This is new. I've never seen anyone hold their own like that when Zoe is being this determined. Or get such a big reaction from her in the first place. Something is definitely going on between these two, but I know better than to ask. And it's clear as we set foot outside, I don't have to.

"Oooh, I can't believe Cheryl Post!" Zoe says, uncharacteristically venting.

Sensing an opening, I ask, "Is everything okay?"

“Everything’s fine if you are fine with everything staying exactly how it is and letting opportunity just pass you by,” Zoe says in an exasperated sigh.

“What do you mean?” I plop the urn on the counter and start my opening routine.

“For weeks, Cheryl and I have been talking about how we could do a real Christmas market. She was all enthusiastic and had so many great ideas and made it seem like this was something she really wanted. So I’ve gone ahead and set everything up, and now she’s backing out on me.”

Boy, do I know what that feels like.

“Well, not backing out exactly. But she seems reluctant to bring it up with her brother. I don’t get it. It’s a great idea. We have everything in place. All the Main Street businesses are very excited. She just keeps saying she needs to discuss it with Hank, but then she won’t do it. And I think that’s the part that has me frustrated,” Zoe says earnestly. “I mean, it’s fine if he says no, then we have our answer. But maybe he’ll say yes? Or maybe she should just go ahead and do it without asking Hank! Sometimes in business as in life, you need to just go for it. You know, ask forgiveness, not permission. But it’s avoiding the hard conversations, not making a decision, that’s where you sell yourself short. You’ve got to ask for what you want.”

Ask forgiveness, not permission. I’ve never heard that before, but I like it.

“To be fair,” I begin delicately, “from what I’ve heard from Cheryl, the Candy Shack is already kind of a big change for Hank.

I think Cheryl feels a little guilty for going off and doing her own thing while Hank stayed here and took care of the family business, so she's just trying not to overwhelm him or, like, tell him how to run things."

Plus, all the other family baggage I've learned but, for once, I know better than to share.

"Hmm, I guess I can understand that." Zoe is thoughtful. "It's true that family businesses *are* their own special kind of complicated," she adds. "Thank you, Amanda, for the insight. I can see you are really coming into your own. And I have been meaning to find a minute to tell you how impressed I've been with your work on this pop-up. You have shown a lot of initiative, focus, and maturity taking this on and, quite frankly, I'm proud of you."

"Thank you, Zoe, that means a lot. I am really grateful you gave me this opportunity," I say modestly.

"Amanda, you are smart, you pay attention to the details, and you are quick to apply what you learn. You have the makings of a great entrepreneur. But I want to be clear: I didn't give you this opportunity just because I like you. I did it because I knew you had the tenacity to figure it out. And offering opportunities to someone like that is a smart investment." She reaches into her bag and pulls out an envelope. "So I wanted to give you your paycheck, *but* there's also a little something extra in there in recognition of the extra effort you have put into making this stand a success."

"Wow," I say, opening the envelope and looking at my check. "That's a really generous Christmas bonus, thank you!"

"Amanda, don't make me take back all the nice things I just said.

Haven't you been listening?" Zoe mock-scolds me. "This isn't a gift. You earned it. And when the Christmas rush is over and you are back to your regular shifts at the coffee shop, our next business lesson is going to be about knowing your worth and negotiating," she adds, smiling. "Also, tomorrow I'm sending Trevor out in the afternoon, and I'd like you to show him the ropes. They are going to start some extended hours between now and Christmas, and you're gonna need some backup."

"Okay, no problem. Thank you, Zoe. Really. I really appreciate everything," I tell her. And I mean it.

"Well, good, you can show me how much by helping out at our Christmas Market, if I can ever convince Cheryl to talk to Hank. You know what, maybe I'll just talk to him myself! There's still plenty of time to make it happen." She puts on her gloves and gets ready to head to her car. "Also, please tell her that I had to run, but that I'll see her tonight at the lodge, our usual table."

"Okay, will do," I say trying to hide my smile.

Usual table, huh?

"And don't be giving me that FACE!"

"What?" I say, grateful to not be the recipient for once. "I'm not making any face."

But I'm totally making the FACE, the one everybody seems to make when Luke and I are anywhere near each other. So I know she's right.

"Uh-huh, you know what I'm talking about. I'm still your boss!" She gives me a little wink and walks away.

Wow! I was not expecting a bonus. I sit on the stool in the shack and take another look at the check Zoe gave me. With this and what I've earned so far, I've definitely got enough to book my train tickets. I can't believe I did it.

Sometimes in business as in life, you need to just go for it.

Zoe said it herself. I know if I ask my parents they will probably say no to me backpacking by myself. But if I just buy the tickets with my own money, and do my research, and come up with a really solid plan, what are they going to do? I probably won't be able to return the tickets. They'll have to let me go. I mean, I'm already going to Europe. What's a few extra weeks.

Ask forgiveness, not permission.

I pull out my phone and open my browser. I've had the site bookmarked for ages and my bank details saved. All I have to do is click a button and the tickets are mine.

Not making a decision, that's where you sell yourself short.

I take a deep breath and hit the "complete purchase" button.

There, it's done. No turning back now.

"Attagirl, show 'em what you're made of," I say, bringing my Coach persona back for an encore, and feel a wave of excitement. I'm going traveling!

"Hey." I look up to see Luke walking over and smiling at me. He clearly heard me talking to myself and being ridiculous, as usual.

"Hey!" I say, jumping down from my stool and leaning on the bar to greet him.

"Well, you're in a much better mood today."

"I am!" I reply sassily. "It's Friday, school's out, and I'm kicking butt and taking names."

"Okay, well, that sounds exciting. I'm fine, thank you for asking," he jokes.

"Yes, sorry, how are you? I guess you probably have some kind of school break too? How's that work with your online courses?"

"Well, yeah, I have to turn in some assignments, but I'm pretty much done. Oh, hang on," he pulls out his phone. "It's Max texting me. We've got plans to go shoot some pool again tonight. Maybe this time I'll let him win a couple," he says, smiling and probably texting the exact same thing to Max, judging by the rapid-fire buzzing of Max's replies.

This is your moment—ask for what you want!

"Speaking of texting. How come all my friends have your number, but I don't?"

"Um, I don't know. You never asked me," he says, still focused on responding to Max.

"So what are you going to do about that?"

"Are you asking me for my number?" He looks up, raising an eyebrow and giving me a very flirty smile.

"Yes, I am. I mean, after next week we won't be seeing each other every day. So we may want to keep in touch."

"I guess I hadn't thought of that," he says, getting oddly serious for a moment.

"And I mean we *are* friends. Well, work friends anyway." I add casually.

"Work friends. That's what we are, work friends, huh?" He shakes his head in mock indignation.

"Okay, fine, real friends. You know what I mean," I start to backtrack. “Geez, Luke, are you going to give me your number or not?” I am smiling with exasperation and handing him my phone. He takes his sweet time adding his number while I lean on the counter and pretend to casually examine my nails so as not to give him the satisfaction of seeing me squirm.

“So I guess I’m going to have to text you.” He hands me back the phone and leans on his side of the counter, giving me that raised eyebrow look again.

He’s so hot and he friggin’ knows it.

“I guess so. But will you have anything to say, I wonder?” I will not let myself fall under the spell of his smolder.

“Someone once told me that for somebody who doesn’t talk much, I have a lot to say,” he says in mock seriousness.

“I guess I have long paragraph texts to look forward to at some point then,” I volley back.

“Hmm, we’ll see.”

“Don’t you have trees to sell?” I nod toward the line of cars starting to pull into the lot.

“Why, yes, it looks like I do,” he says, walking backward a few steps and smiling. “Text you later. Maybe.” Then he turns to meet the arriving customers.

I continue smiling long after I watched him jog toward the tree stand. I shake it off and fix my face before greeting my own first customer. And just like that, the Friday rush begins.

It’s late by the time I finally get home, eat, shower, journal for a bit, and crawl under my covers for the night. Mom and Dad are at Mom’s work Christmas thing and Milo’s hanging with

Celeste's sixth-grade sister, Marlo, next door. Normally, when our sibs hang, I text Celeste to come over here, but I'm not gonna be the one to make the first move. Besides, so much happened today I'm exhausted. My nice warm bed feels amazing. I turn off the light and start to let myself drift.

I can't believe I did it, I booked my tickets! I'm going on an adventure!

That was the right move, wasn't it? It's gonna be fine. I'll tell my parents on Christmas Day. Everyone will be in a good mood. I can let them know that this is what I want for my Christmas present, and it'll all be fine.

It'll all be fine . . .

I am almost asleep when I hear my phone buzz. I pick it up to see a text from

Work Friend Luke

Bro, really? That's how he put his number in my contacts?

I'm already smiling and then I read his message:

I am texting you.

For real?

Yes, I see that.

Srsly that's ur text?

What's wrong with it?

I thought u had stuff to say?

Nope.

Nothing to say.

I can see the three dots. He's still writing.

I was just thinking of u.

I feel the smile on my face kind of spread all over. I reply with a

♥

I'm gonna go to sleep.

G'nite.

Sweet dreams.

I send him one last ♥, and drift off into very sweet dreams.

DECEMBER
19

Chapter 19
ICE BREAKER

"And that's really all there is to it," I tell Trevor, who is probably one of my favorite guys on the Matcha-Do staff. He just turned twenty and is from White Pine, but landed back home after a stint in NYC doing a theater program. Tall, blond, with a dancer's build, he's funny, talented, and fairly low-drama for a drama kid.

Today, he is providing welcome backup at the shack. It's 5:00 p.m., the string lights are glittering, the big fire is glowing, and I've been here all day and I'm beat. We were busy since the moment we opened this morning. I barely saw Luke before the evening tree team arrived to tag him out, and I'm glad to have Trevor take over for me.

"I got this, sweetie, you can go," he says, hip-checking me playfully out of the Candy Shack. "Who's next?" he says turning to the line of snow-kissed, merry people queuing for a warm drink after their tree outing.

"Okay, thanks. Just talk to Cheryl if you need anything!" I gather up my stuff and am about to head to my car when I feel my phone buzzing.

"Hi, Mom," I say, picking up as I walk toward my car. "What's up?"

"So I was just looking at our online banking that, as I'm sure you know, shows me your teen accounts as well? There is a purchase for three hundred fifty dollars for a Eurail pass. Would you like to explain that to me?" Her voice is taut with anger.

Uh-oh.

"Um, yeah, that's mine. I bought those train tickets."

"For what exactly?" she asks tartly.

No point in avoiding it any longer, I may as well tell her.

"Because I want to travel around Europe for the rest of the summer after my program finishes."

"And when exactly were you planning on telling your father and me about this?" She is barely controlling the emotion in her voice.

"I, um, I . . ."

"I cannot believe you, Amanda," she says, cutting me off and no longer holding back. "Not only did you have no intention of doing an internship at my office, making me look ridiculous telling my colleague to expect to hear from you, but you go ahead and make travel plans without even consulting your father and me. And just dropping three hundred fifty dollars without so much as a discussion? I mean, what were you even thinking?"

"I was going to—" I try to interject.

"How do Celeste's parents feel about this backpacking idea?" She continues not even trying to hear me out. "I know they were on the fence about the young leaders program to begin with, so I can't imagine they are fine with this."

"Um, about that," I say sheepishly. "Celeste's not going."

"Well, at least she has some sense. I mean, the two of you backpacking on your own . . ."

"I mean, she's not going at all," I interrupt. "She's not going to do the leadership program. She's staying in Vermont this summer."

"Are you kidding?" Mom's voice is cool. "And when did you find *this* out? You know we agreed to this young leaders program in the first place because you and Celeste were going together."

"Um, Thursday?"

"And I'm sitting here looking at a bank statement that says you bought a three hundred fifty–dollar train ticket on Friday." I hear her take a massive breath, but she says nothing. And I just sit there and wait for her to reload.

"I am so beyond upset with you right now, Amanda. I don't even know where to start. I'm going to have to call the program and see if we can get our deposit back, because I don't see how we can let you go on that exchange program after all this."

"What? That's not fair!" I practically screech. "It's not my fault Celeste canceled on me. You can't make me back out of the leadership program." I realize I'm still standing in the middle of the parking lot, so I walk over to the side of the barn to try not to crash out in the middle of everyone's Christmas tree shopping.

"I can do whatever I want, Amanda, because I am an adult, not a sixteen-year-old who only *thinks* she can. Ugh." She sighs with disgust. "Now I'm starting to see the whole picture, all these hours at the farm, us barely seeing you all month—this was all so you could earn enough to pull off this little maneuver, wasn't it? I just cannot believe you."

"Mom, I wasn't trying to lie to you. But you wouldn't listen, you kept pushing this internship and . . ."

"Amanda, I don't want to hear it. And I don't have time for this discussion right now. It's the holiday party at your dad's practice, and I need to meet him there with all the gifts for his team, and the million other things I have to do while you are hatching your little plans. So we are going to have to finish this conversation later, but you mark my words, all bets are off. If you can't be honest with your parents, then you sure as heck aren't mature enough to travel to Europe on your own."

"But . . ."

"End of discussion. Be home in bed when we get home. We'll continue this tomorrow. I am too upset to keep talking to you right now. Goodbye."

Did she just hang up on me? My own mom?

Oh no. No, no, no, no, no.

"Fudge!" I scream, trying to keep it PG for all the kids around. All this hard work for nothing. I can't believe her. I can't go at all? It's so unfair!

I am spinning out. I feel like I can't catch my breath and I'm starting to spiral into some kind of panic attack. All the kids and families are buzzing around, laughing and giggling. Christmas carols are playing through an open car window. I just need to find some quiet.

I walk past the barn and down the hill toward the pond, where the barn windows cast a warm circle of light before falling off into darkness.

What a total mess. Great job, Amanda.

I do not want to hear from a chorus of inner critics right now. I just need to, like, touch grass or, in this case, snow, and breathe. Relax like I did in the woods with Luke, just look up at the sky and breathe.

I see what looks like a nice pile of snow and am about to plop down when I hear a little *meow*.

"Fairy Barn Cat?"

The little cat steps into the light and meows again, repeatedly.

"Well, great timing. Where have you been? I could have used a little moral support when I was getting yelled at by my mom."

The cat keeps meowing at me but won't come any closer.

"You know what, now's not a great time for your aloof kitty act. Just leave me alone, why don't ya," I say, plopping down in the snow.

But as soon as I do, I don't feel a nice cushion of thick snow but instead hear a hard crack. My butt starts to freeze as icy water flows across my legs. It is a feeder stream to the pond, still flowing under the snow. And I just sat right in it.

So cold, so cold.

I stand up to try and get out of there. I take a step, but the ice under my feet gives out, and now I fully face plant into the icy stream and look up in shock as the little cat scatters off into the dark.

So, so, so cold.

I manage to barrel-roll my way off the ice to stand back up on solid ground, but I'm totally soaked. I've never felt cold like this. The only beacon in the dark night is the warm glow of the lights coming from Luke's loft. Without thinking, I stumble up to the side door and bang on it hard.

Luke opens the door in a T-shirt and sweats, looking like he just took a post-work shower. "Amanda! What happened? Come in," he says quickly, recovering from his surprise at the sight of my wet, bedraggled self.

"I fell through ice by pond," I say through chattering teeth.

"You fell in the pond?" He sounds justifiably concerned and ushers me inside, closing the door and starting to strip the wet jacket off me, as I struggle to step out of my boots.

"No, the stream. But freezing," I stammer.

"Okay, go stand by the fire." He gestures to the cast-iron stove near the old corduroy couch in the middle of the room. "Let me get you some dry clothes."

He bounds up the steps to the loft above the workshop and rustles around for a moment while I hover my hands over the heat radiating from the iron stove. When he comes back down, he has some sweatpants, a T-shirt, a fleece-lined hoodie, some socks, and a fleece blanket, which he drapes over my shoulders.

"Okay, I'll just step into the barn for a second while you change," he says, moving toward the doorway behind the couch where I once almost attacked him with a giant candy cane.

I'm still shivering so much, I just muster a nod, drop the blanket, and start peeling off my wet shirt and pants before he's even out of the door. I'm standing basically in my undies when he catches a glimpse and quickly turns his head and hustles out the door.

I put on all the fresh layers and zip up the hoodie. Then I sit on the couch, wrap myself tightly in the blanket, and stare into the fire like a zombie.

"Hey, you decent?" Luke knocks and peers around the door from the barn.

"Yeah, I'm dressed," I say, my senses coming back online so slowly I'm not even embarrassed by my current predicament.

He looks around. "Where'd you put your wet clothes?" I nod toward the floor by the fire, not wanting to pull my hands out of the warm blanket.

"Oh, your phone." He picks it out of the pile of wet stuff. "I'm gonna turn it off so it can dry out." He rests it on the edge of the couch, then he grabs two folding chairs and a broom and sets up a makeshift drying rack next to the cast-iron stove. He gently wrings out my sopping clothing then hangs them across it to dry by the fire.

As he works, I realize this is one of those moments when I'm grateful Luke isn't a big talker. I'm fine with nothing but the sound of the fire hissing and popping inside the stove and carols filtering in from the lot filling the space between us.

Well, a cold plunge is one way to get your brain to quiet down.

I use the moment to look around Luke's inner sanctum. The

room takes up half of the barn. Across from the couch is a workbench and woodworking area. It's hung with a pegboard and tools, and there are a couple of big table saws. Wedged into the wall above the pegboard are some old Vermont license plates and tin signs. There's a window in the middle with vintage green Coke bottles and a few old plaid thermoses lining the top lintel.

Above the workbench area are low beams that support the sleeping loft where Luke's geometric wooden models hang. The exterior door is tucked under a set of stairs that run up to the loft. In the cozy nook beside the door is a table with a record player and some albums stacked on the floor.

Tacked to the stair stringer are magazine art photos and old-looking postcards of buildings: the Chrysler Building in New York, the Colosseum in Rome, the buttresses of Notre-Dame in Paris, Il Duomo in Milan, the Parthenon in Greece.

I wonder if those are from Hank and Annabelle's trip.

And in the middle is a very faded, framed photo. I stand up and shuffle my blanket-burrito-ed self over for a closer look. I can just make out the image of a group of people: two older men and a young-looking Nancy holding a baby. By her side is a handsome man her age—that must be Joe Post—and two boys who can only be Rob and Hank. The family stands in front of the big red barn.

"Wow, is that baby Cheryl?" I ask, pointing to the picture, my body starting to feel warm and my curiosity overriding my general air of miserableness.

"Yeah, and that's my great-grandpa Henry and his brother, Jim. This was his workshop," Luke says, coming across the room to stand next to me. "They bought the land here after World War II and started the farm. And that's Nan and my grandpa Joe, my dad and his older brother, Rob, and baby Cheryl. The whole Post family. Well, once upon a time at least," he adds almost to himself.

He turns his attention back to my clothes. "These shouldn't take long to dry, but you can wear that stuff home if you need to," he says finding a warm spot to stand by the fire.

"Thank you," I say, returning to my couch nest and snuggling into the hoodie, which smells like him and which I am never giving back. "But I don't think I want to go home anytime soon."

"What happened?" he asks gently, coming to sit beside me on the couch.

"Other than the fact that I have absolutely and totally messed up everything? All my plans for summer, for Europe, for backpacking, for . . . that," I say, pointing to the pictures on the stairs of the great buildings. "My chance to go and see all of that!" I roll my eyes miserably at my colossal fudge-up. "I really like your pictures, by the way, and this whole place is really cool, especially the models," I add in a small pouty voice.

"Thank you," he says, pleased but focused. "I'm still confused, though. You ended up falling in the stream because of this . . . how exactly?" He gives me a teasing little nudge.

"Don't make fun of me," I wail, tipping over in my blanket cocoon to bury my head in his shoulder. "I got in a huge fight with my mom because she found out I booked tickets to go backpacking in Europe without telling her, and I was really upset and was trying to lay down in the snow and breathe to calm down like you showed me . . ." I am still talking into his shoulder to avoid the embarrassment of having to say all this ridiculous stuff to his face.

"But, instead, you laid down in an icy creek," he finishes my thought and puts an arm around me as consolation. "Something like that?"

"Yes. And it's so embarrassing."

"Aww, come on. Lots of people wouldn't think that's embarrassing," he says, making what I consider to be a rather lame effort to cheer me up.

"Oh yeah? Like who?" I sit up to look at him, leaning away from his arm like a giant blanket caterpillar.

"Well, Max for starters. This whole thing sounds exactly his speed."

"I mean, yeah, I can't argue with that," I agree, giving him a half smile and relaxing close by his side. "I'm mostly just mad at myself that I screwed this whole Europe trip up. I thought my leadership program was definitely locked in, and I was trying to find a way to stretch the trip, but now my mom is so pissed she's threatening to make me cancel the whole thing. And I'm, like, devastated. I feel so stupid."

"Yeah, that's a tough one. Have you tried talking to her?"

"No, I think she needs to cool down first. So until then I'm just going to spiral miserably about how stupid I am," I say dryly.

"Nah, come on, don't do that," Luke says firmly. "You're not stupid and that won't help. You just fudged up, you know, like my grandma would say. Don't panic, you just gotta fix it."

"I mean, it's not like I'm *trying* to panic, but I can't just shut it off. This was my dream! I've been talking about this for the whole school year and working like crazy this whole month to make it happen. I don't expect you to understand," I say, getting a little lost in my own melodrama.

"Well, actually, I do understand, believe it or not," he says a little defensively. "I mean, those pictures of Europe, all these art books and stuff, those are mine. I wanted to be an architect ever since I was a kid, building models in here with my dad. He used to show me those postcards and all the places he traveled with my mom, but you know what? They split up. And he needed me to stay, because everyone else left. And this place—that those men built for all of us, and Nan kept going, and Dad kept going—will be mine someday." He looks at the faded family photo. "And I need to be here to take care of it, like he did. So, yeah, I do know what it's like to not get what you want. But sometimes you just have to deal with what you've got," he says flatly.

His tone snaps me out of my self-pity, and I turn to look at him. "Luke, I'm sorry. I didn't realize. I didn't mean to make everything about me. I . . ."

"It's okay," he says, not meeting my gaze. "It's not a big deal. It just is what it is."

"It *is* a big deal," I say fervently. "And if you want to be an architect, you should go for it! I mean, you have a right to a life and to do the things you want. Cheryl's here and your dad seems like he can handle things . . ."

"Huh." He smirks ironically, turning back toward me.

"What?"

"Nothing, it's just you sound like my mom," he reveals. "There's an architecture program at the University of Chicago, where she works. She's been trying to get me to consider it. She gets a deal on tuition, and I could live with her."

"Well, why don't you?!"

"It's . . ."

"Don't tell me it's complicated!" I say resolutely, feeling both sad and outraged on his behalf that he has given up on his dreams because of his uncle, and his mom and his dad's choices. "It's not complicated. If you want to do it, you can figure it out."

"Okay, take it easy." He laughs at my sudden intensity. "I appreciate you having my back. It's just moving to Chicago seems like a big commitment. I think I'd rather start with something short-term, you know like a summer program or a couple of classes. To see if I can keep up. I mean, I haven't been in a real school in a while."

"Wait a second! The program I'm doing in Switzerland! Or well, was doing . . . It has an architecture and engineering track. It could be perfect. If I can fix things with my mom, we could go together and . . ."

"Wait, are you saying you want to travel Europe with me?" He's using his jokey flirty tone, but there's also something sincere, something vulnerable in the way he holds my gaze that catches me off guard.

"I mean, yeah, we *are* friends so it's not, like, a big deal," I stammer, suddenly blushing and feeling very aware of how close he is, and how warm the fire is. And how its yellow glow reflected in his dark eyes make them kind of sparkle. And how I can feel his arm wrap around me again, pulling me closer. And as I tilt my face toward his, I catch myself saying in a breathy whisper. "Yes, I want to go with you . . ." I close my eyes and feel his lips just brush against mine and I think . . .

Yes, that is actually what I want . . .

When suddenly his phone starts ringing, and it snaps us both out of the moment. He grabs it from the pocket of his sweats and looks at it, completely bewildered.

"It's Junjun. I wonder what he wants?"

"The party! I was supposed to help him set up for the party!" I yell, aghast. "And my phone is off. Oh crap, he's probably looking for me. I gotta go," I say, gathering all my wet clothes in a frenzy. "Just please text him and tell him I'm on my way."

Poor Luke sits there on the couch, ringing phone in hand, looking stunned by the very sudden change of mood.

"I'm so sorry." And I really am. I really, really am. "Thank you for the clothes. I'll talk to you later," I say, scrambling toward the door. But before I can get there, I stop, take a breath, and turn back. I lean over the back of the couch, bringing my face close to his, and give him a peck on the cheek.

"Thank you," I say, "for taking care of me."

Then I'm gone, dashing off to Jun's house like Santa in his sleigh.

DECEMBER
20

Chapter 20

ALL I WANT FOR CHRISTMAS

"Amanda, honey, can you come in here for a second?" My dad calls me from the kitchen. It's 8:00 a.m. on Sunday. I've just come downstairs, and my mom and Milo are nowhere in sight.

"Yup, just a second," I reply, finishing getting my things together for work.

I did manage to make it to Junjun's house last night, but most of the setup was already done. He was clearly annoyed that I was late and that I was dressed in oversized sweatpants with wet crusty hair and smeared mascara, but he was too polite to say anything with his family around. I tried to explain what happened, but he didn't really want to hear it.

"Just be on time tomorrow and maybe dress up a little please," he said, lobbing his most intense passive-aggressive warning. "And I hope you and Celeste have worked it out. I don't need any drama," he said, colder than that stream I fell in. I didn't have the heart to tell him Celeste and I still haven't talked.

But right now, I have bigger problems to deal with.

When I walk in the kitchen, my dad is sitting at the island drinking a cup of coffee with another one poured for me.

"Where's Mom?" I ask, taking my spot.

"She went out with your brother, and I thought this would be a good time for you and me to have a little chat," he says calmly.

"Dad, I'm sorry, I know I messed up. But please, you have to let me go on the program, at least that . . ." I start to gush, but he raises one hand calmly and signals that now is the time to listen, not talk.

"Your mom told me everything," he says. "And first and foremost, I want to express that we are both very disappointed that you did not just sit down and talk with us about what you wanted to do. The sneaking around part of this whole thing is probably what we're both most upset about. And I personally don't understand what you were thinking."

"Um, ask forgiveness, not permission?" I say weakly.

"Yeah, you're sixteen, that's not how that works. The reason we have trusted you to date is because each time we have given you responsibility, like with the car and your job, you have used it wisely. It's why we let you do this new job and all the extra hours out at Post Farm, which your mom was not in favor of, by the way. But you have always risen to the occasion. It's also why we were willing to let you do the program in Europe with Celeste. And that was already a huge step. So I'm confounded as to why you thought you had to push for more and why you felt you had to do it behind our backs?"

"I was just worried you'd say no."

"Well, you were damn right!" Dad says emphatically, but then takes a breath, changes tone, and reaches across the table to put his hands over mine.

"Listen, honey, I get it. You're a teenager. You're smart, you're determined, you have big dreams, and you feel ready to take on the world. But for your mom and me, it really wasn't that long ago you were taking your first steps, losing your first tooth, getting your first visit from your very own dentist-approved tooth fairy!" he adds, making me smile.

"I know the thought of you going off on your own this summer has been a big deal for me, but it's been a really big deal for your mom. For her, it's all just too soon, because the next step is college, and she's not ready to have her baby fly the nest just yet."

I guess I didn't really think about it like that, and all of a sudden, I feel really sad because I wish she could just tell me that herself. But who am I kidding? I probably wouldn't have listened. Everything she says sounds like nagging. And I'm not sure when it started to feel like that.

"Anyway," my dad continues, knocking me out of my reverie, "what I wanted to say is that after a lot of discussion, your mom and I have agreed that apart from this particular instance, you have shown a lot of maturity and drive setting up your Candy Shack, and managing your school load with the extra hours, and

I can admit, maybe we have been holding the reins a little tight about Europe, so we've agreed that you can still go on the program."

"Even without Celeste?"

"Even without Celeste. It is an organized program after all, and you have student housing and local support if there's any issues. So it's totally something you can handle."

"Daddy, that's amazing! Thank you, thank you so much. I won't let you down!" I say, standing up and coming around the counter to hug him and give him a big kiss on the top of his head.

"Okay, okay, take it easy, don't mess up what's left of my hair, sheesh!" He smooths his hair back into place comedically.

"And what about the train tickets I bought . . . ?" I ask delicately.

"Now that is a whole other matter. That's the part of this that really dents my dentures. I mean, on what planet did you think we'd ever allow you to just galivant around Europe for a month on your own?" He's getting a little worked up again.

"I don't know, I guess I just got excited, and I thought if Celeste was there . . . and then she wasn't, but I still thought I could do it. I mean, these passes are designed for youth travel, they have all kinds of hostels and meet-ups for teens, backpacking is not a big deal over there, people do it."

"Well, it's a big deal over here," he says, tapping his finger firmly on our kitchen island, "and I'm a hard no on letting you go at all. I don't care how much money you put down on the tickets."

I feel a big empty pit open up in my stomach, realizing my backpacking dreams are not gonna happen.

At least, I still get to go on the program.

"Your mother, however . . . ," he adds slowly, "always a pragmatic negotiator, has convinced me that there might be a compromise that we can all live with, that will allow you to put these tickets to use and also build back our trust."

Am I hearing this right?

"If, *and only if*, you come up with an airtight itinerary, well researched, with train times, lodgings, reviews—footnoted and annotated—*and* you can find someone to go with you, preferably from here, or if you can connect with someone in the program ahead of time, you can extend your stay for two weeks to travel."

At this, my face lights up, and I start to go in for another hug . . .

"Hold on, there is one more nonnegotiable condition. When you get back, you will do a one-month internship for the town, in a department of your choosing, without complaining. Consider it community service to make up for your less-than-stellar judgment on this whole thing," he says gruffly.

"Deal!" I say, and smooch him on the head repeatedly.

"Jiminy Christmas, Amanda, my hair!" he grouses before giving way to a reluctant smile.

"Thank you, thank you, thank you, Daddy."

"Don't thank me, thank your mom," he says solemnly. "You better make sure you talk to her. You owe her a proper apology."

"Okay, I will, as soon as I see her," I say and mean it.

"Now get outta here. Don't you have some hot cocoa to sell?" He waves me off so he can finish his coffee in peace. "And, geez, way to hustle this month, kiddo. I saw your bank balance. I was impressed. I'm expecting something nice under the tree, you hear!" he says as I rinse my cup and run off to work.

"You got it, Pops," I say. "I'll be at Junjun's party after work. See you tonight," I yell, as I run out the door and get in my car to head to the farm.

"You're still in the fight, sweetheart!" I say out loud in Coach's grizzled voice. Woo-hoo!

I get behind the wheel and crank up the tunes. Oooh, it's one of my favorites . . .

Last Christmas I gave you my heart
but the very next day you gave it away . . .

I hear George Michael pining in perfect pop sadness.

Five more days until Christmas and my head is positively buzzing with the news. I'm still going to Europe! I can't believe it! I can't wait to tell Cele—

Oh wait, we're still not talking.

My mood instantly crashes with the realization. I mean, I know I haven't reached out since our big fight. But it's not like she has either! No apology, no note, no checking in?

You know what, I'm still mad at her!

I realize my elation has transformed into anger. She really did almost cost me this whole trip. And it's not like backpacking is 100 percent, either. I still got to figure out who I can go with so, really, she did kind of screw me over.

But I still have the program. That's the main thing. Focus on that.

Maybe I should just be happy with that. She's got her summer thing here. I have my program. Max and Jun will be around doing their things. There's the lake, and maybe Luke would come hang out with us. That would be really nice. I mean, do I really need these two extra weeks? Is it really worth pushing so hard and all the drama with Celeste?

Sometimes you just have to deal with what you've got.

That's what Luke said last night.

I start thinking about our conversation and the calm, quiet way he just deals with things. I mean, I show up at his door drenched, and he just takes everything in stride, dries my clothes. He doesn't bat an eye. He just takes care of me. He takes care of everyone. He put off school and his dreams of being an architect and traveling like his parents did to take care of his dad. How incredible is that?

And how unfair! He deserves to go after what he wants too.

All those books about architecture, and the pictures, all those postcards of great buildings he had hanging in his barn. At least, I finally know what to get him for Secret Santa. They have beautiful art and architecture books at the bookstore on Main Street. I'll find him a good one there.

But that's nothing like seeing the real thing.

Gah! It just boils my fudge! Why should he have to give up on his dream? Why should I?

I'm gonna find a way to get my two weeks of travel, no matter what.

I'm gonna take this trip. And I'm gonna send Luke a million postcards for his collection. I just wish there was a way to take him with me, let him see it for himself.

I wish I could give him that for Christmas.

I did mention the program, and he did say he wanted to find some kind of short-term summer thing.

And who knows, if he goes, maybe he'd want to backpack too? Is it crazy to think that he would want to do that with me?

I kind of can't really process that thought right now. I'm too hyped up. All I know as I'm pulling into Post Farm is I can't wait to see Luke. I have so much to tell him.

But it turns out, I never get my chance.

As soon as I pulled into the lot, I saw Hank by the precuts. He told me Luke was out in the trees all day with the cut-your-own customers, so we didn't get to talk. But he did text me and say he'll be at the party tonight.

After work, I went home for a quick change into my version of party attire: a jade green wrap dress my mom bought in the nineties and, to keep it a little rock 'n' roll, some black micro-fishnets, Doc Martens, and a black wool trench.

And now, as I catch my reflection in the rearview mirror, I feel like I'm looking good. I have on eye makeup, and my hair is up in a claw clip. I even managed some red lipstick, to make a festive pairing with my green dress. Like Christmas colors.

Or maybe trying to be just a little more kissable for a certain someone?

Yeah. That. We like, for real, almost kissed last night. But I don't know what it means. I was so upset about the program and the freezing water. The fire was so cozy. And it all kind feels like a dream.

An amazing dream.

But I think it's stupid to read too much into it. I mean, yes, we like each other. And sure, we like to flirt. But we're just friends. That's it.

Isn't it?

I reach the cul-de-sac where Jun lives. All the houses are lit with Christmas lights and lawn decorations. I instantly recognize Jun's from the two large yellow star-shaped paper lanterns glowing in the front windows. I manage to find a spot to park in front of the stately modern house and start walking up the festively lit path to the grand front door. I pause for a moment, to reach back and straighten the seam on my stockings, when I hear Luke's voice on the path behind me.

"Well, look at you. You look a lot different than when I last saw you."

Luke is wearing fresh jeans and brown suede boots, the collar of his crisp white button-down peeking out from under a navy peacoat. His hair is freshly cut and combed back, his skin shining like he just shaved.

Oh wow, he cleans up nice.

"Well, I don't dress up often," I say sarcastically, "but I can do a little better than your old sweats."

"You look nice," he says sincerely.

"So do you." I smile at him. "Shall we?" I say with my British accent.

"After you, milady," he says, gesturing with a little bow, matching my weirdness, making way for me to step up to the door. I ring the bell.

"Oh, by the way, I wanted to talk to you about last night," I say, casually standing by his side at the door. "There's something I want to ask you."

He turns to me with a slightly surprised and searching look on his face, just as Junjun's mom opens the door and we both snap back to attention.

"Amanda, so good to see you!" Jun's mom says, giving me a big hug.

"Hi, Mrs. Reyes!" I say to the petite, dark-haired lady dressed in a plum-colored tailored jumpsuit and who is the spitting image of Junjun.

"Come on in!" She ushers us into a large, cathedral-ceiling foyer with a big winding staircase wrapping around a beautiful, tall Christmas tree. "And who is this, is this your date?" she asks, smiling at Luke.

Oh no, she didn't.

"Uh no, he's not my date. This is Luke, he is a friend of Jun and mine?" I say, shooting Luke an awkward look and seeing that he's surprisingly unfazed.

"Oh, so nice to meet you, Luke. Come on in."

"Nice to meet you too. Thanks for having me, Mrs. Reyes," he says, shaking her hand.

"Oh, please, you can call me Judy. Let me take your coats, I'll put them in the den. Amanda, you and Luke please make yourselves at home, the buffet is in the dining room. And I think Jun is hanging out by the piano in the living room."

"Okay, thank you, and I love your stars in the windows." I take off my coat and hand it to her.

"Oh, the parol. Yes, they are a traditional Filipino paper Christmas lantern. One of my nephews makes them. They are a nice reminder of home," she replies, taking my coat and then grabbing Luke's.

When she does, I realize I'm standing there in my green dress next to Luke who, it turns out, is wearing a hunter green crew neck sweater under his jacket.

"Oh my gosh, you're matching, you two!" Judy says. "How cute! You're sure you're not a couple?" She winks at me.

Ugh, this is going to be a long night.

But Luke just laughs.

"Now, go find Jun, and get something to eat! We'll do carols in a little bit." She shoos us away to enjoy the party.

"I should have texted you to check what you were wearing." Luke leans close and whispers in my ear, making me chuckle as we step into the lively scene in Jun's living room.

There are two big couches surrounding a gas fireplace with a decorated mantle on the far side of the room where people of all ages are sitting and chatting in Tagalog and English. Little kids wearing Santa hats and Christmas dresses are weaving in and out, and there are a couple of babies being bounced on knees and fussed over by adoring aunties, uncles, and cousins. Smaller multicolored parols with flowing tassels are hanging everywhere, along with garlands of Vermont evergreen and pinecones.

Off to the right through an archway is the dining room with a long table overflowing with Sterno dishes. People are chatting and loading plates with pansit, lumpia, lechon, chicken adobo, kare-kare, and what looks like a million other delicious Filipino dishes.

To the other side of the room is an alcove with a piano and another small couch where Max is sitting next to a petite, stylishly dressed, gray-haired lady: Junjun's grandma, who is looking at something on his phone, while Jun hovers nearby.

"Hey, you made it!" Jun says, spotting us and coming to give me a hug, looking dapper in a chic, maroon velvet Christmas vest. "And you're on time and dressed up. Yay! Wow, you are both dressed up," he says, giving Luke's outfit an approving nod before greeting him with a hug. "Thanks for coming."

"Thanks for inviting me," Luke says, happy to see him.

"I have to say, it's giving more Saint Patrick's Day than Christmas." Jun waves his hand in front of our combined green ensemble. "But I'll take it. You guys look super cute. Did you plan this?" he asks, teasing.

"Totally," Luke says. "It's our official work uniform, Christmas-tree green," he jumps in, saving me from having to answer once again that, no, I did not plan to wear a matching outfit with the guy who I work with and who I almost kissed the other night after I fell into a frozen stream, and I'm not sure if we're just friends or what, but everyone thinks we are a couple.

"Here, come say hi to Lola . . ." Jun brings us over to the couch where Max is in the middle of showing her his latest online content.

"Check this one out, Lola, I put my hoodie on backward, so it looked like I was doing a backwards ski jump."

"Oh no, Max, that looks painful!" Jun's tiny grandma visibly winces at the sight of one of Max's spectacular ski fails. "Why would you post that on the internet? Do people pay to watch you hurt yourself?" she asks innocently.

"Well, not yet but, you know, if I have enough subscribers to my channel, it can be like a full-time job," Max explains enthusiastically.

"Oh, like an entertainer," she says in a sweet, encouraging voice.

"Yeah, yeah, right! Kind of like an entertainer," Max says, nodding.

"Like a clown," she adds innocently, nodding at him and smiling.

"Well, not exactly," Max says, about to keep explaining, but clearly starting to feel the slow creep of a timed-release epiphany.

"Hey, Max, look who's here. It's Amanda and Luke!" Jun says. Then, out of the side of his mouth to me and Luke, "And just in time before Lola has you questioning all your life choices . . ."

"Oh hey, guys, cool outfits," Max says, a little distracted, before going back to watching his video with a pained look on his face.

Oh boy.

"And of course, Lola, you remember Amanda from last night." Jun presents me to his lola.

"Hi, Lola, nice to see you again," I say, leaning down to give her a kiss on the cheek.

"Oh, hi, Amanda, you are looking so nice. Much better than last night. Green is a good color for you. It makes you look healthier. And who is this boy? Is this your steady boyfriend?" she asks innocently.

Not again . . .

"No, Lola," Junjun says a little loudly so she can hear over the party. "Amanda's single. This is our friend Luke."

"Hi, Lola, nice to meet you," Luke says, bending down to shake her delicate hand.

"But, Amanda, why are you single? You are so pretty when you dress up, and look, he's so handsome and very tall." She releases Luke's hand and uses hers to point him out to me as if I should be taking a second look. "You two make a beautiful couple."

"No, Lola, I told you, they're just friends!" Junjun says again loudly.

"I'm not deaf, Ignacio. I can hear you, I just don't believe it," Lola says tartly.

"Ignacio?" Luke says to Jun.

"I'm Ignacio Junior, Junjun," he explains. "It's a nickname."

"Ohhhh," Luke says, a bulb going on.

"If I were you, Amanda," Lola says, bestowing a final word of wisdom, "I wouldn't just be friends with this handsome boy, I would tell him you like him before he gets away. Or some prettier girl snatches him up!"

Tell him I like him?

"Okay, Lola, I'll keep that in mind," I say, smiling awkwardly and looking at Luke who gives me one of his smug little eyebrow raises.

Oh, he's just loving this, isn't he?

And I can't help but smile.

"Maybe I am just a clown. Maybe all of this is a total waste of time. I may as well just accept it. I'm gonna be a car salesman and that's that . . . I just wanted to build something myself, you know?" Max looks up from his phone and stares off into space as if seeing his very own Ghost of Christmas Yet to Come.

"Okay, Max, let's get you some leche flan before you descend into an existential spiral." Junjun grabs Max by the hand and leads him off toward the table.

"I think it's too late," Max says, following along meekly behind him.

When I turn back, I see Celeste walking toward us. She looks lovely in a soft cream sweater, flowy brown skirt, and boots, her red hair billowing from under a sage green headband. But I'm not greeted with her usual warm smile, and I instantly stiffen.

"Hey, Celeste," Luke says. "You just missed Max. He went to get some food with Jun."

"Hi, Luke. Okay, thanks," she says warmly. Then, switching back to her cool demeanor to address me, like the sun going behind a cloud, "Hi, Amanda."

"Hi," I say tensely. "How are you?" I add, trying to lighten up a little but feeling myself getting irritated by her whole frosty vibe.

"Me? You want to know how I am? Yeah, I guess it has been like three days since you were yelling at me in the cafeteria, and I haven't even gotten so much as a text. But, yeah, I mean, fine, I guess?" Her sarcasm is treacly sweet.

"What is your deal?" I fire back in an irritated whisper, instantly escalating the situation. "You want to talk about that right now? I'm sorry, I've been busy cleaning up the mess you made when you bailed on our plans. I haven't had time to text," I spit back.

"Whoa," Luke says, standing between us like a referee in a boxing ring. "I know you two have some things to work out, but I don't think now's the time. Maybe we should just go get some food?"

"We got lumpia for everyone," Junjun says happily, walking up with Max and a fully loaded plate. "Wait, is this what I think it is?" He instantly catches the toxic vibe.

"It's nothing. I'm suddenly not very hungry." Celeste's eyes drill into me. "And actually, Jun, I'm honestly just not feeling well," she says, shifting tone back to sunny sweetness as she turns to him. "I'm really sorry, but I think I need to go home. Max, can you please take me?" She turns to her boyfriend and puts her hand on his arm.

"Yeah, sure, hon," Max says, "whatever you want." He grabs her hand and holds it, clearly concerned, and gives me a vexed look.

"Are you sure?" Jun says, looking at Celeste, noticeably disappointed and trying politely to change her mind. "We haven't even started singing carols yet. And Amanda's going to play!" He quickly realizes from the look that crosses her face that this is not an incentive. "But if you're really lucky, my tito Emil might do his Elvis impression and sing 'Blue Christmas'!" He changes tack to lighten the mood.

"No, I think I want to go home. I'm really sorry," she says gently. "I'll text you later and I'll see you tomorrow at the cabin for solstice."

"Okay, feel better," Jun says, waving as they leave.

"Later, guys. Thanks, Jun." Max waves to us. "Say bye to Lola for me. Sorry we didn't get to hang, Luke," he says as they turn to go, but not before Celeste shoots me one last icy glance.

"No prob, see you later." Luke turns to Jun and me and says, "You know what, I'm gonna go get some food," then makes a quick escape to the dining room.

"Did you really bring this drama to my party?" Jun is still holding his plate of spring rolls like an irritated waiter. "I told you to talk to each other and work it out before you came!" he adds, clearly peeved.

"What do you mean? I didn't do anything, Celeste was totally keyed up when she walked up to me, and I was just trying to enjoy the party," I say defensively.

But Jun is not buying it from the piqued look on his face and turns to set down his plate on a sideboard.

"Oh, there you are," Jun's mom says, stepping up and breaking the tension. "Sorry to interrupt, but I think it's time for some carols. Amanda, are you ready to play?"

"Uh, yeah, of course," I say smiling, "I'd love to."

"Great, I'll start gathering everyone in here." She walks off to herd the many kids and toddlers, aunties, uncles, family, and friends into the living room.

"Come on, Jun." I put my hand on his. "I'm sorry about that. I'll text Celeste later and smooth things out. I promise. Right now, let's go have some fun, okay?" I entreat gently.

"Fine," he says, softening. "But I get to pick the first song. Can you play 'All I Want for Christmas' by Mariah Carey?"

"Can I? All I want for Christmas is to hear you belt it out, baby," I say smiling as I take my seat in front of the keys.

"Uh-huh," he says, now fully recovered and leaning on the piano and looking down at me. "By the way," he adds conspiratorially, "I saw the way you and Luke were looking at each other when you walked in together tonight, giggling in your cute little matching outfits. And I know exactly what *you want* for Christmas." He smiles deviously.

"Knock it off, we are just friends, okay? Like, yeah, he's cute and he's fun to flirt with. But we're just friends."

"If you say so." Jun smiles again.

"Hey, you're gonna play?" Luke walks up with a massive plate of food, looking just deliciously cute in his green sweater. "Cool. It's like I'm here with the band," he says, sitting on a chair beside us, ready to watch the show.

He catches us looking at him and asks, "What?"

Junjun and I just glance at each other and smile.

And I realize that, if I'm honest, yeah, Mariah, all I want for Christmas is Luke.

DECEMBER
21

Chapter 21

LONG DARK NIGHT

I fire off a text to Celeste.

Are u ok?

It's early Monday, the morning of the winter solstice, the official start of winter, and tonight will be the longest night of the year. Right now, it's still dark outside and I'm in my bed, cozy under my covers, the blue light of my phone screen the only beacon in my dim room.

I slept well, but I woke up knowing I needed to text Celeste and try to make things right. There are only four more days until Christmas, and last night my best friend walked out of a party because she couldn't stand the sight of me. Not an ideal way to ring in the Christmas season. So I prop up on my pillow, phone in hand, and wait.

Finally, my phone buzzes with her reply.

Fine

Do u wanna talk?

No reply.

Okay she's really gonna make me work for this.

I'm sorry I didn't call u before

I was busy with work

I don't wanna fight

I was just upset about the trip

Still nothing.

If you don't want me to
come tonight I won't

I want u to come

Can talk then

I'm sorry too

I feel a wave of relief wash over me.

❤️

🌲🌲🌑🌑🌑🌲🌲

See you tonight

I put the phone on the nightstand and nestle back on my pillow, trying to keep the warmth of sleep just a little longer.

There's been so much happening this December, and all of it so fast, I feel like I'm on a runaway train, or sleigh, as it were. I never got a chance to talk to Luke last night, either. We had a ton of fun at the party, and I secretly loved that he got to watch me play. I could feel his eyes on me the whole time. But then he had promised Cheryl he'd help with a big delivery early today, so he had to leave before I was done with the carols, and I didn't get to talk to him about the program.

Or get a good night kiss.

Or that. Yeah. That. What is going on with that?

I can't stop replaying the other night in the barn in my mind. How sweet he was, how nice it was to just talk to him, and how amazing it felt when he pulled me close, his eyes shining in the firelight, and how we almost kissed. Just the thought gives me shivers, tempting me to close my eyes, sink back under the covers, and daydream about it just a little longer. About being together, about what it would feel like if he were mine.

Enough of that, you gotta get up!

I do. I have to get to work. Plus, I don't even know if I'm sure what this thing with Luke is.

All I know is, if I'm going to this party tonight, I need to stop by the bookstore and get Luke his present.

Can't sleep on Secret Santa.

I reluctantly throw off my covers, step into my slippers, grab my robe, and cross the hall to the shower, hoping the hot water will snap me out of it. But my mind stays busy with all the details of the other night as I soak in the steam.

"I do know what it's like not to get what you want. But sometimes you just have to deal with what you've got."

I keep coming back to what Luke said. Regardless of what our almost-kiss means, the thought of him giving up on his dream to be an architect makes me sad. And somehow, it also makes me mad! After everything I've found out and everything he's been through, he should have the chance to go after what he wants.

And I really think the young leaders program could be the perfect solution.

Yesterday, I looked up the architecture and engineering curriculum online, and there are all kinds of incredible professors. They teach the software architects use for 3D modeling, and there's plenty of excursions. It could be exactly what he needs. And there's still time to get the application in.

So I printed it, and I'm going to give it to him when we talk today.

And if he goes, we could spend more time together backpacking.

I mean, yes, there's that too. It would certainly solve my issue. But it could also be fun. He has turned out to be a pretty chill guy. We get along well.

It would be incredible to see the world with him.

I mean, we're friends, so it's like not a big deal.

But it is a big deal. Deep down, you know it is.

Actually, I don't know that. The other night, in the barn, it could have been anything. It could have just been a fluke. Either way, I need to tell him about the program. And as for traveling together, I mean, why not just ask him?

"You'll never know, kid, unless you take your shot!" I say out loud, deciding that Coach, the alter ego created in the far recesses of my busy brain, might be on to something. And my mind's made up.

I snap off the water, step onto the bathmat dripping like Frosty in that greenhouse, and get ready for the day.

I'm a few minutes late to work after my stop at the bookstore. By the time I make it to the lot, it's clear school vacation is in full swing, and it's already busy with groups coming to cut their own trees.

Cheryl has brought out my urns, and there is no sign of Luke. Hank is handling the lot, so Luke must be out in the trees again. I put my stuff behind the counter of the shack and start getting ready for the day.

I text Luke once I have everything set up and a minute to breathe before customers start coming for coffee.

Hey, u busy?

Yes w group.

All good?

I thumbs-up his "All good" but add

Didn't get to talk last night

Wanted to ask you smth

About the other night

He hearts my last line.

Ask me tonight at cabin.

Gtg

Bummer, I was hoping to talk before the party. But I guess it's not in the cards. Speaking of cards, I should get his Secret Santa gift together while I still have a second.

His gift is a glossy hardcover book about the global history of architecture. I didn't get a close look at all the books in Luke's collection the other night, but I don't think he has this one. I put the gift receipt in the front cover, then reach into my purse to grab out the Swiss program application and put it in there too.

This is the right thing to do, right? This is about Luke, not me, right?

Yes. This is for Luke. This is his gift from me. I want him to have this chance. I wrap the whole thing up tight in tissue paper and drop it into a decorative Christmas bag. I'm about to write on the little card on the bag, but as usual, I can't find my pen. Oh well, his Secret Santa won't be a secret for much longer anyway.

The rest of the day goes by in a sweet, marshmallowy, cocoa, fudge, sticky swirl, and by the time Trevor comes to take over for me at five, it's already been dark for forty-five minutes and I'm ready for a change of scenery.

Still finishing up

U can go without me

Meet u there

I read and like a text from Luke, then head to my car to drive over to the cabin. As I pull up, I can see Celeste has been hard at work. There is a wreath of fresh pine branches and holly on the door and a warm glow coming from the windows.

"Knock, knock," I say, opening the door, holding my gift bag, and stepping into a cozy scene.

Celeste is wearing a beautiful dark green velvet dress and has her red hair pulled up into a crown of braids with little white poinsettia clips artfully placed. She's lighting a white candle on the mantle, which is decorated with garlands of pine, holly, and red poinsettias.

Max is at her feet laying logs in the fireplace. He's wearing a red-and-green reindeer pattern Norwegian wool sweater. Junjun is relaxing on the couch in his own fisherman knit, sipping a steaming cup of cider that smells like Christmas in a cup. There is a collection of merrily wrapped presents on the coffee table next to an assortment of cookies, popcorn, and snacks.

"Hey, it's Amanda, Blessed Yule!" Max says exuberantly, looking up from his work laying the fire. "Right, that's what you say on the solstice?" He turns to Celeste for a gold star.

"That's perfect!" Celeste says, smiling at him and then at me.

"Now, if I can just get a handle on my log." Max returns to laying the fire, and Junjun just about spits out his hot cider.

"You did not just say that!"

"Junjun, I'm talking about the Yule log, thank you very much," Max reproaches him prudishly, and any tension between Celeste and me dissipates as we both start cracking up.

"Happy Solstice," she says, coming over and giving me a hug.

"Happy Solstice," I say, hugging her back fully.

"Your mom told my mom that they are still gonna let you go to the program," Celeste adds, "and that you can backpack if you find someone to go with. I was glad to hear it."

"Yeah. They are being very reasonable. It's pretty amazing. And, look, I'm sorry about yelling in the caf the other day. I was out of line. And sorry that I didn't call and check in sooner," I reply sincerely.

"It's okay," she says. "Sorry things didn't work out like you planned."

"It's okay," I say, and we hug one more time, a fragile peace achieved.

"Let's have fun tonight!" Celeste breaks our hug and turns to the room like a schoolteacher to her class. "On this, the longest night of the year, the winter solstice, we light candles and fires to call back the light of the sun, and it is all about leaving behind what no longer serves us and setting intentions for the coming year," she adds, energized.

"Yeah, let's do it!" Max says enthusiastically. "I'm gonna light this baby up!"

"Should we wait for Luke?" Celeste asks.

"He said he's on his way, so I think you can light the fire, and we can do presents when he gets here."

"Okay, well, put your present on the table with all the others, and there's cider in the kitchen."

Max starts up the fire, Junjun puts some carols on from his phone, and I take my coat off, put my present in the pile with the others, and head to the kitchen.

"Hey, everyone, am I late?" I hear Luke coming in, and I lean around the corner of the kitchen and see him walk in holding a very large present wrapped in brown paper and stomping the snow off his boots.

"Luke!" everyone cheers.

"A Blessed Yule to you, bro!" Max goes over and hugs him. "Ooh, who's that for?" he asks, excited like, well, a kid at Christmas.

"Ahh, I can't tell you yet. It's a secret," Luke teases, and leans the present against the wall while he takes off his coat.

Then he catches sight of me and smiles, a bright, full open-hearted smile, just for me.

I feel what I can only describe as an explosion in my chest, and I don't think I have ever been so excited to see anyone in my whole life, and I smile back.

"You want some cider?" I ask, still leaning around the door.

"Yeah, please," he says, walking into the kitchen to say hi. I'm standing over the stove, ladling hot cider into a mug, and he's not sure if he should hug me while my hands are busy. After a brief hesitation, he gives me a kiss on the cheek. I hand him a mug of cider, and he takes a sip.

"You know, I kinda missed you today," he says a little sheepishly, still looking at me intently.

"Yeah, me too." I smile, feeling the strong sensation that something between us has shifted from the moment he walked in the door.

"And I'm glad you want to talk later, because there's something I want to talk to you about too," he says earnestly. "I've been thinking that in a couple of days, you're gonna be done at the farm. You're going to go back to your normal life. And we're not going to be seeing each other every day." He pauses. "And there's something I want to say before that happens."

He's gonna ask me out. For real. We are not just friends. He wants to be together. This is actually happening.

I feel my heart in my throat, my chest heaving. I can't breathe and I can't tell if I'm excited or about to panic. I don't know how to feel.

"Hey, what are you doing in there?" Max calls from the living room. "I want to open presents!"

"Yeah, come on, let's do it!" Junjun chimes in, both clearly dying to see their gifts.

Luke and I glance toward the living room, the intensity between us momentarily broken, and he looks back at me and smiles.

"Come on, let's go," he says, taking my hand and leading me into the living room. "It can wait."

But I can't, what is happening right now?

"Okay, Luke, why don't you go first since we all want to know what that is!" Celeste points to his giant wrapped present leaning against the wall.

"Okay," he says, getting up from where he was sitting next to me and grabbing the large present. "This is for . . ." He stretches out the last word.

"Come on, you're killing me," Max says, bursting with anticipation.

"Max!" Luke finishes. "Merry Christmas, buddy," he says, handing him the present.

"Yes!" Max sets on the wrapping paper like a dog after a squirrel.

"Whoa, bro . . . you fixed it." Max looks tenderly at his old sled, now fully repaired, sanded, and varnished, with a fresh coat of red paint on its steel runners. There are smiles of pure pleasure on both their faces as Max examines all the improvements to his old sled.

"You know, I thought we could take it off of some sick jumps," Luke adds nonchalantly.

"Luke, thank you!" Max gets up and gives Luke a big, heartfelt hug. "I'm really glad we're hanging out again," he adds, clearly moved. "I missed you."

"Yeah, me too," Luke says, hugging him back.

I sneak a glance at Celeste, who is beaming watching the scene, and I see that she clearly is some kind of a magic witch. Because when she put Luke's name in a hat two weeks ago, she managed to pull out the perfect gift for Max: getting his best friend back.

"Awww," Junjun says, "you guys are so sweet."

"You know what," Max says defiantly, "Luke's my best friend! I love him. And I don't care who knows it," Max says proudly with his arm on Luke's shoulder. "And you are too, Junjun," Max adds, a commanding sincerity coming over him. "Celeste, it's my turn," Max says with magnetic confidence. "Junjun, this is for you," and hands him a black-and-gold gift bag.

"Oh wow, is this what I think it is?" Jun peers in the bag, "This is, like, the good stuff." Jun pulls out a sleek black-and-gold sleek travel case full of high-end moisturizers and creams.

"It's the gentleman's collection," Max says proudly.

"Someone told you I wanted skin care products, right? But this is so expensive! You shouldn't have," Jun says, opening the tubes to sniff the wonderful earthy cologne, very glad that Max did.

"No one told me," Max said. "You just work really hard with pep club and yearbook and all your student council stuff, and you always show up to do my filming and help everybody out. I thought you deserved to treat yourself."

"Wow, thanks, Max," Jun says, deeply touched. "I really appreciate that." He gets up to give Max a hug.

"Okay, then, it's my turn," Jun says, racing for his gift as the other guys sit down. "And my Secret Santa is . . . ," Jun says, holding a gift bag and swinging it back and forth between me, Celeste, and Luke like game show host, "Celeste!"

"Yay!" She claps and then reaches into the tissue-filled bag to pull out another bag, this one a beautiful handbag woven in geometric patterns.

"Lola brought it for me. It's made from dyed reed and handwoven in the region where we are from in the Philippines."

"Oh, Jun, it's beautiful, I love it," she says, examining the craftsmanship.

"And there's more inside," Jun says, prompting Celeste to reach in the reed bag and pull out a small box.

"It's a magical cat tarot deck! I love it." Celeste hugs Junjun, then opens the deck and spreads some cards. I catch sight of a familiar orange and gray pattern. "Oh! Look, Amanda, the Judgement card is a calico cat! Just like the one you told me about. How funny is that?"

That's not funny. What does that mean? I feel myself spiraling.

But I don't get to ask because Celeste immediately turns to me, excited to give the next gift. "Okay, my turn. This is for you, Amanda," she says, handing me a wrapped rectangular present.

I open the paper to find a beautiful handbound writing journal covered in pressed flowers and closed with a leather wrap. All my anxiety quiets as I take in the incredible gift.

"This is amazing," I say, opening and carefully thumbing through the painstakingly handmade book. "Did you make this?" I am awed.

"Yeah, I made the paper and bound the book, and the flowers are all from the woods around here. I collected them last summer. I thought you could use it for your travel journal in Europe," she says, looking down modestly.

"I love it." I am moved almost to tears by the thoughtful gift. "Thank you so much," I add, hugging my friend.

"That must mean this is for Luke," Max says, grabbing my bag and handing it over.

"Uh, yeah, that's from me." I turn to Luke who smiles at me warmly, deeply pleased to confirm what each gift given has revealed, that I am his Secret Santa.

All of a sudden, I feel myself go beet red, and a wave of panicky revelation washes over me.

He really likes me.

And I really like him.

We are not just friends.

And I put that application in his present, asking him to go to Europe with me, like it's no big deal.

It is a big deal!

And this is not the way to tell him.

I need to get that application out of there. This is way too weird.

But it's too late, he starts to open the present, and I start to fumble.

"Um, I wasn't sure what to get and then when we were talking about architecture and traveling the other day in the barn, I just had this idea . . ." I continue to babble as Luke unwraps the present and sees the glossy cover.

"Wow, this is awesome," he says, genuinely pleased. "I don't think I have this one. Thank you." He looks at me sincerely.

"I'm glad you like it," I say, feeling like I made a narrow escape. "Um, so what do we do now?" I try to change the subject. But I'm not out of the woods yet, in more ways than one. Luke opens the book and starts skimming the pages, and then finds the papers in the front.

"What's this?" he asks.

"The gift receipt," I say, "in case you want to exchange it."

"No, this," he says, unfolding the application and looking confused.

"Oh, that's nothing. It's what I wanted to talk to you about yesterday, but we didn't get a chance. You don't have to look at that right now."

"Application for Young Leaders: Architecture and Engineering, Zurich, Switzerland," Luke reads aloud as everyone, including him, looks deeply confused. Celeste turns and shoots me a cutting look. "I still don't understand. What is this?" Luke asks again.

"Uh, it's the application to the program I'm going on this summer, but the architecture track. After we were talking in the barn the other night, I thought you might like to apply and maybe go, too, you know. Like I said, that's what I was trying to talk to you about."

"*This* was the conversation you wanted to have. About the other night. This," he says, holding up the application, "this is what you wanted to ask me?" His confusion gives way to stone-faced coolness that feels like a shadow passing over a sunny valley.

"Yeah, I mean I just thought it was something that might be really good for you and you might want to do," I mutter unconvincingly. "And the other thing, from the barn, that happened, I mean, yes, I definitely wanted to talk about that too. We just didn't get a chance."

"Oh, be real, Amanda," Celeste pipes up angrily, our fragile truce instantly cast aside. "I can't believe you are still pushing this? Your mission! Don't pretend that this isn't all about getting permission to go backpacking. I can't go and you need someone to go with you, so you thought you would rope Luke into it?"

"Wait, what is she talking about?" Luke asks, genuinely confused. "I thought your parents weren't gonna let you do that?"

"That's what I've been trying to tell you since yesterday. They changed their mind and said I could go if I can find someone to come with me, so I just thought, 'cause we were talking about the program and since it's such a good fit for what you want to do and would be so good for you . . ."

"That's why you gave me this? That's the reason?" he says, anger flashing through the cold.

"Uh, yeah, yes, that's the reason." I fumble unable to even find words for all the other thoughts and feelings galloping through my mind.

He just sits there holding the application, looking at me stunned, trying to compute the whole situation.

"Well, who are you to decide what's good for me? What I should do? Seriously?" he finally spits out caustically. "Anyway, it doesn't even matter since, based on what Celeste is saying, this is all just some kind of setup. So you can get what's good for you," Luke says, his armor back in place.

"No, it's not like that at all, Luke," I say, feeling like he's on a boat drifting farther and farther away from me on a stormy black sea. "I'm sorry, this was a bad idea. I was trying to talk to you first . . . and you wanted to talk to me too, and we never found time . . ." I am tripping over myself trying to explain.

"Yeah, well, college programs and what's best for me is not what I wanted to talk about."

"I realize that now and I'm sorry. I didn't think this through."

"Yeah, from what I can tell, it seems like you never do," he says, some combination of hurt, disappointed, and resigned. "You know what, I need some air." Luke stands up and grabs his coat. "Thanks for the book." He opens the door and heads outside.

Oh no, I totally messed up.

I feel a pit open up in the bottom of my stomach and I descend. "Hey, Luke, wait up." Max goes after him, stopping at the door to turn and shake his head at me. "I do a lot of oblivious stuff, Amanda, but even I'm not this oblivious," he says before going out into the night.

What just happened? How did this go so wrong? I look around at the remnants of the ruined party and realize that both Junjun and Celeste are glaring at me.

"This is not a big deal. It's just a misunderstanding. I'm gonna go after him." I get up to follow the boys outside.

"Um, I think you've done enough, Amanda. Why don't you leave him alone," Junjun says, peeved with me.

"Jun, this is just a misunderstanding about the summer program between me and Luke. It's none of your business," I say snarkily.

"None of my business?" Jun is suddenly angry in a way I've never seen before. "It's everybody's business! You never stop talking about your summer plans. And how much White Pine sucks and how bad you want to get out of here and go travel. And you never think about how that feels for people who have to constantly listen to it. People who *want* to be here! Do you ever consider what a big deal it was for my family to come here and start over? How hard that is? You never think about that, because you take what you have for granted. All you focus on is what you want, Amanda. You forget to even consider what's important to anyone else."

"That's not fair. I don't do that."

"Oh no? What about forgetting to help me set up? And then forgetting to not bring your summer trip drama to my family Christmas party? What about all that?"

"That's not on me. Celeste started that," I say defensively.

"What?!" Celeste is irate. "Really, I started that? You are unbelievable, Amanda. You're not even listening to what anyone is saying."

"Just stay out of this, Celeste, you've done enough already. Why would you say that to Luke? You don't even know what he and I were talking about."

"Oh, I know what you're talking about. *Your* program. *Your* plans. *Your* mission. The only thing you ever talk about, Amanda, getting what she wants, regardless of what anyone tells you they want!"

I'm so mad, I can't even speak. I just scoff.

"You want to know why I was so mad at you the other day?" Celeste continues cooly. "Because you, like, couldn't even be happy for me, that I found a program *I* like, that *I'm* excited about. Nope! You just keep pushing and pushing for what *you* want. It's like you don't even care how anyone else feels and then you sit there and complain about your mom thinking she knows what's best for everyone, and pushing her plans on you, when you are doing exactly the same thing!"

Three, two, one. Knock out, you're down for the count, kid, you got your bell rung, Coach says in my stunned brain, as I just sit there, the wind knocked out of me, the three of us in shock that Celeste said out loud what I guess all my friends have secretly been thinking behind my back for, what, months now?

"Amanda, I'm sorry. That was out of line," Celeste says,

chastened, realizing she went too far.

"I think I'm going to go home." I grab my coat and head to the door.

"Amanda, come on." Junjun jumps in. "Don't go. We all just lost our tempers."

But I don't listen. I walk out onto the porch. I see Luke and Max sitting on the railing deep in conversation. They both look up when I leave, and I try to catch Luke's eye, but he looks away.

And I walk out into the longest night of the year, feeling the dark close in around me.

DECEMBER
22

Chapter 22
LATER ON, WE'LL CONSPIRE

"Hey, you up? Just reminding you that today's my last day in the office before I am off for Christmas, and Dad and I are going to take Liz from work for dinner. It's her birthday. Milo's going to be next door hanging with Marlo, so you'll have to figure out dinner for yourself. Just order pizza or something," my mom says matter-of-factly, picking some dirty laundry off the floor of my room on her way out. "Amanda, did you hear me?" She sounds a little stern.

"Yeah, okay, fine," I say from under my covers, barely hiding the tears in my voice. But I don't fool my mom.

"Honey, what is it?" She instantly softens, drops my clothes on a chair, and comes to sit at the side of my bed. She gently peels back the covers to find my face buried in the toasty smell of my childhood stuffed animal, a tiger named Ra-Ra.

"It's nothing," I say.

"It's obviously something," my mom says tenderly, pulling back the hair from my damp face to reveal my tear-puffed eyes. Her familiar, loving touch breaks through my last bit of resistance, and I roll over and throw my arms around her waist, put my head in her lap, and start to sob.

"Oh, honeybun," she says, stroking my hair and soothing me like I'm still five years old.

"Mama, I've messed up everything." The remorse train is leaving the station. "I've messed things up with Celeste and Jun, and with you." I look up, the train pickin' up steam. "I'm sorry for all the stuff I did without telling you."

"Shhh, it's okay, I know you are. We're gonna work that all out." The soothing touch of unconditional love emanates through her hands with each stroke of my hair.

"And with Luke," I whisper. "I really messed up everything with him. And, Mom, I realize, I really like him." I look up with an intensity that even surprises me. "And I think he really likes me, but now he probably never wants to talk to me again." I return to sobbing.

"Ahhhh, I see," she says calmly. "Well, you better start at the beginning and tell me everything."

So we sit there, and I do. I tell her all of it, how I didn't like him, then I kinda did, Secret Santa, finding out all the Post family stories, Fairy Barn Cat, Celeste, our fight, why I bought the tickets, the icy creek, Luke's barn, the almost kiss, Jun's party, last night's party, the application and traveling together, Luke's reaction—even what Celeste said about me trying to run everyone's life, just like my mom.

At that, my mom grimaces. But I finish, the litany of my sorrows, and my failures spilled on the floor, and I look up to see her smiling.

"Why are you smiling?!" I say, incensed. "It's not funny!"

"I'm sorry. I know it's not funny." She shakes her head and tries to keep her amusement in check. "But it's just so *you,* Amanda. You have always moved a mile a minute, and that brain of yours is always churning and going. You have to give other people a chance to catch up sometimes. Even yourself."

"What do you mean?"

"I mean, I don't think things with Luke are beyond repair," she says. "I think you have just run circles around this poor boy and he's totally overwhelmed."

"Seriously, what do you mean?"

"Think about it. Three weeks ago, he was alone on a farm with his dad, no school, no social life, just work and sitting in his workshop tinkering, carrying a whole lot of grief and responsibility too. Now, you show up, and you bring all your energy and your fire and crazy big dreams, and your great friends . . . And don't forget, sweetie, you're cute and he's a seventeen-year-old boy, and your chemistry is plain as day."

Well, that explains the FACE.

"Your existence has probably just blown up his entire world." I tense up at that. "In a good way! And *then* you don't ask him on a date, or out for coffee, you ask him to go on an international adventure." She's fully laughing now. "And I'm also thinking about how I'm gonna explain that part to your dad." She chuckles, imagining his reaction. "But let's deal with one thing at a time."

"Ohhh, it's so humiliating. What was I thinking?!" I hide my face in her lap and cringe.

"Oh, come on. It was a little tone deaf, certainly, and definitely jumping the gun, but I can see that you did it because you care about him. And if you talk to him, and apologize for overstepping, and maybe try telling him how you feel, I think he'll see that too."

"Ugh," I moan into Mom's lap.

"And as much as I hate to admit it, Celeste was right. You were pushing your ideas about what's best on him, instead of letting him figure it out for himself. And that is something you get from me," she adds contritely, in a tone that makes me sit up and listen. "I'm sorry that I didn't give you space to figure things out for yourself. That's not how I want things to be between us. I want you to be able to talk to me."

"It's okay. I mean, I know the internship is important for college and stuff," I say, trying to meet her halfway.

"Yeah, sure, but your Swiss program is going to be a really cool talking point. If I'm honest, I think I was pushing the internship at my office because I just want to spend more time with you." She shrugs. "You have to understand, sweetie, this is all moving a little fast for me too."

"It's like you start out when you're young, living your life, building a career, and then when you become a mom, you wake up, and you have these babies, and they are your whole world, and it's hard to balance everything. It's like you're the captain of a ship, keeping everyone afloat on a choppy sea. And you have to run a really tight ship to make it all work. And then next thing you know, those babies don't need you as much—or, they need you in a different way. They start to figure things out for themselves, and it's time to back off and let them sail their own ships. But it sneaks up on you, and it feels like you are running out of time, so you try to hold them close . . ." She fights against her own tears.

I reach out and put my hand on hers.

"But I realize we still have lots of time. Because our home will always be here when you need it. You know, my dad always taught me that if a person is lucky enough to get the chance to go out in the world and develop their skills and talents, then they have an obligation to use them to make things better for everyone, to build community. And I chose to do that here. And your dad chose to come with me. And I'm proud of the home we've built. Just like I'm so proud of you and Milo. But now you need to be the captain of your own ship and chart your own course. And it is time for me to be more like a lighthouse," she pauses to stroke my face tenderly, "so you can see where you came from, and always have a light to guide you, wherever you go."

I'm not sure I can quite understand this, not yet. But I understand one thing perfectly.

"I love you, Mama," I say, hugging her tight.

"I love you too, my baby." She hugs me back. "Now, let's stop crying! You've got work to do. You've got a boy to go win back." She stands up, wipes her eyes, and changes tone. "It's showtime, sweetheart, time to razzle-dazzle 'em!" She claps her hands in her best old-timey Broadway diva impression.

Huh, so that's where I get it from!

I give her one more huge hug, jump out of bed, and race to the shower. I catch her carefully picking up Ra-Ra and placing him gently on my pillow before she leaves the room to start her own day.

As soon as I arrive on the lot, I look for Luke, but he's nowhere to be found. Cheryl has left to do some runs, and the only Post around seems to be Hank.

"Morning, Hank. Is Luke around?"

"Uh, no, not today. He got in late last night and has been working hard. I thought he could use a day off. He went skiing with your two friends there, Max and Junior. He'll be back a little later."

"Junjun," I say.

"That's right." He gives me a long, inquiring, but not angry look.

Oh crap, he knows.

"Okay, thanks. I'm going to go set up then."

And he just nods, still looking at me as I tuck my chin and slink off, disappointed, to the Candy Shack.

It is a glorious morning. The sun is out, the snow a little trampled but pretty, and with only three days until Christmas, the lot is bubbling with holiday spirit. People are starting their vacations, families and tourists are arriving from out of town, and everyone wants a cup of hot cocoa.

I can't find much to be merry about. I manage to feign a smile and a "Merry Christmas" for customers, but inside I'm feeling *bah, humbug*. My eyes return again and again to the spot by the tree stand where I'd normally find Luke but he's not there. It feels like I'm going split in two if I don't get a chance to apologize.

Cheryl turns up during a late afternoon lull and leans on the counter, clearly catching my sad Charlie Brown Christmas tree vibes. "What's with you? I saw Luke this morning, and he didn't seem like himself, either. Something happen with you guys?"

"Yeah, it's kinda a long story. Let's just say, I really fudged up."

"You and me both, sister," she says glumly.

"Why, what happened?"

"Oh, it's Zoe. We had a fight. She's got the Christmas Market ready to go and thinks we could still pull it off on Christmas Eve, as one-day event. But I didn't see Hank going for it this late in the game. So she just reached out and talked to him herself! Without telling me. She didn't trust me to handle things my own way. So, yeah, we got into it. And now she's pissed at me."

"How do you know? Did she tell you?"

"Let's just say her perfect manicure is not so nice when you're staring down that glossy middle finger. Yeah, she's real mad at me. But I'm mad at her too. She was way outta line."

I can't help but laugh.

"What's so funny about that?" Cheryl seems slightly amused herself.

"Nothing, it's just that I have never, I mean never, seen Zoe lose her cool. And she'd be the first to tell me it's never okay to be crass in a professional setting, so this is definitely not business. You must have really gotten under her skin."

Cheryl pulls her buzzing phone from her pocket. "It's Zoe, texting to say sorry and she wants to talk." She breaks into a smile that says more than any apology. "I'm gonna go call her and smooth things out. Looks like you have your chance too," she says, pointing to the road where Luke's truck is about to turn into the lot. She places the call and lifts her phone to her ear. "Hi, Zoe. Yeah, me too." She winks at me and walks toward the house.

My heart is in my throat as I watch Luke get out of his truck, grab his skis from the back, and walk to the barn. He glances my way quickly and catches sight of me but turns his head back and goes in the barn without another look. I feel like the snow queen has just stabbed me in the heart with a shard of ice like in that old fairy tale.

Oh no, that's not how this is gonna go.

My molten fudge core melts the ice dagger. I get up from my stool, march over to his door, and knock.

When Luke opens it, the beautiful, smiling guy from last night is gone. His face is like that old brass cash register before he fixed it up—crusty and dull and shut up tight. I feel the pang of ice dagger in my heart once again, but I press on.

"Hi. Can I talk to you please?" I use my calmest voice.

He regards me stonily but also doesn't close the door.

"I want to apologize for last night. Putting the application with your gift was a dumb idea. I honestly didn't mean anything by it, I just thought it might be something you'd be interested in."

"Okay, fine," he says, starting to close the door.

"Wait."

Don't lose your temper, Amanda. You're here to apologize, remember?

I take a deep breath.

"And what Celeste said about asking you to go traveling with me, just 'cause I needed someone so my parents would let me go? That's not why I asked you."

"So why did you?" A flash of fire behind his eyes breaks through his cold facade.

Don't get ahead of yourself. Choose your words carefully.

"Because I thought it was unfair that you don't get to go after what you want like everyone else. If you want to be an architect, then you should go for it and not let this place"—I gesture to the farm—"and looking out for your dad stand in your way."

I realize from his reaction, I'm not saying what he wants to hear. But I don't know what he wants me to say.

"Is that the only reason you asked me?" he demands intensely.

You know it's not, Amanda. You should tell him how you feel.

"Yes!" I stammer, chickening out.

"Well, guess what?" he says, giving up on me. "This place," he mimics my gesture, "is my home. It's my family's home. It has been their home for three generations. If I want to stay here, it's not just 'cause of my dad, it's 'cause it means something to me. But I wouldn't expect you to understand that. All you want to do is run off to Europe, and you just needed a warm body to go with you."

"Ugh. No! I just said that's not the reason. Now you're just being petty. No one's talking about leaving forever. It's just the way you talked about your dream," I say as earnestly as I can. "I wanted to find a way to give that to you. To make that happen for you. Because you deserve it."

"Yeah, I get it, you were trying to help. You thought, 'Poor Luke, stuck on the farm, not going after his dreams like me, let's fix that for him, like I'm fixing up the Candy Shack.' But guess what, I don't need you, or my mom, or Cheryl, or my dad, when he actually talks, to tell me what's best for me. I'll figure it out myself!"

I hear his words and I get his point, but that cynical, condescending tone does it, because I know that's not who he is. I feel my fudge boiling over and start to erupt like Mount Etna.

"Fine, you're right, it's not my job. And I'm sorry I overstepped." I am seething now. "But I am your friend, right? Or at least I was. And when one of your friends can't see the forest for the effing Christmas trees, then you tell them. As you found out last night, my friends have no problem doing that. So, no, it is not my job to decide what's best for you. I'm not your girlfriend. And even if I was, it's still not my job. But as your *friend*, it is my job to tell you when you are selling yourself short by being a stubborn, friggin' . . . lump of coal!"

I turn on my heel and stomp off toward the pond. I hear Luke close his door, get in his truck, start the engine, and pull out.

Well, that went well. Good job, Amanda.

I plop down in the snow, careful to avoid the stream this time, and fight the urge to scream in sheer infuriation. As if on cue, I hear shuffling beside me.

"Not now, Fairy Barn Cat. Not in the mood."

"Fairy Barn Cat?" It's Hank, looking down at me. "Just wanted to let you know Trevor's here to take over. Where is Luke off to?"

"I have no idea," I say crisply.

"Amanda, how about you come over and sit with me by the fire for a minute."

"Yeah, sure." Maybe Hank can shed some light on how to get through to his ridiculously stubborn son.

"Luke told me a little about what happened last night," Hank says as we each take a stump. "I'll tell you, some of it was a surprise. I didn't know he was interested in doing an architecture program. And the part about traveling together. Well, that sounded complicated."

There's the Posts' favorite word again.

"Yeah, I know it was so stupid," I say.

"It was not stupid," Hank says firmly, his eyes glowing in the fire. "Sounds like it was mostly a misunderstanding. I can see how you meant it to be helpful. And I think he does too."

"You sure? Because I just tried to tell him that and it did not go well."

"What did he say?"

"He said it's not my job to fix him."

"Well, that's funny he should say that."

"Why?"

"'Cause it's not his job to fix me. And I have a feeling that that's what he thinks he's doing by dropping out of school and hanging around, putting his life on hold."

I'm not sure what to say, or how much I'm supposed to know.

"It's okay, Amanda. I'm sure you've heard all the stories by now. I had some hard years. I haven't always handled things well. And sometimes you just stay stuck, even when people try to help you," he says, staring off into the fire. "You know you remind me a lot of her."

"Who?" I ask gently.

"Luke's mom, Anabelle. She was full of big plans too. We took a trip just like the one you're talking about, and it was one of the best times of my life. But things happened back here on the farm, and I had to come home. And she put her plans on hold and came with me. Next thing you know, we had Luke, and it was beautiful. But she always wanted to get her PhD, and I promised we'd take Luke and start our lives like we dreamed of. But I got stuck. And for a long time, I didn't know how to get unstuck. At some point, she realized she had to get on with her own life because I wasn't going to. And she did. And I can't blame her.

"As much as it broke her heart, she let Luke stay here, where he'd have his grandma and Cheryl and these woods, instead of being in a small apartment with a babysitter while she worked and went to school." The firelight casts dancing shadows on his face. "But now, he's keeping himself stuck. Not just like me, but *for* me.

And that's not fair. You being here, Amanda, and seeing him with friends again, watching you two fall in love . . ."

Wait, what did he say?

"It's made me take a clear-eyed look at some things. So what you did, it's not stupid, it was bighearted," he says resolutely. "Maybe a little ambitious—we are tree people after all. We grow slow. But sometimes we all need a little push to get unstuck." He pauses thoughtfully.

"You know that boss of yours, Zoe. She reached out to me about doing an event on Christmas Eve. She said Cheryl wants to do it but has been afraid to bring it up with me." Hank gives me a conspiratorial look. "I'd like to see what we can do about that. I just hope we can get the permits and spread the word in time."

I return his look with a smile. "Well, don't worry about that part. I happen to know someone who works for the town. Very well connected. And come to think of it, I know just the person to help us get the word out online too!"

"I hope it's not too late and I haven't messed this up for Cheryl."

"Well, like your mom used to say, if you fudge up, don't panic, fix it."

Hank bursts out in a great big belly laugh, his eyes twinkling with delight. "Who told you she said that?"

"Cheryl! Why is that wrong?"

"No, Nan said that all right, but she didn't use the word fudge." He's still giggling and wiping tears from his eyes.

It's nice to see him laughing so hard. But I have one more

serious matter to discuss. "There's something I need your help with, Hank. It's in the barn. It's part of a real present for Luke."

"Door's unlocked," he says, waving his hand over the crackling fire, the trees, the whole Post Family Farm. "You just make yourself at home."

So I do.

DECEMBER
23

Chapter 23
FAITHFUL FRIENDS

Since we've no place to go
Let it snow, let it snow, let it snow . . .

It's a cold, bright afternoon and the white sky is swirling with gentle flurries. I'm sitting at my dining room table, Christmas carols playing, our tree glowing, and a mountain of arts and crafts materials spread out before me.

Through the open kitchen door, I see Mom in the kitchen making gingerbread with Milo. Dad is singing along to "Let It Snow," stealing gumdrop buttons from the gingerbread men and dodging a playful whack from Mom's wooden spoon. Just your average two-days-before-Christmas at our house.

"Amanda, come hit Dr. Mathers with this spoon for me and remind him he should set a better example by not eating sweets."

"Run, run as fast as you can, you can't catch me, I'm the

gingerbread man!" Dad steals a kiss from Mom, steals another gumdrop, and bursts into the dining room, my mom in playful pursuit.

"Stay out!" She waves her spoon in warning as Dad circles behind my chair to use his own child as a human shield.

Geez, thanks, Dad.

"Amanda, warn me if he tries to sneak back in," Mom says, shooting him a sly glance.

"No, I'm good," Dad says, giving up the game. "I'm gonna head down to the basement with my saxophone and shed. I need to sharpen up for a very special gig." He winks and tussles my hair before retreating.

"Hey, what's this doing here?" Mom lifts the stained-glass star tree topper from among my piles of craft stuff.

"That's more like it," she says, standing on her tiptoes in her apron, wooden spoon in hand, and placing the star atop the tree. She gives me a kiss on the top of my head and goes back to the kitchen with a smile.

At least after our talk yesterday, things are good with Mom again.

I wish I could say the same for everyone else. I haven't heard from Jun or Celeste. And Luke? I didn't even try texting after our round-two blowup. Everything there is to say about my disastrous Secret Santa idea we've said. And I've decided that if there's a lesson for me in all of this, it's to not keep pushing, but to slow down and give everyone a second. So I'm using my day off to make a tactical retreat and to come up with a plan to fix everything I fudged up.

I'm starting by making everyone their own presents. I know, Secret Santa was my idea, but after all the drama I just want to do something special for each of my friends. I mostly just want to tell them I'm sorry.

I've spent the morning YouTubing how to make a parol, the traditional Filipino paper lanterns I saw at Jun's house. After two trips to the craft store, I have managed to make a pretty respectable one, customized for Junjun.

For Celeste, I went down a Pinterest rabbit hole and made snowy Mason jar candle holders. They're decorated with Epsom salt "snow" and twine, plus a few holiday greens hot-glued on for good measure. I melted some old candles, added clove and orange oil, and poured the wax into the jars with wicks. Voilà, scented Yule candles.

As for Max, Hank and I got the ball rolling on his present last night.

So all that's left is Luke.

"Yo, Brodo Baggins, come in here please."

Milo appears in the doorway, casually licking a spatula covered in icing.

"Geez, take it easy on the sugar, you and Dad are both going to be jacked up later for game night."

"We are simply preparing to beat you and Mom mercilessly at Pictionary," he retorts.

"Whatever, you two always cheat. Everyone knows it. Anyway, that's not why I summoned you. I have a job that requires your unique skills."

"You need me to battle someone?" he asks, holding his spatula like a katana in some ronin duel fantasy.

"No, weirdo, I need you to do something in Photoshop for me."

"Okay, yeah, no problem. Just text me whatever it is and what you want, and I'll do it after I get this next batch of cookies in the oven," he replies brightly.

Well, that was surprisingly easy. Merry Christmas from Milo.

"Okay, thanks, little bro!"

"No problem, Han Brolo," he says, walking back to his cookies.

"Whatever, Bro-bi-Wan Kenobi."

"Nice one," he calls from the kitchen. And I shake my head at my weird wonderful little sib.

The sun is going down by the time I pull up to Junjun's house, beautifully lit and glowing in the swirling snow. I park at the curb and ring the bell.

Jun opens the door.

"Amanda? What are you doing here?" He is surprised and seemingly pleased.

"Merry Christmas," I hand him a gift bag with his present inside.

"What is this? You aren't my Secret Santa. I already got my present!"

"I know Secret Santa was all my idea, but I wanted to get you something anyway. To say sorry for how I've been acting."

"Oh, come on, it's okay. You want to come inside?" He opens the door wider.

"No, I can't stay. And, no, it's not okay."

He pulls the door closed and steps out on the stoop, bundling his arms in his sweater, still holding the bag by its strings. He waits, so I continue.

"You were right. I've been pretty wrapped up in myself and not, you know, checking in with you about your stuff. What Max said is true. You always show up for everyone and listen and help, and I, like, have no idea what you even have planned for summer because I haven't asked. Because I've had my head up my . . ."

"Okay, Amanda, I get the point." Jun rolls his eyes mischievously.

"I've been a pretty crappy friend. And I'm sorry. And thank you for helping me realize everything I have here in White Pine, and how I have been taking it for granted. Especially my friends. I promise to do better."

At that, he smiles and gives me a hug.

"And I'm sorry I unloaded on you, the other night. I will do a better job of telling you how I feel, instead of letting things build up," he says. We hug a little tighter.

"Okay, so that's done!" Jun pulls away and looks into the bag. "What did you get me? Oh, it's a parol! And it has rainbow tassels for the LGBTQ+ student council committee!" He examines the homemade lantern. "Look, there's a camera sticker for yearbook, oh, and Bobby the Bobcat! For pep club! It's a Junjun parol! Did you make this yourself?"

"Uh-huh," I nod, delighted that he's delighted.

"I love it! Thank you." He gives me another hug and laughs.

"I'll show Lola. She's gonna love it. By the way"—he changes tone—"have you talked to Luke since the whole solstice thing?"

"Uh, yeah, it did not go well. I tried to explain that what Celeste said about me giving him the application just so I can go traveling was not true. And I think he heard that, but he's still super mad at me. Did you talk to him yesterday? His dad said you guys went skiing."

"Yeah, we did. But he didn't want to talk about it much." Jun-jun looks me right in the eye. "I did tell him that you are a lot of things, but you are not a liar. So, if you say you didn't give him that application just because you needed someone to go on the trip, then that's the truth. Celeste is the one who got it wrong."

"Thanks, Jun." I am reminded again why he's one of my best friends.

"All he said about it was that he was bummed because he thought you really liked him, and then when he heard what Celeste said, he just felt stupid. Like, you know, the whole thing wasn't about him."

"Oh, it was definitely about him."

But also about me. But not the way Celeste made it sound. I just don't quite know how to tell him that yet.

"Well, maybe something to be clear about if you talk to him again," Jun says. "By the way, have you heard from Max? He sent me the weirdest text saying not to make any plans for tomorrow. He's working on something 'spectacular'"—he uses air quotes—"but that's the last I heard. I hope it's not one of his crazy stunts."

"You'll see." I smile knowingly. "You should be hearing from him later tonight. Just do what he says, clear your schedule for tomorrow afternoon, and tell your family too. Lola Ruth is gonna want in on this."

"Well, now I have to know! I'll keep an eye out. And I'm freezing, so I'll let you go. Mwah!" He air-kisses me on the cheek. "Dang, Junjun, your skin is so smooth."

"You can thank Max for the moisturizer. It's the gentlemen's collection at work!" He turns debonairly and closes the door.

Now to clean up some more fudge.

I pull up to my driveway and park at my house. After all these years as next-door neighbors, you'd think Celeste and I would have a tin can phone or a secret stash of pebbles we throw at each other's windows, but nope. Just the good, old-fashioned doorbell.

Her car is in the driveway, but her parents are gone, so I walk up the steps of their painted lady porch and ring the bell, pretty confident I will get her alone. Or, at least, at home watching her little sister.

Celeste answers the door in plain gray sweats and a full zip hoodie, a fleece blanket wrapped around her like a cocoon. I guess she hasn't been feeling as magical as usual since our fight the other night.

"Hi," I say. "Can we talk?"

"Fine. But Marlo is watching TV inside. Let's sit on the swing."

We take our usual spot on the porch swing, our feet propped on an outdoor coffee table with a glass bowl containing the remnants of some decorative candles and one of those long lighters.

"This is for you." I hand her the bag with her present. She accepts it but puts it on the coffee table without opening it in an act of passive-aggressive theater.

Okay, still gonna make me work for this.

"Look, I'm sorry about everything that happened between us. I'm sorry I was pushing my plans on you and thought I knew what was best, and that I didn't take the time to hear what you wanted with the science program. I am really happy that you found something you are excited about and that you will get to spend the summer with Max."

"Thank you for saying that," she says primly. "It means a lot. And I'm glad you can finally see how your behavior has been affecting everyone."

Say what now?

Her sanctimonious tone immediately gets under my skin. But I do my best to mind the fudge.

"Right, yes. I have been pushing hard about Switzerland. And I'm sorry. But to be fair, it sounds like you were thinking about the UVM program for a while. You could have just talked to me sooner and saved us both a lot of drama." I'm realizing she needs to take some ownership of this whole thing too.

She scoffs. "Like you would have listened."

"You know what, forget it." I stand up and face her, dropping any pretense that this is going to be an easy apology. I don't want it to be. I have things to say. "You are acting like all this is on me.

Like you have had no part of this. Guess what, I'm not the only one who makes everything about me and pushes my agenda on other people."

"What are you talking about?" She glares at me, indignant.

"Why did you feel the need to insert yourself in my conversation with Luke the other night? He thinks I set him up just so I could get permission to travel. You threw me under the bus again!"

"Well, isn't that what you were doing? Pushing your agenda on him?"

"Actually, no, I was trying to do something nice for him. To help him."

"Well, who are you to decide what's best for him anyway?" She fires back defensively. "You told me you barely like the guy."

"Yeah, well, maybe I changed my mind! Maybe he's the most interesting and exciting thing that's happened to me in a long time. And maybe I want to go to Europe with him because I really like him!" I am caught off guard by my own confession, but too mad to stop now. "But how would you even know that? You've been too busy pushing *your* agenda on Max!"

That last part lands like a splash of cold water.

"I do not do that," she says coldly.

"Oh yeah? Tell me this." I cue up my question with the cool precision of a lawyer cross-examining a witness. "Why did you put Luke's name in our Secret Santa draw?"

"What do you mean?" Her guard is all the way up, sensing a trap.

"I mean, the day we did Secret Santa, you had met Luke for, like, two seconds and you decided for all of us that he should be in the draw. Why?"

Realizing she's busted, she finally softens and actually starts talking.

"I saw the way Max was laughing with Luke, and he just looked so happy, you know? Like himself. I watch him with all the guys at the car lot, and with his dad, and it's like he doesn't feel like he can be himself. He has to be 'macho Maximus Rex.' He's kind, and loyal, and caring, but he feels like he has to put on this tough-guy persona around them. And I just thought it might be nice for him to have another friend who likes Max for Max. So that's why I did it. I was hoping it would make Max and Luke be friends again."

I resist the urge to point my finger and go *Aha!* like a TV detective nailing a confession. Instead, I say, "So if anyone set up Luke with this Secret Santa, it wasn't me. It was you."

"You're right. It was me."

What was that?

"I'm sorry."

There it is.

"I know, it's not my job to sort Max's life out for him. I still haven't even sorted my own life out. Like figuring out what I really wanted to do this summer. And I guess I was just distracting myself with his stuff. And I'm sorry. I really should have just talked to you. You are my best friend. And I'm sorry I messed up your chances with Luke. If I had known you liked him so much, I never would have done that."

"It's okay. I don't think I knew I liked him so much." I feel a wave of regret. "But I'm gonna figure that part out. You know me, I always go after what I want."

We sit quietly for a moment, enjoying silence that doesn't feel tense.

Celeste pouts. "I'm sorry we didn't get to do the solstice ritual together."

"About that. Open your present!" I am giddy to show her what I made.

She opens the bag and pulls out the candles. "Oh, these are so beautiful! I love them!"

"Well, since I think we just did a pretty significant clearing out of what we want to leave behind, maybe we can light these and set an intention for what we want moving forward?" I ask sincerely.

"I'd like that."

So we pull out the two candles and set them on the table. I take a seat next to her on the swing, pick up the lighter, and hand it to her.

"I intend to be more honest with myself, and more honest with you, and guard and protect our friendship, which I treasure," Celeste says, lighting a candle.

My turn.

"I intend to do a better job of centering the people around me, and not just myself, so I can show up for my friends the way they show up for me," I say, lighting my candle. "Oh, and being honest with myself. Working on that too."

We look at each other in the glowing light of the candles and smile. But before we can hug again, Celeste's sister, Marlo, bursts onto the porch, phone in hand. "Celeste, you got to see what Max just dropped!"

We huddle around the blue light of the phone and watch.

"Is that a chimney? Is he on the roof of the cabin?" Celeste gasps.

"Uh, yeah, and he's dressed as Santa Claus, and he's got his sled. This is gonna be good!" I'm excited to see what he came up with.

The video opens on a shot of Max in a Santa suit, standing on the roof of the cabin and leaning on the large stone chimney with a hand on his hip, his sled by his side, looking off into the starry night.

"Oh, hello there," he says, turning to address the camera in a ridiculous deep jolly voice. "It is I, Santa Claus!" Then he pulls down his beard and says in his own voice, "Don't worry, kids, it's actually me, Santa's stunt double, maximumdanger, like and subscribe," before snapping back his beard.

"If you're like me and have some last-minute Christmas shopping to do, come on down to Post Farm for the first annual White Pine Pop-Up Christmas Market Christmas Eve celebration. We'll have food, music, and all your favorite Main Street shops will be there."

Now the camera pulls out to a wide shot revealing a giant snow ramp off the back of the cabin.

"Oh no!" Celeste shrieks.

"Sled, don't walk, to Post Farm tomorrow!" As he goes flying down the ramp Max yells, in his Santa voice, "It will be a Christmas Eve to remember!" The last part trails off as he catches air before cutting out to a title card with the hours and directions.

"I'd better call him." Celeste holds out her hand for Marlo to pass her the phone. "That explains why he hasn't been answering my texts. I hope he's not in the hospital."

"Yeah, hope not. Also, I want to find out the response to this video." I say, deadpan. "I have to see how it lands!"

"Not funny," Celeste scolds.

"Nice one!" Marlo says. And I see why she and Milo get along.

DECEMBER
24

Chapter 24
LOVE AMONG THE PINES

It's 8:00 a.m. on Christmas Eve. A yellow sun has risen on a clear winter morn, casting a golden glow on a fresh dusting of snow. I step out of my car on the auxiliary lot in a field across the street from Post Farm, sling my bag on my shoulder, put on my beanie and gloves, and stand, mouth agape, taking in the transformed scene.

Other than the big red barn and the house, I hardly recognize what I'm looking at. The whole horseshoe-shaped lot is lined with booths just like the Candy Shack, each decorated to reflect different Main Street stores.

In front of the barn where I usually park, is a covered stage, sound system, and band setup. The house itself is alive with lights, a fresh wreath on the door, and in the big front bay window, a glittering tree shines, welcoming all.

Meow.

I feel the familiar press of a kitty doing figure eights between my legs.

"Fairy Barn Cat! You're here." To my delight, the pretty little kitty lets me bend down, pick her up, and give her a big fat snuggle.

"Well, just like your tarot card, you certainly ushered in some judgment. Now I'll take some of that calico cat transformation and good fortune Celeste was talking about. What do you think, kitty, can I pull this off? You think I can fix things with Luke?"

I am answered by copious purring and a bop on the nose.

"I got a special present for him here," I say, tapping my bag. "I hope he likes it better than the last one."

More purrs.

"Okay then, wish me luck." I set the cat down. "And enjoy the market, maybe another human will finally see you and I can stop feeling like I'm crazy?"

Meow.

"Indeed," I say, bringing out Sir Reginald Dillpickle, "I thought you might say that. Then adieu. Until we meet again, Milady." I bow deeply to my kitty friend before steeling myself to cross the street and face the Christmas music.

There is all kind of commotion on the lot as I walk up, with people coming and going, loading in and setting up their stands. A crew is rigging lights and speakers by the stage, and just past the firepit I can see food stalls and vendors setting up. In the middle of everything is Max, with a clipboard and one earbud in, directing the chaos like a conductor.

"Okay, Marissa, you guys are in booth three. I emailed everyone the map, and it's also tacked up on the side of the barn." He directs a college-aged woman carrying a box of decorative scarves and soaps.

That must be Helen's infamous Marissa.

"Thanks, Max, loved the video!" she says.

"Thanks, appreciate it. Follow me on my new channel, maximumdangerEVENTS, like and subscribe."

"Will do," she replies.

"Oh, hey, Amanda." Max looks at his clipboard. "You're right on time! Cheryl's super busy with the food stalls, but she said she got someone to start your drinks, and they are in the stand already. And Zoe said Trevor will be coming in early so you can be free-floating and help out with whatever needs attention today."

"Okay, thanks, Max. Sounds like a plan. I gotta say, it looks like being an event planner really suits you. I'm glad this worked out."

"Oh yeah, I love it. Thanks for connecting me to Zoe and Cheryl, they're great. It's like I finally found my calling. Plus, in events you still do some media, so I don't have to give up my passion for content creation, you know?" He grins. "By the way, did you see the jump?"

"Yeah, it was amazing. And the video was very well produced! Some of your best work I'd say. Your acting . . ." I make a facetious chef's kiss with my fingers. "Next level."

"Yeah, it really came together. Luke and Hank helped me. Though I think Luke needs to fix the sled again. It was a rough landing."

"I'm glad you are in one piece at least. Um, where is Luke?" I ask casually.

"I don't know. He's kind of all over helping too. Maybe over by the stage? But you better focus on setting up. We got a schedule to keep." He points to an invisible watch on his wrist. "Can't be slacking."

Who is this and what have you done with Max!

"Oh, Max, there you are." Zoe walks up with her own clipboard. "Cheryl wants you to tell the food vendors that there is space in the front barn for extra storage. Hi, Amanda!" She gives me a big hug, which is a welcome surprise. I guess the fabulous energy of the market has got her in the Christmas spirit. I start feeling it too.

"This is amazing, everything is coming together so well! You and Cheryl must be thrilled."

"Well, we're far from done setting up, but all signs point to this being a blowout today. And we can thank Max here. His video has gotten a ton of traction. I think half the town's gonna come out just to find out how badly he hurt himself with that jump!" She laughs merrily.

"Aww, I'm fine," Max says offhandedly. "Not even some of my most daring work. Though, Amanda, you're right, cinematically I think I've opened a whole new chapter," he muses.

"Where've you been hiding this one, Amanda?" Zoe says giving Max a pat on the back. "He's fantastic, a natural-born entrepreneur. I see big things in your future, Max."

"I appreciate that Zoe, but we really don't have time to chat. I want to get setup locked in by nine-thirty, then we're gonna get the signs out and the parking lot attendants and crossing guard in place to be ready for the opening rush."

"I love this kid." Zoe points at Max and beams. "Okay, let's do it! I'll find you later, Amanda."

I leave them to organize and head over to the Candy Shack, my sweet little shack, now just blending in with the lights and decorations of all the other colorful stands nearby.

"You'll always be special to me, Candy Shack." I feel oddly sentimental.

"Well, it's not like you can't come back and work it next year," Hank says, walking up.

"Hey, Hank! You really whipped this whole event into shape in record time. It's amazing!" I put my bag behind the counter and start the setup.

"Yeah, well, I can't take the credit," he says leaning on the counter. "Cheryl and Zoe are a force to be reckoned with. And between you and me, I think they got their own sparks flying, if you know what I mean."

"Uh, yeah, I think I caught that too."

"Ahh, it's a beautiful thing to see, people finding each other out here at this special place." He smiles, waxing poetic. "Love among the pines," he says wistfully, and I can't help but snort a little.

"Did you just snort?"

"I think I did," I say, laughing. "I'm sorry."

"Well, I guess I'll leave the wordsmithing to you next time." He smiles.

"By the way, Hank, have you seen Luke?"

"I don't know, maybe out in the auxiliary lot getting the parking set up?"

"No, I didn't see him," I say, disappointed. "If you do, can you send him my way?"

"Oh, don't you worry. You'll find each other too," Hank says reassuringly. "I have no doubt about that. Love among the pines!" He proclaims, fist raised, like a joyful rallying cry, and cheerily saunters off into the crowd.

Huh, just as embarrassing as my dad.

I spend the next hour or so totally focused on work, keeping an eye out for Luke, but I can't seem to find him in the growing crowd, and it's making me antsy. By opening time, the market is fully set up, Trevor's manning the Candy Shack, Christmas music is playing over the PA, and tourists and townsfolk are pouring into the parking lot and filtering across the road to peruse the stands. The atmosphere is jolly, joyful, and electric.

But still no sign of Luke.

I'm standing near the shack scanning the crowd when, finally, I see him.

He's walking up from the barn, his coat off, a red-and-black flannel shirt open to the thermal underneath. It's unbuttoned at the collar, revealing his smooth chest and lean neck. He's wearing work gloves and has a freshly cut and bundled Christmas tree slung over his shoulder. He's walking toward the stage across the lot, but he doesn't look my way.

He is so unbelievably hot.

"He's taking his lumberjack look to the next level today." Celeste steps up beside me, clocking my stare.

"Yeah, and it's killing me," I confess.

"You talk to him yet?"

"No, I've barely had the chance. And I don't know if I will, there's so much going on. Not many convenient moments to walk up and be like, 'Hey, you got a second for me to tell you that I'm totally into you, and I'm worried that I completely messed it up and you'll never speak to me again?'"

"Yeah, good luck with that." She cracks a smile. "Amanda, don't let yourself overthink this. Just tell him and put us all out of our misery. Jun has texted me like three times already to see if you've talked to Luke yet. He says Lola Ruth is asking for a play-by-play of how it goes."

I know she's right. I can't overthink this. I just have to do it.

"Okay, I'll do it. But I do need to find the right moment. What about you? You're here early, I thought you were coming later in the afternoon with your folks."

"Yeah, I wanted to hang around to help Max, but I don't think he needs it. He seems to have found his thing. So I'm just gonna wander around and do a little shopping. You know, do my thing."

"That sounds like a plan. I'll be floating around making sure all the vendors have what they need. But my family should be here soon for the show. Come find me, okay?"

"Okay." She waves and makes her way to a booth with vegan soap, botanical extracts, healing crystals, and scented candles. I smile, watching her pulled toward her own passions.

I make my way through the crowd toward the food stands by the firepit and I see Luke, leaning on one of the stands that is *not* the Candy Shack, drinking a cup of coffee and chatting with the barista.

What? He's getting his coffee at the competition!

And I'm oddly inflamed.

Okay, chill, Amanda, just go talk to him.

Sensing this is my opening, I start to walk toward him. He sees me and he doesn't look away. In fact, he's kind of holding my gaze. This is a good sign. But crap, I don't have his gift. It's in my bag in the Candy Shack.

Never mind, just go talk to him, this is your chance.

But before I reach him, I pass booth three and I'm stopped in my tracks by a familiar singsongy voice.

"There you are, Mandy, my favorite barista extraordinaire and young lovely, come on over here!"

"Hi, Mrs. Novak." I feel myself drawn into her orbit like a comet to the sun.

"Why, aren't you just a vision on this fine Christmas Eve day?" She walks over to give me a hug. "Is it my imagination or is there a little extra blush in your cheeks and twinkle in your eye?"

I *actually* blush at that.

"I don't know . . . ," I say bashfully, looking over toward where Luke was standing. He's gone again and I feel my heart sink, but I focus back on my conversation with Mrs. Novak.

"You know what though, you need to upgrade that hat." She points to my beanie. "How's about this one?" She hands me a dark gray, supersoft cashmere cap with a fake fur pompom. "Go on, try it on." And I oblige.

"Now that's perfect, gray to match your stormy gray eyes, like a wild winter sky. I want you to have that, it's a Christmas present from me," she says, patting my hand.

"Oh, that's so sweet but I can't possibly," I start to protest.

"Nope. I won't hear it. Oh! There's one more thing. I've got these darling little felt mistletoe pins. There," she says, sticking one to my cap. "So you'll be ready, in case you run into a certain tall, dark, handsome someone, if you can catch my meaning," she says, giving me the FACE. "By the way, have you talked to him today? I had a feeling he was looking for you."

Does everyone *know I need to talk to Luke?*

"You mean Luke? Uh, no, I've been trying to find him."

"Okay, let me know how it goes," she says, smiling and pointing to the mistletoe. "I told you, I have a feeling about you two," she adds with a wink.

"Okay, Helen," I say smiling. "I will."

"Finally, you called me Helen!" She clasps her hands to her heart as I merge into the crowd.

I head back to the Candy Shack, say hi to Trevor, and reach behind the counter to grab my bag. I suddenly feel overwhelmed by all the merrymakers. I make a beeline toward the south end of the barn, near the pond, to find a moment alone to catch my breath.

And that's where I find Luke, leaning up against the wall under the eaves, staring off toward the mountains.

I walk up and lean on the wall beside him, fixing my own eyes on the view, surveying the rolling hill to the pond, the wild woods where we walked, the Christmas tree rows vanishing into the base of the beautiful winter mountain rising in the distance.

"So this is it, huh?"

"What is?" he asks, keeping his eyes fixed on the horizon.

"After today, I won't be coming here all the time. We probably won't be seeing each other," I add, testing the waters.

"I guess that's true," he says, matter-of-fact, not breaking his thousand-yard stare, which makes me start to panic.

Come on, Amanda, just say what you gotta say.

"So in light of that, do you think it would be possible for me to get a do-over on Secret Santa?" I turn to face him.

He just keeps looking out, his crisp jawline, his dark hair, his beautiful dark eyes all set on the horizon. I can tell he's listening, so I press on.

"Because I have a present for you," I say. "A better one. Something that actually means something to you, not just me."

At this, he turns to face me, and I'm momentarily unbalanced by his proximity, his size, his smell, his closeness, his eyes, and the energy I can feel occupying the space between us.

But I get it together, reach into my bag, and hand him an eight-by-ten-inch frame wrapped in tissue paper.

He carefully pulls back the paper to reveal a restored version of the Post family photo from his workshop.

"How did you . . . ?" he says, surprised and softening.

"Well, Hank said I could go into your barn. I asked permission, don't worry," I say, covering my bases. "And I took a picture of the original. Then I had my brother, Milo, who, as annoying as he can be, is pretty handy with Photoshop, fix it up, and I got a new frame. You can really see everyone now," I say enthusiastically, stepping up next to him to point. "I hadn't noticed, but there used to be a sign on the barn, see? Post Farm." I look up at him as he turns to me, and we find our faces deliciously close.

"Anyway," I say, stepping back. "I thought it might be nice to have, you know, a copy that isn't faded. Because, like you said, this is your family. It's who you are. So it should be fixed up. But I'm not trying to fix you! That's not what I meant," I blurt, terrified I've said the wrong thing again.

"Amanda, relax." He smiles and puts a quick, reassuring hand on my shoulder. "It's okay. I know what you meant. And I'm sorry for how I reacted the other day and the stuff I said. I know you didn't mean any harm. And you were right about a couple of things too."

Wait, what? Say that again?

"You gave me some stuff to think about and helped me realize there were conversations I'd been putting off with my dad. With myself too. That finally happened. So thanks. I guess." He looks deeply at the photo. "And thank you for this," he says. "I love it. It's a beautiful present."

"Really?"

"Really." He nods. And then he looks at me and smiles. That beautiful openhearted smile, just for me. And I feel an explosion in my chest and a wave of relief wash over my whole being, like seeing an old friend after too long apart.

“Oh, I’m so glad, I’m so sorry about everything. I’ve just been feeling so bad . . .”

“But this is only part of the present, right?” There is a hint of playfulness in his tone. “I mean, if I’m gonna give you a do-over, then you have to do over all of it.”

“What do mean?” I say, feeling just a little anxious.

“Why did you give me that application?” he asks directly.

“Oh, not this again . . .” I am almost in despair.

“No, not the program part,” he says calmly. “The other part. What did you want to ask me? About traveling together?”

“Oh yeah, that. I mean, I think you know.” I look into his eyes.

But he’s not letting me off that easily.

“Listen, if this is do-over, then you need to do it right. You have to ask me,” he says, the flirtation unmistakable in his voice as he takes a step closer and holds my gaze.

“Are you really going to make me say it? You know what I want.” I feel an exquisite, agonizing tension start to rise in my body.

“I do. And I know you usually get what you want.” He steps even closer. “And maybe I like being what you want,” he says in a low, warm voice that makes me feel like I’m going to melt into the snow under my boots. “So ask me again,” he says, close enough now that I can smell the peppermint candy canes on his breath.

“Do you want to go traveling in Europe with me this summer?” I ask, looking deeply into his eyes with absolute, unmistakable clarity.

He pauses for just a moment.

This is it, this is what I want . . .

"I'll think about it," he says blithely, breaking out in an enormous grin, his eyebrow raised in his unmistakable smolder.

"Ohhhh, that's a dirty move." I gasp indignantly and playfully slap him on the arm. "I can't believe you," I say, beaming and alive with flirtatious energy.

"Come on," he says, taking my hand and leading the way toward the stage. "It's almost time for your dad to play, and I promised him I'd go to a gig." He turns back toward me, smiling. "Nice hat, is that new?"

I remember my hat and reach up to feel for the mistletoe, but it's gone. It must have fallen out.

Drat, foiled again, Sir Dillpickle pipes up in my brain.

"Let's go." He gives my hand a gentle tug and snaps me out of my thoughts.

"Fine," I say, letting him lead me along, my hand in his. "But I will find a way to get you back for this. And since you made me ask, I do expect an answer." I say, feeling filled head to toe with absolute liquid elation.

"And just so you know," he says, stopping to look at me seriously. "Today is *not* going to be the last day I see you. Not a chance." And we walk on, hand in hand.

The smile on my face is already so big it has nowhere left to go, so I feel it in my heart, and I know for certain that what he said is true.

As we start to make our way across the lot toward the stage, I see Cheryl in the crowd and we stop to say hello. "Cheryl, hey, thanks for getting the Candy Shack set up this morning. This is amazing, congratulations!"

"Ah, thanks, Amanda. Yeah, I couldn't be happier. It's just like the old days when Mom was still with us. And I see you two found each other," she says, nodding to our linked hands.

"Yeah, I guess we did," Luke says serenely.

"Great, now maybe you can help me find Zoe," Cheryl says. "I've been missing her all day, and I just want to say thank you, you know, for helping me do this. It's just blown me away, all of it, she's so amazing . . . Well, you know. I just want to tell her."

"I haven't seen her," I say, knowing that feeling. But Luke, making the most of his height, stands on his tiptoes and points.

"Over there, by the road. I see her. Zoe!" He waves one of his long arms, a beacon amid the crowd.

She catches sight of him, Cheryl, and me and starts weaving her way over, searching along the ground as if for something she lost.

"Hey, Zoe," I say.

"Guys, I know this is gonna sound crazy, but did you see a little spotted cat come through here?"

Ah, Fairy Barn Cat, what are you up to?

"No, we don't have a cat." Cheryl is adamant. "But I was looking for you, Zoe. I wanted to talk to you and say . . ."

"Are you sure you didn't see it? I swear, this cat gave me the craziest look. Like it was reading my mind or something." She is still scanning the ground, which makes everyone else look down, too, except for Cheryl who's looking straight at Zoe.

"Will you stop that for a second," Cheryl says, taking Zoe gently by the shoulders and finding her gaze. "I'm trying to tell you something. I'm trying to tell you that I couldn't have done any of this without you, and this last month working on this with you was amazing, and I don't want it to stop. I don't want you and me being together to stop," Cheryl says passionately while Zoe looks at her, rapt.

"Hey, what's this?" Luke reaches down toward the ground and comes up holding the felt mistletoe from my hat.

"Oh, that's mine. It's mistletoe," I say, and Luke and I share a look.

"You know what, give me that." Zoe grabs the mistletoe and holds it up like the Statue of Liberty's torch as she reaches for Cheryl and gives her a long-awaited and wholehearted kiss.

"Well, Merry Christmas!" Cheryl says to Zoe, pleasantly stunned, before leaning in to lovingly kiss her back.

"Hey, everybody, the show's about to start, if you want to make your way to the stage," we hear Max's voice over the PA.

"Ahem, I hate to break this up," Luke says delicately, "but if you want to join the rest of the party, we'll be over by the stage." Zoe and Cheryl pause in their embrace to smile at us.

"Okay, we'll be right with you," Zoe says in her all-business tone, before turning to Cheryl to exchange a long, meaningful look.

"Come on, I think they may need a second." This time, I tug playfully on Luke's hand and lead him into the crowd assembled in front of the stage. We spot Junjun and Lola Ruth front and center, standing next to Mom, Milo, Celeste's sister, Marlo, Celeste, and Hank.

"Amanda, just in time!" Mom says. "And hi, Luke, glad you two found each other." She smiles at us. And Luke smiles back.

"I'm so excited," she continues. "I haven't been to one of these shows in ages!" She's clapping her hands like a giddy schoolgirl, but when she screams "Bring out the band!" like a deranged groupie, Milo and I exchange bewildered looks, and Luke and Hank start to laugh.

"Hello, White Pine, and welcome to our first annual Christmas Market!" Max takes the stage and speaks into the mic. "I'm Max Pearce and I'll be your emcee today."

"Maximumdanger, woo-hoo," someone screams from the crowd. "Sweet jump!" someone else heckles to cheers and applause, Celeste woo-hooing her head off next to us.

"Ha-ha, yeah, thanks, everyone. Thanks, hon, love you," Max says, singling Celeste out.

"Thanks so much for coming today. This is a great crowd, and we are so excited to introduce our first band of the afternoon. Oh, wait, hang on." Max looks off into the wings and then jogs over to grab something from whoever's back there, before returning to center stage.

"Okay, before we start, the band wants me to read this." He looks at the little piece of paper and squints. "It's a—what is it?" Max says, leaning back from the mic to talk to whoever's offstage. "It's an homage? Okay, if you say so. So this is a homage," Max reads. "Tonight, we invite you onto Santa's sleigh for a journey through space and time to expand your jazz reality and blow your musical mind. Please welcome Dickie Teeth and the Smooth Tones!"

My dad takes the stage holding his sax and wearing all black, with a porkpie hat and a red-and-green Christmas tie, followed by his three best friends who take their places on drums, electric bass, and a Wurly electric piano.

Meanwhile, my mom is absolutely losing it, cheering and clapping and turning to Milo and me. To our infinite horror she says, "Geez, doesn't your dad just look so cute up there in his black jeans? He's so HOT when he's onstage!"

Oh no, no, no, no, no . . .

Luke, Celeste, Junjun, Milo, Marlo, Hank, and I, and even Lola Ruth, turn and give her the FACE.

"What? He's my husband, I can say that. He's a hottie!"

"Thank you, White Pine," my dad says into a standing mic. "You came here for carols, and carols you shall hear, but reinterpreted in the language of jazz by these intrepid souls." He gestures to the band. "This first song you may recognize as 'The Carol of the Bells,' but we call it 'Too Many Notes,' and it's going out to all you jazz lovers everywhere, you know who you are. Hit it!"

With that, Dad lets out a squeal on his sax to wake the heavens and announce that Christmas has come! And it's all a tangle of harmonics from there.

"Is this what it's supposed to sound like?" Lola Ruth asks Junjun with a confused look on her face.

"Yes, Lola, it's fusion jazz," Jun explains loudly over the melodic din.

"I'm not deaf, Jun, you don't have to yell. Although I might be soon, if I keep listening to this." She shakes her head in dismay.

"I think it's far-out," Hank says, clearly in a deep groove.

Two more crowd pleaser–type wedding bands came on after Dad's set, which ran a little long with all the solos, and the revelers continued to ebb and flow for the rest of the afternoon until early evening when the market closed and people scattered to their trees and tables.

And that's how I spent my day before Christmas.

Luke and I stayed glued to each other, hand in hand, the whole time. But when it was finally time to head home, everyone was around. My parents, Milo, Cheryl, and Zoe, even Helen, so we didn't get a chance to say a *proper* good night, just the two of us.

"What are you guys going to do tomorrow for Christmas?" I ask Luke, stealing a moment to chat as my family headed to the parking lot.

"I don't know. I think Hank has something planned, but I'm not sure." Luke has a twinkle in his eye I can't quite discern. "How about you?"

"We'll get up, my mom will make us listen to a Christmas record that her dad got for free with a set of snow tires in 1977, and we'll open presents. Then we'll start cooking Christmas dinner, hang out, play with our new stuff, watch some movies. You know, the usual. But maybe I'll call you, and we can find a way to catch up before dinner?" I am already dying to talk to him again.

"Yeah, okay, we'll see," he replies casually.

We'll see? I don't like the sound of that.

I feel myself spinning up.

"Come on, Amanda, time to go," my dad says, walking over.

"Great set, Dr. Mathers, really revolutionary stuff," Luke says convincingly.

"Amanda, have I told you how much I like this boy? He has a very discerning ear for quality music," Dad says playfully. "See you soon, Luke, and thanks." Dad shakes Luke's hand as I free mine.

"I'll call you tomorrow," I add, and I am pulled away from Luke and the Post Farm with the flow of the exiting crowd, all aglow with the warmth and whimsy of a very merry Christmas Eve.

HO
HO
HO

Chapter 25
THE PERFECT GIFT

"Come on, hurry up, or we're going to be late," my mom pops her head in my bedroom door as I finish putting on some makeup to complement the soft gray cashmere sweater I unwrapped this morning.

It matches my new hat!

"And my wild winter eyes," I say, mimicking Helen Novak as I check my face in the mirror.

"What?" Mom says.

"Nothing." I smirk. "Are you still not going to tell me where we're going?"

"You're not the only one who's good at making secret plans." She smiles. "Come on, in the car in five or we'll be late. And they're cooking up a feast."

With that, I think I have my answer.

***

A half hour later, the four of us—the Mathers Family Band, as my dad likes to say—are pulling up to Post Farm in my dad's car, a bright sun shining on a fine, cold Christmas morning.

The remnants of the market are still visible. All the garbage has been picked up, and the stage is stacked for removal, but the stalls are all still there, closed up for the night.

Hmm, looks like these may be a permanent feature at the farm.

We park and walk up to the house, laden with gifts and sweets and side dishes for the feast. I see the great tree shining in the front window, and my mom leads the charge to the front door, but I interject.

"No, it's okay, we can go in through the kitchen," I say, feeling at home in the place I spent my whole December.

I knock on the porch door and then enter into a warm world of wonderful smells.

"Hi, Merry Christmas!" Cheryl is exuberant, standing side by side with Zoe in aprons, working on what looks like it will be an incredible Christmas lunch.

We all meet for hugs and hellos, and my family hang coats and take off boots by the mat.

"Hey, Mathers, Merry Christmas!" Hank steps in from the hall, beckoned by the commotion.

He's all cleaned up, hair combed, beard trimmed, and wearing his dressiest flannel shirt. Without his trapper hat he has a full head of silver-black hair that will make my dad cry.

We all say our hellos and Milo, the last one through the door says, "Um, Mr. Post? I think your cat wants to come in."

Both Hank and Cheryl look confused and are about to say "We don't have a cat" when Fairy Barn Cat runs between Milo's legs and heads straight to the parlor as if she's lived here all along.

"See, I told you!" Zoe exclaims.

"I guess we have a cat," Hank says. "Come on into the parlor, everyone! I've got the fire going."

My family shuffles through and settles in the parlor, and I hang back to wait for Luke.

"He just ran to the barn to get something," Cheryl says, seeing my searching look. "He'll be back in a minute. Go on in."

"Okay," I say. "Can I help with anything?"

"Oh no, sweetie," Zoe says warmly, "we got it covered." She turns to Cheryl, who gives her an adoring look.

I walk into the hallway, but before I enter the parlor, I take a moment to enjoy the scene. Dad and Mom in the wingback chairs, a roaring fire in the hearth, Hank leaning against the mantle telling a story and pointing out details in the old painting of the farm. Milo on the floor playing with Fairy Barn Cat, who has made herself instantly at home. And Nan's picture on the piano, smiling over all of it.

Through the years we all will be together,
If the fates allow,
Hang a shining star upon the highest bough.

I think of the happy version of that song that I've heard so much since I came to this house. I look at the beautiful shining star on top of the tree in the front window.

Being all together at Christmas. This must have been what Nan was waiting for.

"Hey."

I turn to find Luke standing in the hall, hands behind his back, looking lovely in his green sweater, dark eyes shining.

"Hi!" I say. "I guess I didn't need to call you today."

"Guess not," he says, hovering.

"You were in on this?"

"Oh, absolutely. I'm great at surprises." His flirty tone is already starting to quicken my pulse.

"Good to know," I say, playing it cool. "Whatcha got there?" I point to whatever he is obviously hiding behind his back.

"I'm good at surprises and presents. And this one is for you." He takes one hand from behind his back and holds out a small, long red box.

"Merry Christmas," he says, and I take the box and open it.

Inside is a beautiful wooden fountain pen.

"I made it myself. Well, not the hardware, but the wood part. You know for your journal, because you're always losing your pens."

"I love it," I say, opening the pen and marveling at the smooth wood and the shining silver point of the tip. "Thank you!"

"And . . . ," he adds, "I know it works because I used it to fill this out." He reveals a printed paper form, held in his other hand.

"Is that the application to my program?"

"No," he says matter-of-factly. "It's an application to community college. I'm gonna finish my GED and go back to real school to get a jump on some college credits, so I can start thinking about architecture school."

"That's amazing," I say, excited for him but also registering a little pang of disappointment.

"But this," he says, removing another printed form from his back pocket, "is an application for a passport."

There it is, that explosion in my chest filling me with glee.

But two can play at this game.

"Well, what do you need that for?" I ask coyly.

"Oh, I think you know," he says, stepping forward and shooting me his trademark smolder.

"Well, you know, I usually get what I want. And what I want . . . ," I say teasingly, stepping even closer to him and looking deeply in his eyes, "is to hear you say it."

"Fine. I'll say it. I need a passport because a weird, wild, never-stops-talking, fiery, smart, smoking-hot girl asked me to go backpacking in Europe with her. And I would very much like to do that. Is that what you wanted?" And he closes the distance between us.

"That's a good start, but that's not all I want." I am now even closer, tilting my face up, my lips parting to meet his.

"What else do you want?" His voice is almost in a whisper, closing the last of the distance between us.

"I think you know," I say, my eyes closing.

"Awww, isn't this cute, just like Bromeo and Juliet!"

"Milo! What the actual fudge?!" I yell at my brother who has wandered into the hall and ruined my life.

Luke just laughs and says, "Nice one, little bro, but now get out of here."

"What?" Milo says, shrugging defensively.

"You know what, never mind. We're gonna get out here. Amanda, come on." Luke's mind is made up. He pulls me by the hand, past the joyful sounds of our families in the parlor where Mom is playing piano, through the delicious smells of the kitchen where Zoe and Cheryl are canoodling at the island, and we grab our coats from the hooks and go out into the spectacular winter sun.

"Where we going?" I feel myself pulled along by his warm hand and trot gleefully to keep up. We head into the rows of crisp, aromatic green pine trees, away from the noise and the family and the fuss, and it's just us.

Love among the pines . . .

I start to laugh, snow crystals on the laden branches around us, sparkling and shining in the afternoon light.

"What are you laughing about?" Luke stops and turns to me once we are deep in the trees.

"Oh, nothing, I'm just happy, I guess. It is Christmas, after all. And I love Christmas."

"Well, Merry Christmas," he says, pulling me close. I reach inside his corduroy coat and wrap my arms around his warm body. I feel his strong arms wrap around me and, with a little tug, pull me in tight. He reaches his hand to brush a snowflake from my face. I look into his eyes, he looks into mine, and before I close them I feel his lips touch my lips, and then his mouth open to mine, and we are enveloped in a deep, warm, infinite kiss that sends shivers straight through my whole self, down into the snowy ground below and up to the glistening sky above.

All my many thoughts quiet but one.

Merry Christmas.

SARAH HUTT

is an author and documentary filmmaker whose award-winning work has taken her around the world. Guided by a deep curiosity about the human experience, she works across genres, bringing a documentarian's eye and a storyteller's heart to both fiction and nonfiction. Her passion is crafting stories for young readers that engage, educate, and inspire.

DECEMBER
25
LA LA
LA LA
AAA
MERRY
&
BRIGHT

HO
HO
HO